# The WRONG Promise

## LEESA BOW

THE WRONG PROMISE
The Hendricks Billionaires Series - Book 3
EPUB Format: ISBN: 978-0-6456871-9-4
Paperback: ISBN: 978-1-7635396-3-1
Special Edition Paperback: 978-1-7635396-4-8


Editing and Proofing by <u>Swish Design & Editing</u>
Structural Edits by Madeline at <u>Creating Ink</u>
Cover design by Letitia at <u>RBA Designs</u>


Please join my <u>mailing list</u> to be notified of Leesa's latest releases.

You can learn more about me on my <u>website</u>.

If you're on Facebook, I have a reader group where I chat about books, offer giveaways, and sneak peeks of upcoming books.

*To Shauni,*
*My beautiful lotus flower.*
*I watched you rise in the darkest of times, created a new path in life, and owned it. You were challenged many times, and yet you continued to bloom.*
*Thrive.*
*You'll be forever my inspiration.*

ZARA

I SHOULD BE EXCITED.

I should be out of my mind excited because, after years of self-doubt, my best friend is finally happy. She's treating our friends and me to a weekend retreat at a hotel that has an acclaimed restaurant where the stars secretly dine and a five-star spa service, yet I can't shake the disheartened ache in my stomach.

I'm thirty-five, single, and third-wheeling with my best friends. I love Penny, and Hugh and his wife, Sienna, but they're all happy and... I don't know how to be.

"Thank you for coming." Penny pulls me into a hug.

"No, thank you. This place is amazing. One would be crazy not to want to stay here."

"I know, right." She rubs one hand over her rounded stomach. "When Franklin spoke to Jobe about ideas for a weekend away, he suggested coming here."

Oh, did I mention both Penny and Sienna are pregnant?

And until last week, I also didn't know Jobe owned this hotel.

Franklin is her husband, a man I disliked for months for breaking Penny's heart but who has since proven to be the perfect husband. His younger brother, Jobe, on the other hand, I still dislike with every fiber of my being.

"It's truly amazing," I say while looking around the foyer at the oversized rose crystal statue and the massive chandelier hanging directly overhead.

Her smile grows. "This is his way of preparing me for the baby... being pampered and surrounded by my friends. What else does a girl need?"

"Nothing. You deserve it all." I take her hand and squeeze it. It's hard to believe we grew up together in San Diego, and our families often struggled to get by. We spent days thrifting not to be trendy but because it was all we could afford.

Franklin's voice sounds from behind us, echoing across the luxurious hotel foyer. "Come and join us for dinner later."

We turn to see who he is talking to. Oh, for the love of God.

*Anyone but him.*

Jobe is striding across the marble floor toward his brother, his expression severe like we're keeping him from a million-dollar business deal. I refrain from rolling my eyes and take in his dark hair, suit, and body. Those dark eyes meet mine, and his forehead furrows as though he wasn't expecting to see me.

*Asshole. I'm Penny's best friend.*

Penny places a hand on my arm. "You don't mind if Jobe stays the weekend, do you?"

*Yes.*

"Of course not. He's part of your family." *And he owns the hotel, so...*

Jobe is like Franklin, a shrewd businessman. The first time I met Franklin, I liked him. The first time I met Jobe, he was a stuck-up, wealthy, arrogant snob even though he is the same age as me. Three years later, my opinion is unchanged. While I understand their stern demeanor, unrelenting focus on their goals, and how tough decision-making earned them their successes, it carried into Jobe's personal life.

Like I said, asshole.

Penny has warmed to her husband's brother and tried to convince me he's all sweet and kind on the inside once you get to know him.

I remember the first time she met him and how shitty he made her feel, as though she wasn't good enough for his brother. They didn't move in the same circles, and Jobe didn't like it.

*Hurt my friends, and there is no second chance.*

Even if he has paid for us to be here for a weekend of five-star treatment and pampering, it's probably loose change for him.

"Are you sure you're okay with him here? I know you're not a fan," she says softly.

Understatement of the year.

I shrug. "It's a big place. I can find somewhere not to hear his annoying voice."

She laughs. "Hugh and Sienna should be here soon. Hmm. What shall we start with? A relaxing massage?"

*Send me in the direction of the bar.*

"A relaxation massage sounds divine."

She loops her arm through mine. "Can you believe I'm going to be a mom in thirteen more weeks?"

I close my hand over hers. "Yes, and you are going to be

the best mom." Penny is kind and has so much love to share. Being a mom will come naturally to her.

We walk together, arms looped, toward the spa. Being with her is like being reunited with my twin. The world is right again. Everything around us is in harmony. Moments like these are what I miss most since we only manage to catch up once a month these days.

"And you're going to be the best aunty. I need you to promise to be part of my child's life. Because you've always been a big part of mine."

We smile at each other. For as long as I can remember, we have had each other's back. "I promise to be the best *aunty* I can be."

She leans her head against mine for a moment before we are greeted by a woman wearing a white shirt and trousers. She ushers us into a room with the background noise of birds and the sounds of nature.

The air carries hints of lavender, sandalwood, and lemon. I inhale the scent and let out a sigh.

"I'll text Frank and ask him to bring us a green vitality juice with spirulina."

I swallow. Not the drink of choice I had in mind.

Hugh and Sienna arrive in the afternoon. Penny orientates them to the hotel facility, and they decide to do the couple wellness package, starting with facials. Penny looks at me. "Are you ready to be pampered again, Zee?"

"I am heading outside to soak in the mineral spa bath. You guys go ahead without me. I'm saving the facial for tomorrow."

She tilts her head to the side. "Why not have one each day? We're only here for the weekend. After how your boss treats you and your week at work, you deserve all the pampering."

I smile at my friend. "The month from hell. Actually, it's been a year."

She places an arm around my shoulder. "Exactly. Do this with us."

I have never been spoiled by luxurious gifts, nor am I one to indulge myself. It has taken years for Penny to accept it. Despite her now lavish lifestyle, she still fights for what she believes in, like protecting the environment and curtailing his family's private jet usage, but she has caved to Franklin's extravagant gifts.

"Yes, please join us. We'll send the guys into another room," Sienna emphasizes, rubbing her stomach, which is a slight bump compared to Penny's very pregnant belly.

Our girly conversations will be hijacked by baby talk, and at the moment, I need to clear my mind. Talk myself into being excited. Weekend retreat. Going to be an aunty. Happy for my friends. Not sad and sorry for my single self. "Seriously, you all enjoy it as couples. I'm changing into my bikini and allowing the spa and sunshine to clear my head."

Penny hugs me again. "If you change your mind, we'll be here."

I wave them goodbye and head to my room to change. I know Penny is looking out for me, but this weekend is for her. A special time to relax before the baby comes. She needs to have some time with Franklin and experience the retreat as a couple as his work consumes his life. And it's nice to do the couples thing with another duo. Besides, I have been eyeing the hot tub from the moment I arrived.

After adjusting my bikini straps, I tighten the belt on the bathrobe. Then, once outside, I position my sunglasses over my eyes and inhale the air that has a little warmth remaining at the end of the day.

Springtime is nice, but I'm so ready for summer.

Six white, rounded pools rise up from the green, soft grass. Palm trees and tropical plants surround the area. It's like a mini paradise. From here, I see the infinity pool that I intend to use later. Dropping my robe onto a pool lounge, I climb into the hot tub, rest my head back on a cushion, and close my eyes. All I hear is the gentle rumble of the motor and the bubbling water around my body. While champagne would be the perfect visual complement to this moment—all class and relaxation—I'm still not at ease.

It's like Penny and Hugh have crossed a monumental threshold in their lives, and I'm stuck back here, uncoupled, not expecting a baby, unable to truly follow them.

My stomach balls up as tears threaten.

The worst part is I've spent so many years convincing myself I like being single that I can't imagine being happy in a relationship anyway. And I don't want children. Not in an I-can't-have-them-so-I'll-tell-myself-I-don't-want-them kind of way. I actually don't want children. Every time I make peace with it, other people judge my decision. So there's really no way I could ever fully cross that threshold and live the same happy family life as my friends. I'll always be outside their bubble.

Damn. This is not clearing my head. I focus on relaxing my mind completely.

I have no idea how much time has passed when I hear footsteps behind me. I sit up, and with the sun low in the sky, I shade my eyes to see who it is.

*Ugh.*

"Penny sent me to say dinner is at six." Jobe's gaze bores into me as he holds out a crystal flute of what I assume is champagne. "I thought you might want this, although it's recommended not to have glass by the pools."

I make a splash, moving too fast to sit up, and he jumps

back, almost spilling the drink. "Pass it here. You obviously can't be trusted with fine glassware," I joke.

He smiles and hands me the glass, his hand brushing over his tie, white shirt, and suit jacket.

"Thank you. I appreciate it. You can add psychic to your resume." Jobe Hendricks just made me smile. One for the *Guinness Book.* "Are you now part of the staff to please your brother and Penny?"

He frowns at me. "Please them how?"

"Well, for one, you have offered the entire facility for Penny and us when it could easily accommodate a hundred guests. It's a tick in her good books."

He nods slowly, his dark hues reminding me of his older brother's eyes as they consider me. Those brown eyes lower to where my chest is now out of the water, and then his unapologetic gaze meets mine. He is so damn unreadable.

I detest the man, but the champagne was thoughtful. Do I want him to find me a little bit attractive? Of course I do. I need some validation in my life that I'm a teeny bit desirable, even if he is the last man on Earth I ever want to say it. One look to confirm it is all I need. Yet, there is nothing. The standard Hendricks' poker face.

"Penny is a caring, beautiful woman, and she somehow manages to extract the good in people," he says. "She draws it out as though she is a magnet for kindness."

I already know this since she is *my* best friend. "Ah-ha, and if you do anything to hurt her, you'll have me to deal with."

Jobe smirks. "Firstly, I'm trying to please her because it also pleases my brother, but in saying that, I genuinely like Penny. Best sister-in-law I've ever had."

"Only sister-in-law," I correct.

"Secondly, I'm curious. How would Zara Indigo Hart deal with me?"

*What?*

He grins at my shock. "I am privy to the guest list."

Right. "My mom is the sole person who says my entire name in that tone, and you have no reason to be upset with me."

"I have some right to be offended since you assumed I would hurt my brother's wife in some way."

"Not assumed... warned. You have a reputation of being—"

Jobe's eyes hold mine prisoner, and I'm unable to finish my sentence. "You were saying?"

"Direct." It's the first word that comes to mind other than not-so-nice adjectives.

He nods slowly. "Enjoy your drink, Zara Hart. I'll see you at dinner."

Not if I can help it.

I sip my champagne and watch him walk away.

*Great ass.*

It's obvious he works out, and an image of him hot and sweaty and *not* in a freaking suit jumps into my head. No. I am refusing to think of Jobe Hendricks as hot, even if he is annoyingly good-looking.

I should be pondering why he is being nice to me.

*Is it for Penny's sake?*

It doesn't matter. I refuse to give him another thought.

ZARA

DINNER IS a healthy choice of divine foods suited for a wellness health spa such as this, and while every dish is delicious, I'm surprised this is Jobe's spa retreat hotel. I assumed, with his bad boy edge and fit body, he was more of a nightclub type of guy. He doesn't have to practice a certain lifestyle to understand that it is a good business investment.

This hotel is a prime example of that. It helps the Hendricks are one of the wealthiest families in the country, proving he understands what it takes.

*Invest in what you know.*

With no investments but my own happiness, I'm not business savvy at all. I barely manage to save anything from paycheck to paycheck, but I live well. I enjoy my online shopping and girls' nights out. I guess one could say my wealth isn't anything monetary.

While the men continue their chatting, our girly conversation is again hijacked with baby talk. It's not that I oppose the discussion. I am excited for both of my friends, but it has been our only conversation this evening, which I had hoped they would have discussed in entirety during their facial treatment.

*Stop. This is one of the most exciting times in your friends' lives.*

*Try harder.*

"I can't wait to see Hugh and Franklin change poopy diapers," I say with a smirk.

"I'm with you," Sienna adds. "Even the word poop has Hugh running for the hills."

Penny stares up at her husband. "I think he's going to be fine," she says gently. Franklin guides her head gently onto his shoulder, and she smiles at me. "I can't wait to see him cradling our baby. I dream about it every night."

Around the table, the discussion overflows with love, and the picture they paint is not hard to imagine. And yet, it's too much. I catch myself before my face drops. The divide between my friends and me is changing our future. I know I promised to be a part of their child's life, but we are heading in separate directions, and it scares the hell out of me.

Jobe stands. "A toast to Penny and Franklin. To many happy days and sleepless nights." He glances at Sienna and Hugh. "And to you both. May your future babies be nothing like their fathers."

That garners a giggle from the girls.

"And for those of us who can drink, may I serve you something a little harder than what the wonderful staff has prepared?"

I raise my hand. "Yes, please."

Franklin glances at Penny. "Perhaps a nightcap?"

I check the time. It's only eight o'clock. Far too early to sleep.

By the time I finish my glass of champagne, Penny is standing and Franklin is downing the last of his whiskey. She rubs her rounded belly and offers me a weary smile. "I'll see you all in the morning. Breakfast is served from six o'clock." She takes Franklin's hand. "I now need pampering in other ways."

Franklin is right behind her and wraps both arms around her middle, leaning down and whispering something in her ear. Penny giggles.

*I. Am. Not. Jealous.*

"Night, lovers," I call after them. "See you in the morning."

Sienna and Hugh stand. "We are also taking advantage of the super king-sized bed," Hugh says, and leans down, kissing my cheek.

"TMI," I tell them.

"It's good to see you again, Zee." He gives me a brief hug, glances at Jobe then eyes me. "Are you staying?"

"Have you ever known me to leave a bar before nine o'clock?"

Hugh leaves a supportive hand on my shoulder. "I could stay for another drink with you?"

"No, I'm having one more and heading to bed myself." I stand to hug both my friends, then look at Jobe. "May I buy a glass of champagne from the bar?"

He downs the rest of his whiskey and stands, walking to the small bar area. I watch as he speaks to the staff, who opens a bottle and places it on the bar, disappearing to the back.

Jobe gestures for me to join him at the bar, and I take a seat on the classy, white leather rounded-back barstool. When I take in the open bottle in front of me, my eyes pop.

*What the actual fuck?*

Dom Pérignon. Not any bottle, the Gold Vintage.

"I-I didn't..." I stutter. "I can't afford..."

Jobe smiles. "It's on me." I check behind us, noting the room is now empty. All the staff has disappeared. Not that it matters. He can take what he likes.

"You were struggling," he says, matter-of-factly.

"How so?"

"All the baby talk. I saw the look on your face."

My shoulders sag. "I'm trying to be a good friend. No, I am a good friend, and I'm excited for both of my friends. The fact I haven't dated in a year doesn't mean anything. It's an exciting time in their lives. I can only imagine how overwhelmed they are with their lives changing, well, like forever. And in a good way, of course. I've never seen Penny this happy, and that makes me happy. I'm so glad she met Frank. I mean, who knew you could find your soulmate setting a proposal beach theme for your friend and it then being a disaster? What do they say? You never know when—"

"Take a breath and drink," Jobe interrupts and hands me a glass. "Your happiness is *a lot*. I'm not sure if it's for the baby or Penny has found happiness with my brother?"

I down a few mouthfuls. God, it tastes amazing. "Both."

"And it makes you feel..." He waits for me to answer.

"Happy, of course."

"Hmm." He loosens his tie and slips it off, then rolls it, placing it on the bar.

Swiveling on his chair, he faces me, turning my stool so his knees imprison my thighs.

My stupid heartbeat picks up a notch.

His dark eyes assess me. "How do you really feel? And don't say happy."

*Nervous this close to you.* "I'm going to need more than one glass of champagne for me to speak my mind to *you.*

Not that you'd understand. You spoke your mind far too scathingly when you first met Pen."

"Ah. I see I'm not forgiven for that." His smirk bugs me as though he knows exactly what he is doing. "Then I'll start. I love my brother. I'm closest to him out of any of my siblings, and their happiness brings my family unbelievable joy. Especially my parents. He has always been someone I have respected, as no one does it better than Franklin. Ask my father. He was the perfect student and a ruthless businessman. He has made my father proud."

I frown at him. "And you haven't?"

"I partied my way through college and messed around for years. Until my father spoke sense and gave me the rope to do something I enjoy since hedge funds and business analytics never inspired me. Beautiful homes and beautiful things enthuse me. I like speaking with people face-to-face and convincing them they need something more in their lives. Although, of late, the business has taken me further away from this and more to real estate investment trusts and buying office towers. Another challenge I enjoy."

I narrow my eyes at him.

"I would never sell them something of poor quality, and I usually deal with millionaires and billionaires, so to my clients, it's just another house."

"You'd never sell a house to me." A statement, not a question. I take another mouthful of truth serum.

"I think I could if you had the equity. I am a convincing man when in the zone."

A single laugh erupts from my throat. "Thankfully, I'm not in your market, and I doubt I would ever succumb to your sales pitch."

*Or you.*

"It's not a pitch, Zara. More a way of life and understanding the client's needs. I take my job seriously."

I believe him.

Looking at the bottle of champagne, I pour myself another drink and top up his glass. I raise my crystal flute. "This is good, by the way."

He undoes the top two buttons of his white shirt. "Do you want me to ready the next bottle on ice?"

*What?*

"I'd be happy for a G and T."

He gives me a disapproving side-eye before moving behind the bar, where he ignores me and opens another bottle, placing it in ice. Jobe places two coupe glasses on the bar.

"Oh, the fancy boob glass."

Jobe's eyes hold me captive, and then his gaze lowers. "I don't believe it's shaped to fit yours."

Raising a brow, I take the glass and fit the opening over my left breast. It barely covers the area around the nipple. "You're right." Placing the glass back on the counter, I add, "Best I use that glass now."

Jobe's dark expression causes my stomach to flip. "Not a chance." He slides the glass to his side. Straightening both his arms, he leans on the counter, staring at me in a way I can't think about anything else while prisoner to his mesmerizing eyes. "Enough about my work and fake happiness. Where do you work, Zara?"

What were we talking about? "I'm an executive assistant to the HR manager at an environmental preservation company. Penny helped me secure the position three years ago. Before that, I worked at an insurance firm. In other words, nothing exciting."

"What excites you?"

What's with all the serious questions?

"Workwise? Nothing at the moment. What I would love is to climb the career ladder into HR. But there's no chance of it happening in this company, so I'm bored and ready for a change." I down the remains of my glass. "Sick of LA if I'm being frank."

"You're not Frank. Or Penny, for that matter." He gives a cheeky smile as he fills my boob glass with the newly opened bottle of Dom. "You're Zara Indigo Hart and stop reflecting on the blue nature of indigo and find your purple."

I frown. "Blue as in feeling blue? And what do you mean by my purple? Because it sounds cheesy coming from you."

He raises his glass as though to salute me. "While it sounds random, a friend recently educated me on color. All part of the décor in real estate. For instance, blue is calming and serene, yet it can improve concentration and stimulate thinking. A color to improve productivity, so I had my offices painted in different shades of blue." *It sounds wanky to me, but I say nothing.* "You, however, need some excitement." *Not arguing there.* "Bring the purple of indigo in how you think about the future."

I lift the glass to my lips. "Well... if we're talking about a stand-out color, my superpower is to blend. I'm a chameleon." I shrug. "If I could go anywhere in the world right now, I would..."

*Purple... royalty...*

"Work in England." It feels like a game, and I answered right.

He nods slowly, pushes off the counter, and straightens. Jobe is not as tall as Franklin, but still my gaze lifts to meet his. "Good choice."

I laugh, mocking him. Or, if I'm honest, mocking myself. "It won't happen."

"Why not?"

"Um, I know no one and have no work prospects. No

visa. And my passport has expired because my life sucks." I sound sad even to myself, so I down my drink in one go.

*Woah.* I close my eyes, letting the buzz wash over me. I better slow down.

"Give me your cell."

"What?"

Jobe's hand is outstretched, waiting, so I unlock my cell and hand it to him. He taps away, then holds it to his ear. I watch as he retrieves his cell from his trouser pocket. "I've sent you my details." He hands me my cell. "What's your address and email? If you're serious, I have a contact who can make it happen."

"Say what?"

"Do you want a job in London?"

*Do I?* I don't want the job I've got—there's nowhere to go from here—yet my career matters to me. I might not want a family, but it doesn't mean I don't deserve purpose. And this could be the clean break I need to get it. "I'm tempted." I blow out a breath. "Can you really make it happen?"

He glances up from his phone and raises one eyebrow. "Ask yourself why before you make a decision."

I shake my head as if my thoughts are muddled.

*Shit. Shit. Shit.*

"Why? Because I also deserve to be happy when around me, my friends' lives are exploding with excitement. Their lives are one continual fireworks show, and I can't even crack a spark of fun. I'm living vicariously through their joy, and I want a turn. Even better, an adventure. And I damn well deserve it."

Jobe picks up his cell and taps away as I give him specifics. "Do you want me to hit send on the email?"

I lean on the bar and look him in the eye. "London," I murmur, pondering the idea.

He walks around the bar and stands between my thighs,

holding the cell close to my face. "Read it. If you're happy, then press send."

I skim over the words. *Wow.* He highly recommends me. I raise my hand, and he yanks his cell away.

"Promise me you're making a decision based on *your* happiness and not running from something else."

"Why are you doing this and being so nice to me?"

"I'm in the business of helping people attain their needs."

We consider each other for a moment. Is he talking about other things?

"Zara?" He holds his cell closer. "I'll delete it if you're not sure."

"It's what I want." I hit send and scream. Then I throw my arms around his neck and hug him. "I could kiss you."

"Have you forgotten how?"

Why would he say that? Oh, I mentioned the lack of dating earlier.

Our eyes lock, and there's a surge of heat in my chest. My arms loosen around his neck. Tonight, I'm drunk and up for the challenge because a girl never forgets *how* to kiss. Only what it feels like. "Of course not," I murmur and edge closer to his lips. I pause and glance up at his eyes, which tell me he feels something too.

My lips gently brush with his, the movement slow and even. His facial hair bushes my mouth, and it ignites something deep, my pussy clenching, appreciating I'm with a man. Suddenly, we are lip-locked, his hand on the back of my head as his tongue darts in and finds mine. There's no escape. I moan as desire rips through my body. It's been too long, and right now, my body wants action regardless of who it is with.

I pull away, breathless, only for a moment before Jobe

straightens, and I cling like a monkey, my legs wrapping around his waist. I'm enjoying this more than I should.

The softness of his mouth, the taste of whiskey and champagne on his tongue, and the way he kisses make me breathless. An equal measure of desperate longing and desire.

*Lust. It has been too long, my friend.*

His voice is dangerously low. "You taste fucking good."

My stupid heart reacts again, beating erratically. More to his warm skin surrounding mine than to him. *Jobe.* Pushing the thought aside, I allow my hands to roam, feeling every hard muscle beneath my fingertips.

"It's a pity you're not my type," I whisper.

He pulls back.

Reality hits, and I can't help feeling the disappointment of space between us as I slide down his body to find my feet.

"And you're not mine," he says softly. "If we were a thing, I'd have invited one or two other guests to join us. Regrettably, I cleared all bookings for Penny to have the place to herself."

*Ugh. The man is an animal in bed...*

My brain finally catches up. "I'm the possessive type and extremely jealous. You would never be happy with someone like me. *I don't share.*" Maybe that's my problem. Am I too much for men?

"Your words don't scare me, Zara."

I'm staring at his lips, afraid to meet his gaze, knowing what I would find if I did.

"I'm not trying to scare you. I'm warning you. You would not enjoy being with someone like me."

I finish drinking the remains in my glass. I'm not wasting a drop of Dom. When I twist on my chair to leave, Jobe is standing behind me.

His dark eyes bore into mine. "Do not tell me what I enjoy," he growls out.

Making another questionable decision, I jump into his arms. My tongue is already sliding with his before my brain catches up and acknowledges what comes next.

Pain above my left eye orientates me to morning.

I'm acutely aware of the sun shining into the room.

*Ugh, why did I drink so much?* It's supposed to be a healthy weekend with my friends to reenergize our bodies with all the pampering every girl desires.

I sit upright in my bed, a tidal wave of horror hitting me.

Jobe is not beside me.

I fall back onto the pillow and cover my painful eyes with the back of my hand. Slowly, I lift the silk sheet and...

*Shit.*

I am completely naked.

And my pussy has a delicious throb.

I close my eyes and force myself to remember details. *Desperate kissing.* I scan the room for my dress and recall him telling me he'll buy a new one.

*Did he tear the material?*

Three ripped condom packets are on the side of the bed.

I clench my eyes shut, visualizing the memory of his shoulders framing my face. Orgasming loudly.

*I am so embarrassed.*

The alarm on my cell sounds, and I quickly silence it.

Jesus, I just fucked my best friend's brother-in-law, and I don't even like him.

*What the hell is wrong with me?*

Especially when I can't remember details.

*Can he?*

He left before I woke up…

A sign of instant regret? Is he mortified as I am? Or should I interpret it as a cold rejection?

Oh, for the love of God. I now have to face him at breakfast.

After showering and dressing, ready for another day of pampering, I take the stairs down to the restaurant. Before walking through the French doors, I hold my breath, then let it out when there is no sign of Jobe.

"Morning," I sing and straighten my hair as though it has a freshly fucked style despite my shower.

"Morning, babe. What would you like to eat?" Penny's cheeks glow with motherhood agreeing with her.

"I'll have what everyone else is having."

Blending again. My traitorous stomach growls. I cannot drink the ginger and green juice today. "I'm not late, am I? Jobe's still not here?" I question innocently.

"No, he had to rush back to the office for a crisis meeting," Franklin says offhandedly, as though it happens all the time.

My shoulders relax, and I push the weird disappointment out of my head, taking it as a change of luck with something going my way for once.

My cell pings with an email.

*Dear Zara,*

*We received your email and intent to work with us in our London office.*
*We will look over your credentials and be in contact within the week.*

*Yours sincerely,*
*Anthony Warburton*

Oh, my God, it's happening. He was good on his word.

Heat creeps up into my cheeks, remembering more about last night. I take a deep breath to compose myself before taking a seat beside Penny, tucking away my phone. The way Hugh is staring at me, he notices something is up.

*Are you okay?* he mouths.

I nod with a smile.

I love my friends, but I'm ready for my own journey.

I am more than okay.

# 3

ZARA



HOW DOES ONE MEASURE HAPPINESS?

Research suggests certain theories, yet I am testing them in my own way. I'm living with the freedom of anonymity—not shadowed by my own past, by the person back home everyone knows me to be. People in London only know me at face value based on the woman I present when we first meet. A new country, a fresh new start, and a new timeline of happiness.

The warm feeling in my chest is an indicator of where the scale of happiness is stuck. Firmly on yellow. Sunshine in my heart.

Prior to leaving LA, my friends warned me about the dreary weather, and even though it's the first week of October, in my mind, it feels like a hot summer day. I've been here for a month, and already I'm loving everything about the city—the architecture, friendly people, and traditional bars.

Before starting my new job, I toured the sights from daylight to dark. On my first day, I rode on a red double-decker bus, and then stopped off at The Tower of London, Big Ben, and Westminster Abbey. Then I spent a week visiting castles. There is plenty of sightseeing, and with the recommendation of my new work friends, I'll be traveling around the country every weekend for the next ten years. Living in London signifies my deep love for royalty, so I eagerly absorbed the history. This is my new home, and I refuse to be ignorant about the country's heritage.

I'm stuck in fascination mode, and everything about the country is like a shiny new toy. It's only been three weeks since I began working in the heart of the city and within walking distance from my hotel. Some nights are split between visiting an old-time pub and the cocktail bars closer to my hotel. The other half of the week, I stay in my hotel room to work on extra projects for the company and gain my footing in this new role while trying to set myself apart from the team in the event that a promotion opportunity arises. If I'm going to do what I said and accelerate my career, I need to be committed and stay up as late working as I do on pub nights.

While I love trendy cocktail bars, like the ones I frequented with my friends in LA, the old-time bars give a timeless feel since they have been around for centuries. As long as I'm not expected to quote Shakespeare, I have slipped into discussions relatively easily, especially since topics with my work colleagues have moved beyond questions about living in Los Angeles and why I moved when Hollywood was at my doorstep.

A career change and making a name for myself as a

professional is my response because every time I think about home, tears threaten to unhinge me, and I question my decision.

*Penny.*

*Hugh.*

Every morning, when I open my eyes, I think about them, their families, and how happy they are. Taking the risk and creating a new life is hard when all I want to do is hug my best friends.

*And Penny's baby.*

Being mindful of my happiness and not feeling like the worst best friend is more difficult than I thought.

It's the end of the working week, and before I step inside the pub, out of the wind, my cell chimes in my bag.

It is Piper from the office.



It's my first official invite that excludes meeting work colleagues for a drink after work. And, it is my first free Saturday where I haven't busied myself exploring the city. After I text back, I'm still smiling as I walk into the grand old-time bar.

The bartender fixes me a gin and tonic, which I down quickly and ask for another before I leave the safety of the bar to find a seat.

*Oomph.* I stumble when some idiot bumps my hip. Thankfully, I somehow managed not to spill a drop.

"Sorry, love. Ahh... here she is. U.S. of A." Oscar grins at me before eyeing my drink.

Oscar is tall, dark, and handsome. And not my type. He introduced himself the first time I wandered into this bar after the cheers of happy people drew me inside.

He is a gentleman, perfectly groomed with not a hair out of place or any sign of a shadow on his jaw. Oscar's voice is soft and caring. Sometimes, it's too gentle for me to hear over the boisterous patrons in the bar. Something about him screams he wouldn't cope with a broken heart, and it's a known fact I fall for the bad boy. But this move is about stepping into my own light—no more blending, not even with the way I used to be—so I promised myself not to rule anything out.

"Still afraid to try the ale?"

"I tried it a few nights ago and still not a fan."

He smiles, clinking his drink with mine. "G and T it is. Do you drink anything else?"

*Does a bear shit in the woods?* "Wine. Cocktails. Champagne."

He chuckles. "If you try the ale again, start with shandy."

"Noted." I look over his shoulder, but the table I was eyeing is now taken.

He turns to where I'm looking. "Do you have a table?"

I shake my head.

"Are you here with anyone?"

I offer a strangled laugh. "Not tonight, though my work colleagues have invited me to watch the game tomorrow."

"Look at you fitting in with the locals. I assume it's not at *the game*?"

I frown at him. "You shouldn't assume."

He chuckles. "It's incredibly difficult to get tickets and prices are high, but yeah, there are ways to buy them. So at someone's house or a sports bar? I could name the bars in the area that are screening it live."

"Notting Hill." I clink my glass against his. "You can drop any detective skills, Big O. Unless, you are working for the FBI and haven't told me?" I say, and smile.

He grins, though it's more about his pet name—Big O.

The reference is to his height and not to what every woman wants between the sheets. Oscar is six foot six, and my own personal drone to what is happening in the bar. "Not a chance. And it's MI5, here, Americano." He nods toward the back of the bar. "Let's find you a table."

Thirty minutes later, we are laughing about the differences between our countries, more so with the extra gins I have consumed. "You know something, Big O? I should be drinking champagne to celebrate. I have officially lived here for one month today."

"If you want champagne to celebrate, then I'll get us a bottle even though I like it as much as you do the ale. But you're not in any state to be walking home alone tonight."

I smile at my friend. "You don't have to do either. I can buy my own drinks, and I'll get an Uber home."

"You're not paying for your celebratory drinks." He slides out from the table and heads toward the bar.

I eye his tight ass hidden beneath the perfectly tailored suit. Like me, he is here for Friday night drinks, though we haven't shared our place of work. Should I be more careful? I pull out my cell to take a sneaky photo because I should have someone I spend time with on my camera roll.

A text from Penny lights up the screen.

> Can we please FaceTime? I need to speak with you and make sure you're okay.

> Pen, I need you to stop worrying. I am fine. I'm not going to pretend I don't miss you, but I'm happy here. I'll send you my location so you know where I am. I'll send you another when I get back to my hotel. Give Summer a big hug from me x

After sending my location, I drop my cell back into my bag. It's the same every Friday night. Before Penny met

Franklin, we would meet on Friday nights along with Hugh. Nothing stood in the way of our meetups, not even my boyfriends.

However, guys never stayed with me longer than six months. Every relationship has ended the same. We were too different, even though I tried to change to be more like the girl they envisioned me to be in their mind. I even changed my freaking diet and pretended to like the same foods as they did. I'm not made of relationship material, accommodating the other person, ultimately making me unhappy. Miserable, actually, and I'm not going back to being that girl.

Finally, I understand I have to love myself before anyone else can love me. My new life is about self-discovery along with the adventure of living in another country and building my career.

The champagne bottle pops, and cheers sound from nearby tables. Everyone is so happy here.

Oscar fills my glass, and we clink our glasses. "Cheers." He smiles at me.

*What are we cheering?*

"It's my understanding that scones are not scones, and biscuits are not biscuits," I say and raise my glass.

"Life lessons." He grins and downs his glass, then wipes his mouth before a shudder rolls over his broad shoulders. "Next lesson, what food are you ordering?"

Before I answer that I'm not hungry, I acknowledge the test.

"Chips, not French fries."

He refills my glass. "Bangers are?"

"Pork sausage. Now, I have a question. What is it with everyone taking a vacation to Thailand? Why Thailand?"

He laughs at my disbelief. "First, it's holiday, not vacation."

"Oh, right, I remember."

"Exotic destinations are appealing."

I shake my head. "Like Mexico?"

His brows tighten. "I consider Thailand to be different from Mexico. I prefer Madeira."

In conversation with my coworkers, I discovered many of them have traveled to far more countries than me. I have traveled around the US, Canada, and Mexico but never pondered venturing farther until a few months ago.

"Mark it as a place of interest," he suggests. "What's the next destination on Zara's want-to-explore list?"

"Oh, more castles and formal gardens, and I've not been to Scotland."

"An *Outlander* fan?"

"Only since my flight over. I binge it when I can't sleep."

"Does live music interest you?"

"Hell, yes."

"There she is." He grins. "I thought you'd aged twenty years while I was at the bar."

Our discussion leads to our favorite bands and another bottle of champagne.

The girl at the table beside me begins dancing around us. Because of the lack of space, she bumps into me. Instead of getting annoyed, I jump up and dance with her. Carefree, I move my hips to the beat, laughing along with her as though we have known each other for years and not the ten minutes we've been dancing. While her youth is noticeable, I don't care that I'm thirty-freaking-five and should be acting in a more mature, classy way. It feels good to be free of judgment. As much as Penny and Hugh like to enjoy themselves, they'd never in a million years get up and dance with a stranger in a bar—and so, in my typical blending fashion, I wouldn't have either. But here, I'm coming out of my shell, and it feels fantastic.

Oscar claps his hands and smiles at me as he stands, whispering, "I'm heading to the loo."

*What a weird word.*

I don't need to know his every move, though I appreciate he is looking out for me. With my hands in the air, I twirl, the liquid bubbles giving me more confidence than I naturally have. The cheers of other tables incite us to keep dancing. Eyes closed, I imagine all my fears leaving my body, as though I'm expelling it through my fingertips, and like invisible gas, it's circling above me, and I'm lighter for it.

I have to stop reading fantasy books.

Smiling, I open my eyes, and my entire body freezes. A few feet away, Jobe Hendricks' dark eyes hold me captive.

"What are you doing, Zara?"

# 4

ZARA

"Dancing. What does it look like?" I counter in my sweetest voice.

He gets up in my face. "How much alcohol have you consumed?"

*How much alcohol have you consumed?* sounds out in my head, mocking him.

"Not enough to forget how annoying you are." I glance at my table, and his gaze follows. "Why are you even here?"

Jobe grabs my wrist. "Apart from a business trip? I think you know why."

I yank my arm from his grasp. "I'm having fun, happy *as promised.*"

His expression softens. "And *I promised* Penny I would check in on you and make sure you're safe."

I roll my eyes. "Please. Does it appear I'm in immediate danger?"

I slide onto the chair, pick up my glass from the table, and down the remainder of the champagne.

"You never leave drinks unattended at a table," he says bluntly.

"Ugh, my friends are nearby."

He laughs once as though I'm clueless, and it grates on my nerves.

"Okay, let's get you home."

Before I object again, Oscar appears at the table. "Is everything all right?" he asks directly to me.

I nod. "Oscar, this is Jobe, my girlfriend's annoying brother-in-law." Oscar smiles at him and holds out his hand. "Oscar is a friend."

"Who wasn't here watching over your table." Jobe shakes Oscar's hand. "How long have you known Zara?"

"Well, mate, I met Zara here one night, and we've caught up several times since."

"So not well enough to be friends."

"Hey." Oscar raises both his hands. "I'm only looking out for her. No offense, Americana, I like you, but you're not my type." Weirdly, my shoulders relax. "And neither are you," he states matter-of-factly to Jobe.

I smile to myself. "Not many are." Jobe gives me his best scowl, and I force down the smirk threatening to spread.

Oscar picks up his drink and downs the last of it. "He's looking out for you, love. It's not a bad thing."

*What?*

Ugh. "I didn't ask him to look out for me."

"No, but Penny did, and I need to report back that you're home safe after I found you in a bar, intoxicated, with no one we trust."

"Back off, Jobe. I'm not a kid." I push past him. "See you next time, Big O."

Out on the cobbled street, I tighten my jacket around my

chest. The nights are not as warm as back home this time of year. I inhale a deep breath to clear my head as I walk toward the main street.

"I'm doing what she asked," Jobe says, now keeping in step. "Don't kill the messenger."

"Your message has been received. Now you're free to leave." I turn, ignoring him, and scan the streets for a taxi. When I don't see any, I retrieve my cell to order an Uber. Jobe covers my screen with his hand.

"Please, Zara. I have a driver waiting. He'll take you back to your hotel."

"Fine. Then will you leave me alone?"

"If that's what you want, then yes."

"Finally," I murmur.

I'm still mad that I never heard from him again after that night. Guess I'm really not his type. I'm too embarrassed to mention it, and since he has never said anything, it's easier to pretend it never happened.

Jobe calls his driver, and a few minutes later, a black Mercedes pulls up beside us. Jobe opens the door, and I slide in. The driver doesn't turn around even when I say, "Hi."

"Where are we going?" Jobe asks.

I tell the driver my address. This time he acknowledges me in the rearview mirror with a simple nod.

We drive in silence for the few minutes it takes to arrive at my hotel, where Jobe slides out and holds the door open for me. "Thank you." I offer him a slight smile.

"Do you want me to see you to your room?"

One thing I have learned is not to make the same mistake twice.

"Zara," he prompts when I turn to walk away from him. "Penny is not the only reason I'm here."

"Why *are* you here?" I question sharply, looking back at him.

"Because I feel some responsibility for you being here alone."

"Don't. It's what I wanted. I'm making friends, and it's the adventure I craved."

He runs his fingers through tousled, dark locks. "You left LA before I got a chance to say—"

"You don't need to say anything."

*Because you had a chance to before I left, yet you chose not to take it.*

Jobe frowns, and I sense he wants to say more.

"Night, Jobe. Enjoy your time in London."

The following day, I meet my friends at a bar in Notting Hill, and they order a round of beer. I'm in struggle town, shuddering after swallowing every mouthful. If I persevere, I'm going to puke. Admitting defeat, I order a gin and tonic.

The bartender hands it to me, and I almost jump over the bar when men shout behind me. "They're just cheering, love," the bartender explains. "You Americans love footy, right?"

"Yeah. We do." But this is not football. It's soccer. I head back to my friends, now standing in front of the screen. Scrap that. George is yelling at the screen.

"What happened?" I ask Piper. She's probably my closest work friend, despite our obvious age difference. Our desks are next to each other in the office, and she's forever offering me homemade muffins that she baked herself. It's a simple kindness but so genuine it warms me.

"Umpire's decision was questionable in George's eyes," she answers.

So, the game is similar to the NFL.

"Is this your team?" I ask because she barely cheers when another goal is scored.

She shrugs. "I'm here for the beer." She drains the last mouthful, so I join her at the bar and order for both of us. "Thanks. Are you enjoying your new job? I mean, you're with all of us, so how can you not." She grins at me.

"True." I smile. "Although it's different, I'm adapting. Everyone is nice enough, and I'm not stressed, so that's a bonus."

She toys with her long, straight, blonde hair that is almost to her waist. "A nice way to say you're bored."

"Not bored." *Yet.* My extra work in the evenings is enough to keep me engaged for now. "I'm adapting and learning company protocol. Though career progression should be on all our radars."

"Not all. Some of us are working until we finish our degree."

I stare blankly at her.

"We're studying part-time. Work full-time to make ends meet."

"Oh, I get it." *How old are you?* I don't come right out and ask. "Is George also studying? He looks like he's around thirty."

She choke-coughs. "He's twenty-seven and acts twenty."

"What about Anna?"

"Twenty-five."

God, I'm ten years older than her.

"Anna and I are studying law at the same university, although she is a year ahead of me."

It's my turn to choke on my drink.

"Lydia is married with kids and is mid-thirties, or is it forty? She comes out with us once a month, if that." She talks as though Lydia is old. Jesus, what the hell am I doing with my life?

My cell dings in my hand before I get a snap of my friends screaming at the screen. It's Jobe, and I don't know whether to be happy or not.

Do you want to meet for a drink tonight?

I should type, *No.*

I was hard on him last night. I should show some gratitude for helping me to break into a new career in another country. Not contacting me after that night meant I really did achieve it on my own without his assistance. It feels good to be in charge of the next chapter of my life, even if it means hanging out with these *kids.*

Sorry I was short with you last night. How long are you in London? I'm with work friends watching the game and might not make it back to my hotel in time.

Where?

Notting Hill. Maybe tomorrow night?

"Your boyfriend?" Piper assumes.

"Far from it." I pop my cell in my bag. "My friend's brother-in-law. He travels to London for business and checks in on me *for her.*"

Piper frowns. "Checks on you."

"Yeah, like I haven't been mugged, and I'm... I don't know... not ruining my life somehow."

"It's rather odd."

*Tell me about it.*

"My friend and I have been besties since elementary

school, and she married her soulmate and recently had a baby. Which isn't a life I want, but staying close to her was going to make me feel like being a childless woman is a fault rather than a choice." I clear the lump from my throat. "I decided to do something fun with my life. I needed an adventure, only she wanted me to be part of her daughter's life. I will be. Not now... I didn't want to stay and regret not taking the chance to work abroad."

"You made the right decision," she says, eyes wide. "I'm going to take a gap year for a working holiday in Europe. Mainly Italy," she draws out. "Better lovers, you know?"

I don't know at all.

"I'm never getting married..." She trails off and frowns. I pivot on my bar stool to see what has caught her attention. It's a guy wearing a suit. "Though, I could do him."

What the...

Jobe scans the room. His eyes lock with mine, and it's not his usual dark and broody look. There's something else, and my stomach does a little flip.

He strides toward me. "Zara."

"This is my *dad,* Jobe," I tell Piper. Her eyes pop, and her gaze flicks from Jobe to me. "The one I was telling you about."

"Ri-ight." She turns to me. "Why are you complaining?" she whispers.

"You don't know him."

"If he wants me to, then..."

I cough to stop her saying anything else and introduce her. "Piper and I work together along with the rest of the team over there." I point to my work friends, still gathered near the big screen.

"May I buy you a beer?" Piper asks in a sexy voice.

He frowns at her. "I. Er..." Jobe's glaze flicks to mine, and I hide a smirk.

"Jobe has exquisite taste in booze. Best allow him to buy his own whiskey."

The crowd erupts into cheers, the happy shouting so loud I barely hear what Jobe says.

Piper runs off to jump around with her friends to celebrate the win.

"I never understood this game," Jobe scoffs.

"Same. But the celebrating part looks fun."

Piper bounces back to us. "We're heading to Soho. Want to come?" I glance at Jobe. "Both of you are welcome to join us," she adds.

"It's up to Zara. I can cancel the dinner reservation." He eyes me as though he would prefer not to go.

"Count us in."

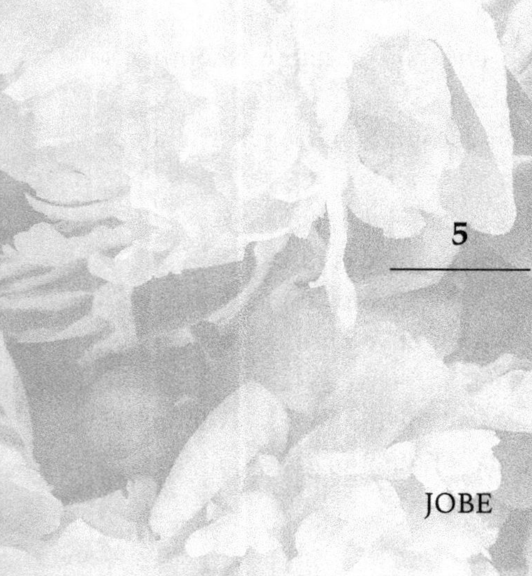

**5**

---

JOBE

THERE IS BARELY any standing room at the cocktail bar, not exactly what I had in mind when I came to see Zara. We were supposed to be at a Michelin-star restaurant having a quiet dinner.

The table is in the far back corner, where we are squeezed around it, and the closeness of everyone has my teeth on edge. If I'm going to be surrounded by fucking kids, I'm going to need something strong to cope.

Needing an excuse to escape, I offer to head over to the bar and buy the drinks, where I wait forever to be served, then make my way back to the table. In the crowded space, I juggle too many brightly colored cocktails and a neat whiskey—not my label of choice, but it will do.

A girl bounces around in my face. "Hi. Is one of these for me?" She offers a sultry look as though I'm simply going to hand one over. After waiting twenty minutes to order, if she lays one finger on the glass, I'll fucking walk out.

She gives me a wink as though she's only playing and squeezes past me, knocking me off balance, and some of my cocktail spills out onto the floor.

*Why am I here?*

When you have a sister-in-law begging for you to check in on her best friend with tears streaming down her cheek, then you do it. Admittedly, I also wanted to desperately see Zara. The unspoken words between us about a certain night are driving me crazy.

She's pretending it didn't happen, and that hurts. I wanted to offer an explanation of my sudden disappearance to ensure her it wasn't rejection. It's quite the opposite since a woman has never spooked me as much as Zara did.

When I get back to the table, Zara is waiting alone. "Everyone left. They said it's too busy and went somewhere else."

She stares at me as I set the drinks on the high table. "You didn't go with them?"

She shrugs. "I didn't want to run out on you while you were at the bar buying me and my friend drinks. It wasn't the right thing to do."

"Thank you," I offer, sliding both cocktails in front of her. It's typical of Zara to do the *right thing*. It's why I need to ask for a favor. She drains the cocktail through a straw in seconds. I raise an eyebrow. "Can you at least sip it? I'm not keen to get back in that line."

Zara drains the second glass just as quickly. "Drink up," she says. "I want to leave."

"Are you serious?"

"Yeah, it's not really my thing."

*Nor mine.* "Where did your friends go?"

"It's not that. I want to go home."

I throw my whiskey back and stand, holding out my hand to take hers. I know if I don't keep hold of her, I'll lose her in the crowd. It's only when we make it to the doors that I let go of her hand to wipe down my suit jacket. There's enough alcohol spilled over me to fill another bottle. It will need to be dry-cleaned or tossed in the damn trash.

We walk to the street, and I tap on my cell to call my driver. "Thank you for coming," she says gently. "I could see you were struggling in there. I should've said no to my friends, but I wanted to test you, and it was wrong of me."

I finish speaking to Ben, then end the call and ask, "Test me how?"

Zara shrugs.

"Don't do that."

"What?"

"Pop your shoulders. A flippant attitude is disrespectful." She rolls her eyes. "And so is that. Tell me... what's on your mind. It's better than the guessing game we have going on." I wasn't one to beat around the bush. It was more productive to get straight to the point.

"Do you really care about me?"

"Of course, I care about you."

Her eyes assess me before looking away to the busy road. A red double-decker bus drives past, and the sight makes her slightly smile. She looks at her feet and then back at me. "You're here for Penny, and while it's sweet, I have told her I'm fine. Now I'm telling you I'm doing okay and don't need a minder because it's frustrating the hell out of me."

Ben pulls up, and I open the door for her. Zara just stands there like she doesn't want to get in. "Zara?"

"If you're here because of Penny, then I don't need to see you anymore. But if you're here because you want to be, then..." She pulls her coat around her shoulders and looks down the road.

"Then what?"

She fucking shrugs again.

"Get in, Zara. We'll talk about this at yours."

"Don't go to mine. There's barely any room. I have no food, and to be honest, I'm starving. I'm happier to drive through a burger joint."

"We are not driving through a takeout restaurant." I close her door and stride around the other side. "To my penthouse, please, Ben."

Her eyes round. "You have your own penthouse here?"

"Of course I do. Where else do you think I stay?"

"The Ritz?"

I chuckle. "Good guess."

She stares out the window for the remainder of the drive, taking in the lights of the old-world buildings, the architecture signifying royalty. It's why I enjoy being here and how it differs from home.

"Are we in Westminster?" Zara murmurs.

"Millbank."

"Isn't this where Robert Pattinson lives?" I wait for her to explain further, and she rolls her eyes. "The hot vampire in *Twilight*."

"It's a beautiful part of the city," I note, not entertaining her question as Ben parks near the entrance to the building I call home while in London. Instead, I offer, "We'll take a walk in the daylight. I think you'll like it." Sliding out of the back seat, I offer a hand to help Zara out, closing the door behind her. She then follows me inside, past reception, where we take a private elevator to the sixth-floor penthouse. "There are five bedrooms, so you're welcome to crash here anytime."

"Thanks." She frowns. "Does anyone else live here?"

"No. Why?"

"Five bedrooms. That's huge, considering I'm staying in a hotel room where you can barely swing a cat. I assumed with the lack of skyrise apartments there is a housing shortage."

"Everything has a price." I pour myself a whiskey, one I'll enjoy. "The Italian restaurant downstairs is open until midnight," I offer, handing her a menu. "You said you're starving. Choose something."

Zara shakes her head. "No thanks. I probably won't stay long."

"Stay long enough to eat." I pluck the menu from her and add, "I'll get you the prawn linguine. It'll be a hell of a lot better than fast food." With a quick dial, I place the order downstairs. "A cup of tea while you wait?"

She smiles. "I'm still not a tea drinker."

"I thought you were blending…"

"Ha." She turns in a circle, surveying the penthouse living room. "This is fancy, although I'm not surprised. You're a Hendricks, so only the best."

Her annoyed tone irritates me. "Is that a problem for you?"

"No." She shakes her head, and her tangled emotions are immersed in the solitary word. "I don't know why I'm here. I really should go."

Before she takes the first step, I'm in her face. "I assumed we were going to talk." I take her hand and lead her to the bar. The moment I stare into her brown eyes, I'm captivated. Noir chocolate eyes. Sexy. Mysterious and a touch dangerous. It's what attracted me to Zara the moment we met. Her sass is a bonus. I force my gaze away from her lure and mix her a gin and tonic. "Come and sit with me. It's too beautiful a view to adore alone." Removing my tie, I loosen the top buttons of my shirt. "Come."

Taking both glasses, I lead her onto the terrace.

Zara inhales but doesn't say a word. I felt the same way when the agent showed me the apartment a year ago. The breathtaking views of the Thames and Houses of Parliament remind me of the abundant wealth in London, and I'm adding a nice portfolio to the Hendricks family name.

The hundred-foot private stone terrace is supported by huge round stone pillars, giving it a modern castle feel. Ficus trees trimmed into perfectly round balls offer the final touch of opulence. It's a stark contrast to my home in LA and a refreshing one, a small piece of the pie I'm after since London is one of the top luxury capitals of the world.

I point to the chairs. "Sit with me."

Zara takes a few mouthfuls of her gin before sitting. "Bringing me here is a form of bragging. If you wanted to talk or have company, we could have gone for a walk along the river."

"You want to take a walk?"

"Not now," she says bluntly, wrapping her arms around her waist as she stares toward Westminster Bridge.

I stand and slip off my suit jacket, draping it around her shoulders. "What's next for you, Zara?"

"For dessert?"

I smile at the first suggestion that comes to mind. "No." I take the seat beside her, lean back, and swirl the whiskey in the glass. "In life."

"What everyone else wants. World peace." She shakes her head as though it's a dumb question.

"My question was directed to London. I was under the impression you needed a change, and when I helped set up a job, I assumed you would take it as the first step in a career change. Yet I get the feeling you're on a gap year from college and working to pay for your party lifestyle."

"What?"

I take a sip of whiskey without looking at her, as I know I'm getting on her nerves. "You're still living in a hotel and probably blowing your money."

"What do you want me to do? I knew no one, and affordable rent was hard to find. I'm making new friends and asking if anyone wants to share a place with me." Now she's really pissed. "For your information, I am taking on extra projects and working on them some evenings. You simply don't see it. Besides, we don't all have access to the Hendricks' limitless funds." She throws back her drink and stands, tossing my jacket on the chair. "Thanks for the evening. It's been pleasant as always." She glares at me when I don't respond. "You're an ass."

In perfect timing, the door buzzer sounds. I get up and sidestep her, purposely ignoring Zara's remark. "You might change your mind about me being an ass after you taste the dish I ordered."

"You know what you can do with your dish..." she calls out as I leave to answer the door.

I laugh to myself. We'll see. I tip the pasta into fine China and get her some cutlery, tossing the bamboo fork in the trash. "Despite what you think of me, try it before you say no." I hand her the bowl and take a seat beside her.

She mumbles what sounds like 'thank you' before taking a bite and closes her eyes, making a pleasurable sound. "Oh my God, this is divine." With each mouthful, she releases a groan, sparking something inside me.

I wait for her to take the next bite to say what is on my mind. "I have an offer for you since you're a friend of the family."

She swallows the pasta. "Yeah? What is it?" she asks quickly without looking at me.

"You could stay here, rent-free. Save your money and climb the corporate ladder since you're more qualified than anyone else in that office."

She chokes on the last mouthful. "What do you know about my office?" She pokes her fork toward me. "I have been working hard late at night and some weekends to appeal to my boss as a dedicated worker and in good stead for the next promotion." Her eyes round. "Wait. You want me to live with *you*?" she questions condescendingly. "Are you mad? We'll argue all the time, and you'll get evicted," she says and laughs as though imagining it.

I wait for her mind to calm before saying more. "While the offer is to stay here rent-free, I would need a favor from you in return."

"Here we go. I knew you wouldn't do something that didn't help you in some way. What is it? I want to know, even though my answer is never in a million years could I live with you."

*Ouch.*

"Firstly, you wouldn't be living with me all the time. I'm here for a week once a month. So you get three weeks to yourself. While I am here, we'll still live our own lives."

She tilts her head, listening yet not convinced. "I can do the math."

"I'll work long hours, which is to your benefit. But there will be rules like no parties. It's the building's rule, not mine."

"It's irrelevant, but you haven't mentioned the favor?"

"I'm building relations while merging with a finance company here. To keep it short, I liaise with Harrison as he manages everything. However, his father, Sir James, owns everything and oversees it to the point of having the final say." I check she is keeping up. "He's a family man, and for some reason, he doesn't trust me."

She laughs, and I give her a moment to revel in her glee. "Oh, my God, you're serious. I think I like Sir James already."

"Good. Because I need you to pretend to be my

girlfriend and accompany me on dinner dates with Sir James' family."

Zara's eyes widen, and her mouth falls open. "Are you high?"

It's the reaction I was expecting. But I'm desperate for Sir James to consider my offer, and for that to happen, I need to appear settled in my personal life. It seems the man can smell a playboy a mile away, and he thinks I'll treat his company with the same abandon as my lovers. "Before you say no, let me show you around the apartment. You'll see how we'll easily manage residing together with our living quarters so far apart. Think of it as a business agreement and helping each other out."

I stand to lead Zara inside, but she doesn't make a move to follow. "I don't care how luxurious your penthouse is. I can't pretend to be your girlfriend. It will be a disaster, and Sir James will see through the lie. It won't end well for either of us."

ZARA

The man is insane.

Jobe is many things, and desperate isn't one of them. "Surely, you have a string of girls lining up for dinner dates." I imagine beautiful models and actors—at the same time— as I have listened to the rumors surrounding his personal life back home.

He gives me a typical Jobe look, then indicates for us to head inside, locking the terrace doors behind me. "I need someone I trust. Someone the family can count on."

"Why are you bringing the family into this? You're talking as though it's a personal favor from Penny because it's me."

He pours another drink. "I'm sure Penny has told you about our father's expectations. This is building the Hendricks' portfolio. *I* do not want to be the one to mess it up."

"Sounds like most of the pressure is on me, and none of

it has anything to do with me. Besides, fancy dinners are not my thing. I'll embarrass myself, then embarrass you. Your plan will backfire." My heart speeds up thinking about it.

*God, why am I even here? I should go…*

"Hey." Jobe is suddenly inches away from my face watching me carefully as though he is alerted to my pending anxiety attack. "You need to give yourself more credit. You're beautiful, lively, and perfect to be my partner."

I snort a laugh, but his voice is serious. "You really think I can do it?" I don't know why I said that because I'm not considering it even though Jobe has a convincing way about him.

"I trust you, Zara, if nothing else. I know you won't bring any harm to the family."

*Shit. He struck my Achilles.*

I shake my head. I'm so confused. If we were back in LA, I would say no without hesitation. For the last few minutes, a voice in the back of my head has been saying to stay and experience opulence even for a week until I find somewhere to move with my work friends.

"Think about it," he says gently. He leans closer, and I hold my breath. Only he moves past my face to my ear. "I *promise* it will all be pretend. Besides, you do owe me one," he whispers.

I close my eyes as his breath caresses my neck and quickly compose myself. "For sending one email?" I shoot back because my credentials did the rest. Yet, he does deserve some thanks in return. "One night. I'll do it for one dinner date. If, and I mean it's a big *if,* I find it tolerable because I can't imagine it being at all fun, then we try it on a week-to-week basis. If I want out, then you tell your boss we broke up."

He frowns at me. "Then I'll ensure it's fun."

I snort and laugh again. "You're delusional, Hendricks."

He smirks as if he knows a secret I'm not in on, and I don't trust what he's going to say next. "If you stay here a week, I'll make a wager you'll want this arrangement to work."

*Arrangement.* "I'm not bought that easily."

Jobe shoves his hands into his trouser pockets. "Everything has a price, Zara." When he grins, I want to slap it off his face.

"I'm doing you the favor, not the other way round. We are still negotiating the terms of the arrangement, and I'm still at the *it will never happen* end of the scale."

His expression shifts, and I hate the way he is staring at me. It's like he wants me, and it's giving all the wrong information because, like he said, it is merely a business agreement between us.

"All right, let's start with a tour of where you'll sleep."

"For one night," I repeat more to myself than him. Then, I pour myself a drink before I make the dumbest decision of my life.

Five bedrooms.

Seven bathrooms.

*Seven.*

What universe am I in?

My hands have a nervous tremor, so I grip the rail as we descend the circular staircase with what appears to be a gold railing. I glance up at the ceiling, which is double the height of any room in my hotel. Everywhere I look, there is classical elegance. While the amenities are modern, the old-world charm remains with the wooden paneling and original decorative plasterwork. Floor-to-ceiling glass French doors open from the kitchen to the stone terrace.

"I decided to keep some of the original design though I asked Penny for some insight in remodeling some other rooms."

*Please stop talking about Penny like she is ammunition to convince me to stay.*

"Down this hallway is the cinema room and the study."

I lean on the kitchen counter. "I don't need to see everything tonight." I let out a long, overwhelmed sigh.

"I have not shown you where I sleep."

"And I don't need to see your bed," I shoot back. "I want to go to mine. It's been a long week."

He nods slowly, his dark eyes watching me carefully. "You have the pick of the other four bedrooms. The pool and gym can wait for tomorrow."

"I haven't made a decision." I head the opposite way of Jobe.

He hasn't won *yet.* Then I catch sight of the skyline view and lose my breath at the beauty. If the mattress is even half as soft as this carpet, I'm done for.

And the Italian food was like heaven in my mouth.

Oh, God.

He's totally won.

Unfortunately, it was the best sleep I've had in a month. The perfectly soft mattress and divine sheets had me dreaming of another life.

I roll over and check the time on my phone. It's after seven, and the battery is almost dead. A remote control is on the bedside table. Curious, I press the button, and the drapes slide back, allowing sunlight to shine into my room.

Shards of light hit the mirrors on the wall and dresser, causing pretty reflections to dance around the room. It feels magical compared to my small hotel room. I push up and fluff the pillows behind me, taking in the direct view of the Thames River and the bridge.

*Could I live here?*

It's hard not to imagine a new life here. Walking along the Thames, meandering around Kensington Gardens, dining at the beautiful restaurants. Then I remember the deal.

I live here rent-free if I agree to be his fake girlfriend when he has dinner meetings with Sir James. He mentioned the dinners are held once a month when Jobe is in London. The rest of the time is mine to live here and do as I please.

It's appealing, yet equally scary when I think about the dinner dates with London's high society businessman. I don't have the skills to be the woman he wants me to be.

Suddenly, I'm distracted by the aroma of bacon and eggs wafting into my room.

*Is it coming from here or outside?*

My windows are shut.

*Is Jobe really cooking?*

I jump up and eyeball my dress from last night. There's something about putting on the same dress from the night before that makes me reckless. I open the wardrobe, and a white bathrobe hangs on a hook. I swear it's like being in a five-star hotel. The fabric is every bit as soft as it appears as I tie the band and head out to face the grumpiest man on the planet.

Before I have one foot in the kitchen, I freeze.

Jobe is shirtless, wearing only a pair of jeans and barefoot.

I have *never* seen him like this.

I definitely haven't seen his naked torso in daylight. Part of the cabinetry conceals my presence, and I take a moment to watch him reach up into a cupboard. His shoulder muscles are contracting, his abs taut, and even from here, I can count the definition between each muscle in a neat line from his chest to his…

I gasp, seeing a spray of dark hair peeking out from the band of his jeans since the top two buttons are undone.

He turns. "Morning, Zara. I take it you slept well." His smooth voice wraps around me like liquid caffeine waking me the fuck up.

Did he have someone stay over? God, part of me hopes so because he can't look this sexy *all the time* for no reason. But if I'm going to stay here, I don't want to see his just-fucked face. I don't want to be staring at his tanned, ripped body or clothes that expose a raw man all the time. It's not something I can handle. We are not that close, nor do I want to be. Hell, we aren't even friends.

I clear my throat. "I slept okay."

He stops flipping bacon in the pan and smirks.

"What?"

"Going by your hairstyle, I'd wager you slept exceptionally well."

Shit, I didn't even bother to check myself before the aroma of a cooked breakfast drew me out of the bedroom. I finger-comb my hair and ignore his subtle chuckles. "Excuse me, but I rushed out of the bedroom in confusion as to who could possibly be cooking or that the apartment might be on fire."

He raises one eyebrow. "Not a black stripe to be seen when I cook."

I lean one hip against the counter. "You cook regularly?"

"I need to eat, Zara," he says with sarcasm.

"I assumed you had a chef."

"I do have a chef in LA. He has worked for me for the past ten years. He also taught me how to cook, as I found it therapeutic. So much so he now works part-time. He has a young family, so it gives him time to be at home. I didn't change his salary as he will come to my aid any time I need him. When I can, I cook for myself."

The bread pops up from the toaster, and I jump. Nervously, I tighten my robe. I don't know Jobe as well as I thought.

*He cooks.*

He is paying his chef in LA even if he's not working for him, as he knows it benefits his young family. That speaks volumes about him.

"Can you please butter the toast?"

Could I be a tiny bit wrong about him being an asshole?

"Zara?"

Huh? "Oh yeah, sure."

He grabs glasses and pours the orange juice, placing breakfast on the table. "The juice is cold pressed. I did it earlier while you were sleeping." He hands me the tongs. "Ladies first."

We serve up our plates before I take a seat. A groan slips from my mouth after the first mouthful of bacon. "This is good."

"You sound surprised."

"Very. Though I'm curious if this is an act of convincing me to agree to your plan."

"I assure you it's not part of my plan, but if it's what it takes for you to say yes, then consider your breakfast cooked every Sunday morning while I'm here."

I take another bite. "You know, this could seal the deal," I say with a laugh.

He leans back into his chair and assesses me. "Done. Shall we go to your hotel and pack up your clothes after lunch?"

I choke on my food, causing pieces of bacon to shoot from my throat and onto my plate.

His eyes widen, but there is a hint of a smirk. "We can't have that lack of etiquette in front of Sir James."

Oh, God. I'm going to make a fool of myself in front of full-blown aristocracy. I'm trading my rent for my dignity, not exactly what I had in mind when I decided to reinvent myself in London.

This is going to be a huge mistake.

7

———

JOBE

Zara has packed her LA life into three suitcases.

I can't envision bringing so little to live in a foreign country. Apart from a few framed photographs of her family and friends, one including my brother and Penny holding their baby, the rest is mainly clothes. It intrigues me how Zara sold off most of her possessions, her past life meaningless to her. If it's a new life she craves, I'm going to help her achieve it. And I want to show her the privilege of not being committed to a relationship.

"We need to write down a set of house rules," she says, placing her luggage in her room.

"Later. You need to unpack, and then I'm taking you out for dinner."

"Already?"

"You'll need heels and a nice dress. Not to mention familiarity with the restaurants where we'll be with Sir

James, so it won't be overwhelming when we are on our first date."

She unzips her case.

*For the love of God, what a mess.*

"So tonight is not a proper date?"

"Tonight is practice." I walk out of the room because her mess overwhelms me, and that is no easy feat.

I open my laptop to a never-ending list of emails. Several are from Hayley, my PA, in Los Angeles, telling me to take action on certain emails as soon as possible.

Hayley has worked for me for the past eight years. Her work ethic exceeded my expectations and in time, I knew I could count on Hayley even as my partner to important functions and gala balls. People judge without intention when I continually attend meetings and special occasions with my PA or alone. They doubt my responsibility and integrity, and some older businessmen, like Sir James, have a dated opinion that my personal life reflects on business matters. If I cannot be loyal to one woman, then how can I be trustworthy in business negotiations?

My cell buzzes on the table with email alerts from Hayley. Why is she working this early on a Sunday?

I have everything open in front of me. Hayley is almost as competitive as me. It's why I pay her well. If I land this deal, her bonus triples.

I send her a text.

> Any news on Sir James' previous business partners?

She replies within seconds.

I lose track of time following up on emails and attending to business. When I glance up, Zara is standing in the kitchen, and I no longer have the desire to work.

"Wow," I murmur as though I have lost the ability to speak.

Her gold dress glimmers under the lights, the fabric hugging her curves and falling loosely from the hips. The cut is perfect, with a slight dip to show her cleavage, but still classy.

Where the hell does she wear this?

I close my computer and stand. "Gold suits you." Her eyes are outlined in black lines, with long seductive and mesmerizing lashes.

"Thank you. I bought it when I first arrived and haven't had a chance to wear it."

I stare at her plump, red lips as she speaks. I'm doing everything in my power not to take her face in my hands and kiss her. I've never forgotten the way she kissed me on the night we pretend to have forgotten.

"What?" I snap out of the trance.

"Is something wrong?"

"No, I'm remembering..."

Her gaze flicks over my face. "Remembering what?"

I shake my head. We can't do this now. My attraction to her on that first night will distract me from what we are really doing here.

"I'll call Ben and ask him to meet us out front in ten minutes. Would you like something to drink before we go?"

*Because I fucking do.* I need to pull myself together and remember this is a convenient arrangement for both of us.

I pour myself a whiskey, then change my shirt and tie. Walking back into the room, I'm finishing knotting my tie when Zara smiles as she approaches me. Then, with delicate hands, she helps me tighten it.

"If anyone were to own a gold tie, it's you." She grins, her eyes dancing with humor.

"Why do you find it amusing?"

She shrugs. "Franklin and you must own hundreds of ties. Girls love shoes, and you both like ties."

"It's not the only thing I love. Besides, what other use do you have for shoes?"

It takes her a moment to realize what I'm implying. Her makeup conceals the blush to her cheeks, but I see the shade of red on her neck. Her lips part, and I hope she is imagining being tied to the bed.

I know I am. With my gold tie, in fact.

"I assume you own other accessories. Otherwise, I'd be disappointed in the rumors." I like the way Zara thinks.

"Rumors are just that. You have first-hand knowledge, after all."

Her ruby-red lips part, yet she says nothing.

I throw back the rest of my whiskey and head to the door. I wait for her to walk out before locking it behind me. In the elevator, we remain silent, but when the doors open, she holds my arm to stop me. "What are we doing?" Her eyes are wide and afraid.

"Having dinner like I promised."

"I'm going out to dinner with my best friend's brother-in-law. Behind her back. This is wrong."

"You could tell her," I say wryly.

"I... no way."

I pretend to be insulted rather than hurt by the sting of her horrified tone and say nothing, waiting for her decision.

"Okay." She attempts to rally herself. "Yeah, okay."

I place a hand on her lower back as we walk out onto the street. Inside the car, I check my emails for Hayley's update. Nothing.

The restaurant is a small drive from my penthouse, and paparazzi line the pavement.

"My God, what's happening?" Zara murmurs.

"The White Orchid is where the stars like to dine. Just smile and walk past. They're probably waiting for Kylie Minogue or Elton John."

"For real?"

As we step out, I nod to a cameraman I've seen many times and turn my head the opposite way when his camera flashes. Zara remains tight to my side, and when I check on her, she is focused on the ground ahead. I pull her close, an instinct to keep her safe. "It's okay," I say gently as I guide her to the door. I should not feel this content being on a fake date with Zara, yet my gut is telling me it's exactly what I want.

Inside the foyer, the waitress leads us to a table by a window. I keep hold of her hand until we are seated. "May I get you something to drink?"

I glance at Zara skimming over the menu, and then her eyes round. Taking the initiative, I ask, "Would you like a bottle of Dom?"

"I-I... um..." she stutters.

"One bottle of Dom Pérignon and a glass of Blanton's La Maison du Whisky."

Zara is watching me. "I could have drank the house sparkling wine."

"Not here. We're practicing for the next date, and if you prefer to drink anything else, then I need to know. Because a boyfriend knows what their girlfriend likes to drink." Fuck, that sounds good coming out of my mouth.

She rolls her lips while my words sink in. "It's expensive, and I know it's what you would drink out with your friends, but I don't. Besides, if I had to drink a bottle on my own, I'd get smashed and say the wrong thing..." She pauses and looks at me.

*Does she remember?*

The magnetic heat of our bodies moving together. The broken cries as she begged me for more. The way she burrowed against my side, practically purring, when we finally stopped to sleep. And if she remembers, is this her way of telling me she thinks it was wrong?

I clear my throat as the waitress returns, popping the champagne. I gesture to Zara. "For the lady."

Zara takes a sip while I swirl the golden liquid in my glass. She is watching me, my gaze locked with hers. "Have you always drank whiskey?"

"I prefer Michter's. Franklin favors Blanton's, and for years, it was a debate in our family about what was best. So now, I enjoy Blanton's after drinking with him for years."

She nods. "What else should I know about you?"

"About me or Hendricks Reality?"

Her shoulders rise and fall. "*You,* Jobe. I wouldn't care for your work as much as I care for you *if* I were your girlfriend."

I stare at her for a few seconds, mulling over her words. "I disagree since my work means setting up a future for us. You'd want to secure the contract as much as I do."

She shakes her head. "I wouldn't. The value of money doesn't mean to me what it does to you. This is exactly why I'm wrong for the job. Sir James will see through me. See through us." She links her fingers near her face as though she's begging then rests her forehead on her knuckles before looking up at me. "You need to find someone who can act as I suck at make-believe."

I signal to the server to fill her glass, and then I give her a minute. "You're not wrong for the job. If I start talking about my family, you can add to the conversation. It will come naturally to you. Tonight, we'll talk about our favorite foods at our favorite restaurant."

The waitress appears, and judging by Zara's expression, she is far from ready to order a meal. "Can you please give us a moment longer?" I ask and wait for her to leave before I continue. "Do you want me to order for both of us?"

She raises her perfectly sculpted brows. "Then you wouldn't know what I like."

I smile. "True." She lifts the menu from the table, and I can see she's going to need some guidance for this to work. "Zara. Leave the menu on the table."

She places it down and frowns.

"Here are some quick pointers. Never lift the menu from the table. Raise it with some touching the table." She's still frowning and tilts it at a perfect angle. She picks up her glass to take a sip while reading the menu. "It's preferable you drink from the same spot of your glass so you don't leave a lip ring."

The comment causes her to roll her eyes. "My lipstick does not leave lip rings." She smacks her lips together as though to prove a point, and when she puckers them, I find myself smiling.

*Fuck, she has no idea how hot she is.*

"If you get excited, never clink your glasses with others. I know you like to 'cheers,' but it is fine glassware. The less noise, the better."

"How do you know I like to cheers?" she asks.

"I've seen you with Penny when you're out."

Her face falls, and I realize mentioning Penny's name

can be a trigger for her. I focus on more tips to distract her. "Do you like oysters?"

"Feeling horny, Jobe?"

Jesus, how am I going to get through a night with her when my thoughts flick back to our night together? "If there are no forks on the table..." I continue, in an attempt to be serious, "... do not ask for one, as it means the oyster is loosened, and you can simply use your knife."

"Easy."

"Keep the rim of your plate as clean as possible."

"Got it. Now, can we talk about the menu?"

We talk about the appetizers and mains and our preferences. Zara likes steak, seafood, and pasta—everything I do. "It should be a piece of cake. You're not fussy at all."

She pops a shoulder. "I used to be. Ate what my boyfriends preferred me to eat. I'm done with that shit and happy the way I am. I'm all about enjoying the things I love."

I smile at her. While I love seeing her new confidence, I'm curious about what douchebag had her feeling she wasn't good enough. And her choice of words tells me I should mention cussing. "With me, you may cuss as much as you wish. When we're with Sir James, we need to be mindful."

"Of course."

The waitress returns, and I order prawns and oysters, then the lobster for our mains.

"Practicing our fake relationship is going to cost you."

"It will cost me more if we fuck it up," I whisper.

"Do I need to remind *you* about cussing," she says in her posh voice.

*Cute.*

"How much is this deal worth to you?" She takes a sip of her champagne, eyeing me.

"A billion or so."

She coughs, choking on the champagne, and it sprays from her lips. "Oh, no, no, *no*. I'm not doing this. I'm not going to be the one to blame." She stands and dabs the champagne droplets on the table with her napkin. "Pretend our arrangement was never mentioned because I'm out."

"Sit down, Zara."

"Don't tell me—"

"We are meeting Sir James tomorrow. The arrangement is already in place."

She folds her arms. "I'm not doing it."

"You're making a scene." She glances around and slowly lowers into her velvet-backed chair, downing the entire contents of her glass. She goes to refill, and I place a hand over hers to stop her. "Wait for the server, please." Her chest is rising up and down faster than normal. "You're going to be fine. I wouldn't have asked you if I didn't think you could do it."

She closes her eyes and slowly shakes her head. "It's not worth it. I know the expectations of your family. I don't live like that."

"Some risks pay off."

Her eyes round. "A billion-dollar risk?"

"Everything will be fine. Be yourself. Be patient. If you're nervous, then tell me, and I'll guide you through it."

The lobster arrives, and Zara has finished her third glass of champagne. "I'm no longer hungry." She moans.

"Eat, Zara. You can't survive on champagne alone."

Waiting for her to take her first bite before I continue eating, I feel like a piece of shit for making her nervous. Zara has potential, and I need to show her that taking a risk can be beneficial to more than your own means. Her long lashes flutter as she forces herself to swallow every mouthful.

She's clueless about her task being significantly easier than my end of the deal. While in London, how am I going to live with Zara and manage to keep the relationship between us platonic? Right now, I want to take her in my arms and tell her everything is going to be okay.

Then do a hell of a lot more than that.

# 8

ZARA

WHEN I AGREED to help Jobe last night, I didn't know what I was expecting, but it wasn't being the pawn in a billion-dollar deal.

Arriving home, he asked about my dress and shoe size, then stared at me like I was dessert. The anticipation faded before anything else was said when he turned his back and walked toward his bedroom.

He was gone when I woke.

Now, I'm sitting in a café across the road from my office block, though this morning, I need something stronger than coffee to get me through the day.

Piper walks into the café at the same time she has every other weekday. "Have you been here a while?" She adjusts her bag's strap over her petite shoulder and lays a box on the table.

"Yeah, I couldn't sleep. Are these mine?"

"Chocolate muffins today." She smiles at me. "Do you want another cup?"

"Sure. Thank you, and I need a sneaky bite now."

She slides into the chair opposite me. "What time is our first meeting?"

I check my emails. "Ten o'clock."

"If Grant asks me to do any more of his shit jobs, I'm resigning. I've been here long enough to get a promotion."

"I think he likes you," I offer with a smile.

"What? He grunts every time he speaks to me as though I'm wasting his time."

"Some men are like that. If he's getting your attention with shitty behavior, then he'll keep being an ass."

She fiddles with her long, blonde ponytail. "So, how do I get him to stop?"

I take a bite of her muffin and groan with pleasure. "Ignore him, so he needs to change his behavior to get your attention, or you tell him you don't appreciate the way he speaks to you. If he continues, then go to HR. You don't have to put up with his crap even if he likes you."

Our coffees arrive, and she takes a sip. "He is kind of cute."

*No, he's not.*

"What's the office policy here? Are relationships allowed?"

"Why wouldn't they be?"

I'm not about to give her a lesson in heartbreak or losing your job because your male colleague dumped you and fake excuses were made for your dismissal. She is more than ten years younger than me and has a life of lessons ahead of her. However, I will warn her when the time is right.

I finish my coffee and stand. "I'm heading up as I need to start work. I'm finishing early as I have a ..." What is it? "I'm meeting a friend for dinner."

"That sounds like fun."

"I'd rather stand barefoot on tar in one hundred and twenty degrees."

She screws up her face. "How many?"

"Oh yeah, whatever it is in Celsius." I need to study that more as I haven't yet worked out the British metric system.

"So why are you going?" she asks, wiping milk froth from her lips.

I let out a sigh. "I agreed to the arrangement before I..." *Before I knew how much money was involved? Before I thought it through?* "It's only one night," I say more for my benefit. "I'll see you in the office."

When I walk into Jobe's penthouse that evening, there are boxes on the floor and dresses hanging on a wheeled rack.

*What the...*

He is nowhere in sight and presumably not yet home from work. I retrieve my cell from my bag to text him.

> Why is there a rack of dresses here?

Before I get a chance to walk into the bathroom, he has sent a reply.

> If you like any, keep them. Accessorize with the shoes, jewelry, and bags.

What is happening?

I throw my phone on the bed and head to the shower. By the time I have finished applying my makeup and styling my hair, there is still no word from Jobe.

I keep wiping my hands on my robe when I play out

tonight in my head. What if I say something that's inappropriate? Surely, this is doomed before we even start.

Out on the terrace, I stare at the view of London and the people walking near the river. The stone terrace calms my erratic mind. In the street below, I watch as a black sedan stops, and Jobe emerges from the back seat, then disappears from view, heading inside. A minute later, the door whooshes open, and he stops in his tracks when he sees me.

"Did you choose a dress?" He rushes past me toward his room.

"Good day to you too."

"We have ten minutes to be downstairs," he fires over his shoulder.

Jesus, if he's stressed, who is going to calm me?

JOBE HAS BEEN TALKING ON HIS CELL SINCE WALKING OUT OF his room. He mouthed, *lovely*, when he saw me, then continued his conversation, leaving me to sit in awkward silence.

By the time we arrive at the restaurant, he is still in a heated conversation as he leans over to open the car door. When I don't move, he stares at me expectantly. "Zara, we're here," he says, moving his cell away from his face.

"I know, and you haven't uttered a word to me. I'm not ready to go in."

He looks intently at me. "I'll call you later," he barks into the phone. "Don't do anything until I give you further direction." He pops his cell in his suit jacket and slides back into the car. "What is it?"

Those sexy dark eyes search my face. Is he really this clueless? "You haven't spoken a word to me. Barely acknowledged my dress and if you liked it."

"I said you looked lovely," he counters.

"I need to look better than lovely," I snap. "If we're going to pull this off, then the conversation between us needs to happen before we leave the house. I'm not a professional actor and don't have a switch I flick on or off to be in character mode."

He yanks the door closed. "Ben, please continue driving for a few minutes."

"You said you'd be here for me, and yet you've ignored me since you arrived home."

"I haven't ignored you, Zara. I'm still working. It sucks, but this is my life. I don't have a finish time."

I glance down at my hands, where I'm fidgeting with the purse strap. Maybe I'm being immature, but he could have acknowledged me and the work I put in to make myself presentable. Is it so hard for a guy to tell a girl she looks beautiful? Even if she isn't beautiful in his eyes, the time it takes to get ready for a date should be recognized.

His large, warm hand covers mine to still my fingers. "It's going to be fine. Stop worrying. Be yourself, and everything will work out the way it should."

"Will it?"

"It will. He'll be besotted with your beauty and then charmed by your personality." He smiles, and while I thought I wanted to hear the validation, it doesn't calm me in the least.

"Am I a ploy? The takeover is a business matter, not a show-off-your-shiny-toy at a business meeting." I'm not sure why I waited until now for my feminist side to show her face.

He rubs the side of his jaw before meeting my gaze. "We agreed on this. He needs to see how much we're in love, so he believes there is an element of trust and commitment in my character. Your beauty is a benefit. Not a ploy. While we'll discuss some business matters, it's the light conversation about family that will seal his belief, and no one knows my sister-in-law better than you."

I'm stuck on the part where he says we need to act as though we're *in love*.

"But I like being single," I murmur. I have embraced it and have no desire to start an unhealthy relationship again.

"And so do I," he shoots back. "Everyone has the potential to act and pretend to be someone they're not. Remind yourself of your douchebag ex-boyfriends and how they fooled you at the beginning of your relationship."

He manages to make me smile by calling my exes douchebags and for taking my side. But he has a point. Everyone plays pretend at some point in their lives.

Ben pulls up at the restaurant, and Jobe waits for me to acknowledge him. "Are you ready?"

I take a deep breath in and nod. "I'm ready."

Jobe exits the car and opens my door, taking my hand and keeping a firm hold on it as we walk toward the restaurant doors. He's handsome in his ivory suit and white shirt with a black tie. I also never told him how gorgeous and ridiculously hot he looks, though I'll never admit those exact words to him. "You look handsome, yourself," I whisper.

He turns to me and smiles. A smile that melts panties and surges hormones all over the world. Tonight, it's enough to ease my nerves. He squeezes my hand, a comforting touch as we follow the server around white, cloth-covered tables with tall candles as centerpieces in brass holders.

A round table is set for six. Three men are already seated and stand as we approach. Jobe makes the introductions and the two other men, one being Sir James' son, Harrison, shake my hand. The other is Clive, a business partner.

As I approach Sir James, he smiles and doesn't appear at

all threatening. He's about my size, almost a foot shorter than Jobe. He has thinning gray hair and a medium build. However, his designer gray suit suits him. His demeanor oozes sophistication.

"Zara," he says gently and raises my hand, kissing the top of it. Did Jobe expect him to charm me? "I eagerly awaited meeting the lady who has tamed Jobe Hendricks. Why has he kept you a secret?"

I smile nervously and sneak a glance at Jobe. His nod is subtle. "We decided to wait a few months until it felt right to be together in public. You know how the tabloids fabricate material."

I stare at Jobe with starry eyes. I might actually be good at this acting thing. Jobe comes to stand beside me and wraps a hand around my waist. My breath hitches, but my fake smile remains broad.

"Come darling, the staff is waiting for us." With a hand on my lower back, Jobe pulls out my chair for me to sit and takes the seat beside me. Sir James sits on my other side.

*Stop shaking. You can do this.*

"My apologies for my wife's absence. She became unwell today and decided to rest in bed," Sir James shares, leaving me as the only female at the corporate business world table.

*Fun.*

The server comes to take our order, and I casually ask for a bottle of Dom Pérignon Oenotheque Champagne Rose, as though it's my choice of drink every day. The men order expensive red wine, except for Jobe. He sticks with his favorite whiskey.

In silence, we peruse the menu for a few minutes, and I notice there is barely any noise coming from the other tables.

*I must not drop my cutlery on the floor or even on my plate for that matter.*

I repeat it in my head because there's a high probability I will and bring attention to our table. Jobe leans close. "Order the seafood. It's also Sir James' favorite," he whispers.

His breath dusts my neck, and I tilt my head toward him. One little tickle leaves me wanting to be closer to him. *Focus.* I see what he's doing, and I'll follow Sir James' lead. He needs to trust me.

Leaving the menu partially on the table, I decide on a few dishes that caught my eye last night. Jobe was right in dining here last night as I'm not as uncomfortable being here a second time.

When the server arrives, Sir James orders first. If it's a hierarchy of importance, then I assume I'm to order last. When Sir James finishes, everyone looks at me.

"And the lady?" the server asks.

"Oh." Sir James ordered the steak—the most expensive one on the menu. "I'll have the same as Sir James, please." I smile at Sir James and catch Jobe's shocked expression in the corner of my eye. I know it's not about the cost but the fact I deliberately defied his advice.

Well, buckle up, Hendricks, because I got this. After a couple of glasses of Dom, I'll be nominated for an Oscar.

"How is Rachel?" Jobe asks Harrison.

"Doing better. Four weeks until our son arrives." He smiles at us and then looks at his father, who isn't paying attention. Sir James is having a quiet conversation with Clive.

"You know it's a boy?" I pipe up and hope I'm not overstepping a line.

"Yes. After two very loud girls, it will be nice not to be the only male in the house."

I laugh. "Yes, girls are not quiet. How old are your daughters?"

"Four and nine. Although Phillipa, the oldest, acts as though she is going on nineteen."

I laugh again. "Girls always want to be older than their age. Do you have any photos?" His eyes dance with delight as he hands his cell to me. "Oh, they are beautiful. You must be very proud."

"I am. They keep me on my toes for sure."

I rest a hand on Jobe's thigh, and he leans into the back of his chair as though he can finally relax.

I smile at Harrison. "I can't wait to have children. All my life, I've wanted twins."

Jobe subtly coughs up a mouthful of whiskey and tenses beside me.

*Liar, liar, pants on fire.*

Suddenly, Sir James is interested in our conversation.

"I know it's early days between Jobe and I, but I believe in making your plans clear from the early stages of a relationship. No pretenses. Be transparent from the beginning."

Sir James sits forward so he has Jobe in his view. "You didn't mention this."

"No. I'm aware it's what Zara wants. If we're together in another six months, then we can discuss it further."

I peer at Sir James, rather pleased with myself. "He hasn't run away," I say with a grin.

Sir James' lips part into a smile. "No. Even though you were clear with your goals, I like your honesty, Zara."

"Jobe is wonderful with children. Franklin, Jobe's brother, and his wife, Penelope, have a daughter. She's only a few months old, but if Franklin was on a business trip during her pregnancy, Jobe would be the one helping her in any way he could. Penelope is my friend. It's how Jobe and I met."

*Shit, am I saying too much?*

"And seeing how wonderful he is and a fabulous uncle to his new niece, I'm convinced he'll make a wonderful father."

"Okay, darling," Jobe pipes up. "No one wants to hear about me having a soft side. I have a serious business reputation to uphold."

"I would like to hear." Sir James leans back into his chair, wine glass in his hand. "There is much I don't know about Mr. Hendricks."

I'm unsure if he says it in sarcasm, but it gives my motor mouth a green light. "One night, we couldn't settle Summer, Penny and Frank's baby," I add and glance around the table, making eye contact. "Jobe walked the hallways until she was asleep on his shoulder." I glance at Jobe and smile as I rub his thigh affectionately. He's frowning, and his eyes tell me he's unamused by my storytelling skills. I'm sure he's a little nervous about what I'll say next.

*Relax, honey. I've got this.*

There's something empowering about captivating everyone's attention at a dinner table. "Diapers." I wave my hand. "Not a problem."

"I assumed this a chore for the nanny?" Sir James asks.

"Right? Penelope is grounded and is a hands-on type of mother. She has also requested we all stay involved in Summer's life, and we rotate babysitting duties so she recognizes us from a young age." I'm smiling broadly as the words roll off my tongue since it's not a lie. The immensity of the truth hits me.

It was all my best friend wanted, and I ran out on her.

My throat burns as I'm hit with the reality of my own words. I pick up my drink and take a few sips while the rest of the guests watch on.

Jobe leans into me with a calming hand on my back. "Zara misses them. She is on a working visa for twelve months in one of my partner companies. Fortunately, she gets to travel home with me for short breaks to see my family and her friend."

I nod vehemently, agreeing with his lie. "It's true. I miss them, but I also want to take the opportunity to absorb everything London has to offer while I'm here. Once I return home, I'll have no regrets for when I settle into motherhood." I take another sip of my champagne, but it's bitter on my tongue.

*Why is this such an easy lie for them to swallow? That every woman must yearn to be a mother.*

For the last two years, I've come to terms with remaining single for the rest of my life, and I'm happier for it. It's been significantly harder to find peace in not wanting children. The societal expectation is so intense. No one even assumes that it's a choice. Instead, it's always a given. My chest aches at having to act the opposite of my truth.

For the next half hour, I remain quiet while the men talk business, delicately breaking my bread and buttering the piece I'm about to eat while leaving the remainder on the plate.

My etiquette is on beat.

The main meals are presented, and I'm relieved the night is coming to an end.

Sir James asks for the bill, then we all stand. Jobe thanks the men for their hospitality and mentions he'll see them tomorrow.

While Sir James and he continue in quiet conversation, I continue the rouse and step to Clive and shake his hand. "It was lovely to meet you." Then I step sideways to Harrison. "Thank you again. I hope everything goes well for Rachel. I can't wait to see photos of your new baby boy."

"Thank you, Zara. I'll send the photos to Jobe as soon as he's born."

I smile. "I'd like that very much."

Then I'm standing face to face with Sir James, and our eyes meet. There is no judgment, which surprises me. "Thank you, sir, for a lovely night. It was an honor to meet you." I hold out my hand to shake his.

Sir James takes my hand, then covers the top of my hand with his other one. "The pleasure is all mine. It was a delight to meet you, Zara." He looks at Jobe, then back to me. "Don't be a stranger. If you need anything at all while Jobe is away, please reach out to us."

*Wow.*

"Thank you, that is very kind."

"Jobe, please pass on our contact details to Zara."

He nods and shakes all their hands once more.

As soon as we are in the confines of his car, Jobe lets out a long breath. "Did you have to bring babies into the conversation, Zara?"

"Are you serious?" After everything, these are his first words? "You wanted me to act. And since women who don't want children are judged harshly in any social circle, I did what I thought you wanted me to do, even though I hated it. Even though it hurt. I came to London to find myself and to embrace the part of me that doesn't want what women are expected to want. And there I was, back to square one *for you.* You could at least say thank you."

He is silent for a long time, then quietly offers, "Thank you."

Something about his apology calms me. "I didn't mean to go overboard, especially since it's furthest from the truth for both of us."

"He did like you, and you certainly fooled him. It seems this deal needs to happen faster than predicted. Otherwise, we might need to act like a wedding is on the cards."

"Or we break up," I mutter.

When the car stops in front of the penthouse, we wearily head inside, neither of us speaking a word. The elevator doors open, and we end up in the kitchen together. Surprisingly, Jobe pours another glass of whiskey instead of going to sleep as I assumed he would since he'll be in the office tomorrow.

"Can I get you a drink?" he asks without even a look my way.

"No, thank you. I think I've consumed enough champagne for one night. I'd hate to say the wrong thing again."

He swirls the whiskey in his glass, something I notice he does when he's pondering or before he's about to speak. "Zara, can you sit with me a while?"

*God, please don't be nice to me.*

It's much easier when he's being an ass.

Then, at least, I'm not tempted to do something I'll regret.

# 9

———

ZARA

THERE IS something about his tone, raw and emotional, that makes me agree to stay up and speak with him. "Give me a moment to change out of this dress." Changing into my sweatpants and a T-shirt, I remove the jewelry and carry the dress to the living room, hanging it on the rack. "What are you going to do with all these gowns?"

"Did you try them on to see if they fit since you'll be wearing all of them?"

"All of them?" *How long do we have to play this game?*

"If they are not your style, then go shopping, and I'll give you my card to pay for them."

*Give me his card.* He makes it sound so easy. Instead of being grateful, I'm annoyed. "I'm sure I'll find something. Please thank your stylist for me." Tonight is not the time to express myself. I need to make peace if we're going to live together for one week a month. It's not a big ask, and I need to show him more gratitude.

Part of my frustration is not being in a financial position to make decisions with the ease he does. I assumed by coming to London, I would gain control over my life, and yet again, I'm leaning on him to help me until I find somewhere else to live. I'd heard London was an expensive city, and I now know why multiple people live in those tiny townhouses.

Tomorrow at work, I'll start asking for advice on the best places to live and if anyone knows of someone looking to house share. Thank God my new job provided free rent in the hotel to help me settle in. However, I'm excited to have a beautiful kitchen to start cooking meals in instead of ordering takeout most nights.

Walking around the couch, I take a seat beside him.

"Sweatpants?" he asks.

"Don't judge me. There's nothing better than sweats at the end of the day when you want to relax." He raises an eyebrow, staring at me like he can't relate. "Wait... you don't own any?"

"I have worn some to train or run in, but no, they are not lounging attire, although Byron would beg to differ."

"If we are going to be a couple, then you need to wear sweats. Couples who dress down together stay together," I joke.

"I don't think that's a thing," he mutters.

I backtrack fast so he doesn't get the wrong idea. I know we'll never be a couple. We are opposites in every way, and we frustrate each other equally. "Luckily, we don't need to worry about it, so you can laze around in your designer suits."

He's staring as though he wants to say something but pauses as if deciding against it. After a heavy pause, he finally begins, "We need to discuss some other matters. I can arrange for a chef to speak with you on meal preference if that's what you'd like. It will make nights easier for you."

"My nights…" I'll be alone and have plenty of time to cook for myself. "Thank you for the offer, but I'd rather arrange my own meals and shop for my own food." He nods slowly, and whatever is on his mind, I wish he'd say it. "Anything else?" I press.

"We should set some ground rules for appearance's sake so there are no loopholes to be caught out."

"Loopholes?"

"If we're *together,* then we act so in public even when we're not. If either one of us behaves badly and is photographed, there is every chance Sir James will see the images. So let's prevent that entirely. And before you say anything, the man has contacts."

"Contacts like spies?" I say in jest.

"Yes. So when you're with your friends, please act as though you have a boyfriend."

I narrow my eyes at him. "For how freaking long? I didn't come here to be locked away, pining for my man to come home."

"Please be mindful, that's all I ask." He sips his whiskey and stares toward the terrace.

"You need to follow the same rules," I bite back. "Even when you're in LA because if either of us are going to be photographed in public, it's going to be you."

Jobe turns and holds my gaze. His intense mood crackles the air between us. "I have every intention of honoring my end of the agreement. This business deal is my priority over everything else."

I swallow hard, understanding the meaning of his words, and clarify, "No casual sex, not even in your home, because *you* could be photographed."

"Let's see how long we both last," he mumbles into his glass before taking a sip.

"Piece of cake for me," I shoot back. "My record is six months, thirteen days, and eleven hours." I grin, hoping he finds some humor in my sad sex life, though I can't tell him about my current time since he was my last.

Instead, his eyes round. "Months, not weeks?"

I laugh. "One of us is going to suffer more than the other. But since you're the one to gain the most, I think it's a small sacrifice." I push up from the couch. "Anything else?"

"None that I can think of. Hayley will email you with some more instructions."

*Email me...*

"I'm looking forward to signing the *fun* contract," I mock. Move over *Fifty Shades,* Jobe Hendricks has reinvented the pleasure wheel.

"Night, Zara." He sips his whiskey without turning my way.

"Night, fun-slayer."

THE FOLLOWING DAY, I'M HAVING LUNCH WITH MY COWORKERS, and the conversation leads into the weekend. I want to hang out with them, but I'm going to have to figure out a way to drop hints about the fact I'm seeing someone. If I'm going to play this game for him, it needs to appear real.

I mull over that for a moment.

Why am I playing his game when all I have to do is find someone else to live with, and I won't need to stay with him? The sooner I have a conversation with my friends, the quicker I can move out. Ugh, my stomach. It's the same dull feeling I get when I let someone I care about down. My stupid subconscious wants to do the right thing. It's not that

I owe Jobe a thing. But I do care about Penny and Frank, and if they knew what Jobe was doing to secure the contract and I ruined it, I'd feel bad even though it's wrong to lie about our relationship to Sir James. I'm damned if I do and damned if I don't. But if I had a choice, I'd choose to do it for Penny—even if she is unaware of my good deed.

Hopefully, it makes up for running out on her.

Is my happiness selfish?

*It's only for one year...*

Anna and Lydia laugh out loud. *Shit, snap out of it.* I fake a smile and nod, listening and hoping to catch up on the conversation as it veers to the coming weekend.

"Are you in, Zara?" Piper asks. "It's going to be fun."

"Before I say yes, tell me more about the place," I say, acting interested.

"It's a beach house," Anna adds with a shrug. "Not your average beach house, as my sister's boyfriend is loaded. But we can stay all weekend, and go for beach strolls, and have some fun at night. Bring the booze you want to drink, and we'll go grocery shopping there."

"How far away is it?"

"It's Sandbanks. So about two hours." They stare at me again as though I should know this information.

"Sorry, I'm still learning the location of places."

"This is prime real estate we get to stay in. Compare it to Miami."

"Then it should be fun," I add.

Anna turns to George who is acting far more enthusiastically than me. "Are you bringing Corey?"

"No, he's acting like a little bitch lately."

Anna giggles. "Then it's set. No partners."

Sounds like the perfect weekend.

Back at the office, we separate as we head into private meetings. I'm not sure what's happening because after Piper returns to her desk on the opposite side of me, she slumps forward before logging back onto her computer.

"Is everything okay?" I whisper.

She pops one shoulder. "I guess you'll hear soon enough, even though we're told not to discuss anything with coworkers. The company is downsizing before a major change. Tim didn't go into detail. He wanted to give us notice and an option of being made redundant. I haven't been here long enough to reap benefits, and although I'll have a job, it might be a different role." She shakes her head. "I can't afford a demotion or to lose my job. I might need to search elsewhere because I have one more year of university remaining, and I have to stick it out until I graduate," she says in a hushed voice.

Tim appears at the front of the room and calls George to follow him into his office.

I lean closer to Piper. "Do you think anyone will lose their jobs today?"

She shakes her head and closes her eyes. "I hope not. It's unaffordable to live here and not work."

*Hmm.* "Are you from here?"

She shakes her blonde locks. "Sheffield."

For her to move back home is out of the question. "Who do you live with?"

"A friend from university, but she graduates this year, so I'm not sure what's happening there either. The timing sucks."

Part of me is grateful to be with Jobe albeit temporarily, so now I can put the wheels in motion for us all to move in together. "What about Anna?"

"She lives at home. Her parents live in Croydon."

I do a subtle eye roll.

"What?"

"Croydon is the name of a certain ex-boyfriend." One I have tried to forget.

"Oh. It's okay, great for sports and if you're a foodie. We should go there sometime with Anna when her parents go on one of their many international holidays."

"I'm up for *any* travel," I emphasize. Even to Croydon because I need a better image than the one in my head reminding me of one certain fuckface ex-boyfriend.

She smiles. "Anna wants to stay at home until she finishes university. It takes her less than an hour on the train, so it's financially viable for her. On weekends, she stays with either George or me."

We could all benefit from a shared apartment.

I continue reading emails until George returns to his desk, three rows ahead of me. He sits quietly and resumes working. I can't tell if he perceived the news as good or bad.

What if I'm terminated because I'm the new girl, my role is relatively new, and before the probation time has lapsed? If I'm fired so soon after starting, my extra work won't have time to pay off with a promotion to the human resources department.

"Zara." I glance up to Tim standing near my desk. "Can we talk in my office, please?"

"Sure." I sign out of my computer and follow him along a hallway, my heels clicking with every step. His assistant glances up from her desk and stares at my feet. It sounds like I'm wearing tap shoes and ready to dance when my insides feel like I'm heading to my career funeral.

He closes the door behind me, and it's the first time I have seen his office. The walls are dark gray with timber structures accentuating thoughtful architecture. His oak desk faces the window that overlooks the London skyline.

"Please take a seat."

"Thank you." I sit forward in the black leather chair and

cross my legs, taking a deep breath to compose my nerves. It's not my first rodeo in a boss's office to discuss my value as an employee. In my head, I run over reasons why I deserve to hold my position and my value to the company. Remind him of my experience.

"I'm sure your coworkers have mentioned that Warburton Investments is about to experience some changes. While these changes were in motion over the past year, the process accelerated over the last month, and a sister company will be joining us."

"Sir, is the merger going to affect my new role?"

His eyes widen. "Yes and no."

*Fuck.*

"Your role, among others, will be reduced." He holds my gaze, and I assume the others he mentions are Piper, Anna, and me, and others. "However, in another month, we'll have Board changes and require new executive assistants. Since you have experience in HR and have been delivering exceptional work on additional projects since you started, you are currently best suited for the position."

*What?*

I'm gaping at my boss. I can't find the words to thank him as my brain was fired up, ready to defend my value.

I never expected this.

"There will be an interview panel as we are required to advertise the position, but the Board wants you to work alongside Gretchen, who is the CEO's executive assistant."

I nod three times to make a point. "Thank you." Butterflies upset my stomach. "Sorry, sir, I'm shocked. I expected my coworkers to be considered before me."

"You'll be privy to information not yet shared with other employees. We need it to remain confidential until a formal statement is released."

"Yes, sir."

"When I know more, I'll let you know, but right now, while I'm following the rules, I'm also a bit in the dark."

I nod. "I understand. Will you be announcing my new position to my coworkers?" It's the last thing I want in case of backlash or losing friendships if anything goes south.

"Not as yet, though tomorrow I'll formally introduce you to Gretchen."

I nod and leave the room, closing the door quietly behind me. Then I take a deep breath of relief while excitement replaces nervousness, knowing my hard work has paid off.

When I arrive home from work, I change into casual clothing and take a walk along the Thames. Finally, my life is falling into place. With an extra spring in my step, I smile at strangers as they pass. It's not until the air turns chilly that I head back to Jobe's penthouse, unsure whether I'll see him tonight.

I unlock the front door and tepidly walk in, looking around for him with my every step. The apartment is quiet, too quiet.

Opening the refrigerator to decide on what to cook, I grab some vegetables, but when I turn around, I'm startled and jump, almost dropping my dinner's ingredients.

Jobe is sitting on a barstool at the counter. His eyes meet mine, though he doesn't acknowledge that he's scared the shit out of me.

"Zara."

"Jobe."

"Are you cooking dinner?"

"Would you like me to cook you dinner? I should have

asked but when I didn't hear from you, I was unsure whether you were here or returned to LA."

His eyes narrow at me. "I wouldn't leave and not tell you."

*Oh.*

"I had a good day, so I finished up early," he says with his poker face, and it's hard to tell if he's happy about it or not. There is always someone who needs him, so maybe it's a good thing.

"I also had a good day." I smile as I lift the frying pan from the drawer.

"Anything specific?"

I still for a moment. I don't want to share and jinx myself. "Nothing notable. The day went smoothly, and I had lunch with my coworkers. It was fun."

Jobe is watching me intently. So I shoot him another smile because his stern face is not going to ruin my day. Thankfully, his cell vibrates on the counter. "Sorry, I need to take this."

A wave a hand at him. "Go ahead."

I start chopping vegetables, then find the condiments and dried herbs.

I mouth, *Do you want me to cook you any meat?*

He shakes his head and whispers, "No, thank you."

Is he staying or going out for dinner? He's still in his trousers and his shirt with the top buttons undone. No tie. The definition of his pectoral muscles is peeking out from his unbuttoned shirt, reminding me he has one hell of a muscled torso. I suck in a quick breath as a memory of that night together hits me. A memory of me running my fingers along his sternum, lower and lower. *Oh.* I've remembered snippets of conversation and banter. And how good I felt *after*. I'm feeling good now.

Jobe is suddenly beside me, reaching to the shelf for a

packet of rice. He's close enough for me to inhale his sexy cologne. I'm feeling really good. Damn the timing of my hormones. I'm staring at those hands, imagining how he could pleasure me, then I notice...

*Microwave rice.*

"You eat that?"

He grins. "Doesn't everybody?"

"Noo," I exclaim. "I cook it like a pro."

He adds the herbs to the vegetables, and I step to the side, giving him some room. Who knew I would enjoy watching Jobe Hendricks cook? "I never took you for a two-minute rice man."

"I think you need to stop assuming you know me."

"Touché."

"I hoped tonight we could talk some more." His beautiful dark eyes hold mine captive. It's a moment where Jobe Hendricks looks raw and emotional. Not the arrogant guy he's known to be.

"About what?"

His eyes flick over my face as though I should know. "Us."

**10**

———

JOBE

Zara places our plates on the dining table.

"What about us?" she asks in a quieter tone, and I sense her nervousness on the subject. She takes the seat opposite me and won't look at me.

"I decided not to have Hayley email the details. Instead, we could have a conversation about it."

She glances up with a frown firmly set on her pretty face. "Since we're adults, I'm sure we can discuss it without it being in writing," she says sarcastically.

"Business partnerships are made by signatures at the bottom of the page," I remind her.

She rolls her eyes. "I guess you're going to have to trust me."

*There is my problem.*

"I trust your honesty," I say, pausing because vulnerability isn't a comfort zone of mine, but after the way I made her feel last night, this needs to be said. "It mustn't be easy to share the fact that you don't want children. I understand that many people hold the deluded belief that you are less of a woman without children. I don't think that at all. In fact, one of the things that attracted me to you was we both agreed we didn't want babies." I take another bite.

Zara ogles me. "You find that attractive?"

"I found it refreshing we had something in common. Penny's baby weekend was a nightmare for you. At dinner, you had *kill me now* written all over your face."

"It w-wasn't *that* bad," she stammers.

"Zara. It has nothing to do with you being a good friend and everything to do with you wanting to find happiness elsewhere." She nods slowly as though this is something she struggles with. "If you believe babies should be a topic of conversation, then maybe we should plan what we'll reveal about our future at the next dinner."

"Which is when?"

"Friday night." She chokes on her food, and I raise a brow. "Is there a problem?"

Her expression turns desperate. "I thought you were here for one week a month?"

"On average." Where is this going?

"I'm heading to a beach house on Friday with my friends."

"Zara. If I need you, then it's a priority. It's not a big ask. You can *party* with your friends anytime."

"Don't make it sound like I party all the time. It's Sandbanks, and they don't do this every weekend. It's about fitting in with my new friends."

How do I make Zara understand she doesn't need other people to fit in? She has a magnetism about her that pulls people toward her. I'm beginning to understand these friendships are important to Zara to feel better about herself. I don't understand it, but moving forward, I'll support her. "So we go to dinner then I'll drive you to meet your friends early Saturday morning."

"You'll drive all that way?"

I grin at her. "It's what boyfriends do." Our eyes meet and lock and fuck, with one look, I'm being drawn closer to her and into her world.

"I feel bad asking you to do that."

"We're both making sacrifices." I also want to check out her friends but not for Sir James' benefit.

Pouring a whiskey, I move to the couch, making room for Zara as she grabs some chocolate from the shelf before sitting beside me. "London has the best chocolate in the world," she says with a mouthful. "I keep it on my tongue and let it melt."

Christ. If these conversations continue, I'm going to need fucking earplugs because now I'm thinking of where I could put that melted chocolate for her to lick. "Let's move on to the details of our relationship. Timelines. Anniversaries. Future plans. What we both like and dislike."

She springs up from the couch as though I've upset her. "I'm going to need a fuck ton of chocolate for this conversation."

Forget the earplugs. Give me a damn eye mask so I don't have to look at her mouth sucking the chocolate.

Friday night, we walk into the penthouse after dinner, and I head straight to the bar to pour myself a whiskey. Zara heads to the room to slip out of her gown.

Sir James has taken a liking to Zara, and his wife, Natalie, chatted to Zara like they had known each other for years. With it only being the four of us, the night went better than I anticipated.

Standing in front of the glass doors leading to the terrace, I stare out to the Parliament houses. We have a gala ball in early December, two months from now, and it's probably the last formality for Zara to attend. It should be a relief, but I'm finding excuses for us to stay together for longer.

I stare into my glass and swirl the golden liquid. London has become a sexual nightmare. At dinner, Zara tested my limits. Her acting, every touch of my thigh, and fuck-me-now look in her eyes crossed boundaries. My head is foggy. My dick's fault. *My* stupid idea, so I am the one to blame. It doesn't help that the only taste my dick wants is the one fuck I cannot touch.

We messed it up once. If we become enemies, then Penny will never forgive me. Pretending is as good as it gets.

"I'm pouring a gin." She strolls into the room wearing her sweatpants. *How does she make baggy pants look sexy?*

She prepares a drink, then hops onto the couch and crosses her legs, keeping a tight hold on the glass. "I think tonight went well."

"It went very well." I sit at the other end of the couch, away from her roaming hands, but it's me who can't be trusted. She's a temptation I can't give in to.

Zara holds up her hand, and I high-five her like a child. "We make a good team."

I smile at her enthusiasm. "I believe we do."

"Who knew how awesome we'd be together." She laughs and takes a sip of her drink. Her words hit me straight in the gut, as though I was thinking it, and now she has brought my words to life. "I mean," she doubles back after seeing my face change. "We're good at acting."

"How much of it was an act?" Because she was testing me.

She frowns. "What are you saying? That I was coming on to you?"

"Could you kiss me now with no one here to witness it?" I hold her gaze, challenging her. For most of the night, Zara left a hand on my thigh, caressing my muscles, her fingers sliding high, dipping down to the inside of my thigh. My dick twitched with every touch, and I wondered if she was teasing since they couldn't see her hand. And once, she leaned in and kissed my lips. A peck, but it surprised me.

"It meant nothing, Jobe."

"Prove it. Now." Christ, what am I saying?

"You're overreacting because I'm better at showing affection than you." She downs the rest of her gin and stands to pour another.

"I, at least, could control my hands."

She turns and stares at me. "We're supposed to be a couple. Couples touch each other."

I glare at her. "Take a seat, Zara."

"You don't get to tell me what to do."

"Take a seat. *Please.* I need to hear you say there is nothing going on between us."

*Otherwise, because of your little performance, I'm on the verge of throwing you over my shoulder and taking you to my room.*

She laughs sarcastically and stands in front of me. "Oh, please. You're not that irresistible."

I take a long breath to withhold an urge to prove her wrong. "We have one upcoming event we need to get through without complication."

"I'm not complicating anything." She plops down beside me.

"Touching my shoulder, my arm, my hands, even my chest is acceptable. A quick squeeze of my thigh is okay, but you left your hand there most of the night."

A subtle smile crosses her lips. "You liked it."

"Of course I liked it. I'm a fucking man," I growl out.

Her smile grows wide. "You're the one struggling because you haven't had sex, and you liked me touching you."

"Your point?" I snap.

"I'm better at this than you." Her confidence is infuriating.

"There is no winner, Zara. We need to get through this together, and I'd prefer not to blow in my pants when I'm out at dinner." I throw back my whiskey, frustrated that I had to explain myself to her.

"Best give yourself a hand before going out."

"You wouldn't like it if I almost made you come in public." That finally seems to get through to her.

She stills and eyes me warily. "I guess not."

"You want to be a winner, Zara? Fine. You win. You have more restraint than me. So use it on yourself and promise not to touch me like that again... in public."

Her eyes widen at my last words. "Okay. I'll see you bright and early in the morning."

I stare into my empty glass, debating on pouring another. She is right about one thing—I need to give myself a hand, especially if I'm to get any sleep tonight. Another whiskey it is.

With my drink in hand, I walk outside to the terrace. The view usually calms me. Tonight, all I can think about is Zara's hand almost on my groin. The flutter of her lashes when she smiles at me. The way her eyes sparkle when I say something that makes her laugh.

I have allowed her to blur the lines of our agreement when everything about us is a lie.

We're barely even friends.

This started as a favor to Penny when she asked me to

check on Zara to make sure she was okay. I had to take it one step further, and now I'm feeling things I don't understand.

As I head inside, the wind catches the door, and it slams shut. I stop in my tracks and listen, hoping it didn't wake her. Fuck, now I have an image in my head of Zara sleeping.

Is she naked?

*I remember... I remember everything. The subtle curve of her hips, her full breasts, her rounded ass that I wanted to smack and fuck. She is intoxicating to the point I can't think straight.*

Heading to my room and stripping off, I turn back the bedcovers and grab the lube. I close my eyes, imagining it is Zara's hand wrapped around my dick. *Her hot mouth is all over my chest... my mouth sucking her pretty pussy.* Jesus, I'm building fast. My hand quickens. *Her hips grind as I taste her.* I raise my hand to my lips as I imagine tasting her. *Sweet as honey.* "Yes, baby, come for me," I murmur. *Her breath quickens as she moans my name. She's now on top of me, riding me, her hips moving in sync with mine until I hold her still and pump into her. She lets out a cry as she comes...* I shoot all over my stomach.

"Zara," I whisper. Only it's not enough. I need *her*.

Saturday morning, I'm up at the crack of dawn to drive Zara to Sandbanks.

An hour out of London, I stop for gas and when I return to the car, Zara is busy texting. She looks around. "Does it still feel weird to you?"

Us on a road trip together? Strangely no. "Meaning?"

"How different things are. Drive on the left side of the road. You stopped for petrol, not gas. They call foods different names."

"Every country is different."

"Yeah. It's taking me longer than expected to adapt. Except for the chocolate," she says and giggles. Her cell buzzes. "Hey, we're almost there... sure... okay, see you then." She pops her cell in her bag. "Can we stop for some groceries? Piper forgot some things."

While Zara is shopping, I make some calls of my own, including the contact of a condominium I rented for the weekend.

"How well do you know everyone?" I casually ask when we're back on the road.

"My work colleagues?" She stares out the window. "You met them at the pub."

"Anyone else staying the weekend?"

"Yeah, Anna's sister and her boyfriend. I'm not sure who else. Piper said it has nine bedrooms. In*sane*."

"How did you find the house?"

"Anna's sister's boyfriend's family owns it."

After following her direction, I stop out front of a double-story white building on the beachfront. "I'm impressed."

She smiles. "Piper said it's the Miami of England here." She offers me a parting smile and says, "Bye, Jobe. Have a nice weekend."

"Call me if you need anything."

She stares at me for a moment, and I expect her to give sass like saying, *sure, Dad*. Instead, she smiles. "Thank you, Jobe. I appreciate it." I wave and watch her stride up the path to the front door, my eyes glued to her sexy ass, wishing it was mine.

After dinner, I head out for a stroll along the waterfront to clear my head. While I used the time to work and then check out the local real estate, I'm now thinking about Zara and what she's doing.

For whatever reason, I don't seem to be able to stay away and find myself heading in her direction. The closer I get, the louder the music becomes, a clear sign this isn't the place for me.

Hands in my pockets, I stare at the front door and contemplate leaving. I'm not leaving until I know she is okay. *Knock. Knock.*

"Hey, dude," a guy with long, black hair answers the door, reeking of weed. I glance over his shoulder, and smoke wafts around in the room behind him. "Can I help you?"

"I'm with Zara." *So move aside.*

His blank expression takes a while to comprehend my words.

"The American."

"Right. C'mon in, man." He opens the door. "Head straight out the back."

In the front room, another guy and three girls are smoking weed. Jesus, this music is depressing. And fucking loud. My eardrums are about to burst, not to mention the amount of smoke making me squint.

In the kitchen, five girls are dancing. But that's nothing. The back room is where it's at. It's crowded, and I can't hear my thoughts with the *thump, thump, thump* in my head. People are spinning as they dance in front of me, blocking my way.

*Why the fuck am I here?*

*Why is she here?*

I weave around men and women, but there is no sign of her. A chick grabs my arm and pulls me close, grinding her hips against mine. What the fuck? "Where is Zara?" I yell.

"Upstairs." Her ass grinds my hip.

"Thanks."

I get out of the maze and head up the circular staircase. Voices carry toward the back of the first floor, so it's not much relief from the noise, but it is something. Piper and Anna are sharing a chair closest to the doorway.

Piper takes one look and then glances across the room. "Zara, your *father* is here."

Hysterical.

I step into the room so I can see Zara. She is leaning against the counter of a smaller kitchen alongside another six or so other people. Others are making out on the couch opposite us.

"Jobe." Her eyes round. "What are you doing here?" She looks at her friends and then back at me.

"I was in the neighborhood."

It takes her a moment to register, so I go to her. "Is everything okay?"

She wraps her hands around my neck and kisses me on the cheek. "Girls, this is Jobe, who I was telling you about."

It takes a moment to catch up. She's behaving like she has a boyfriend, just as I asked.

I slip behind her and lean on the counter, wrapping my arms around her as I pull her back to my front. I lean in close. "What is this place?" I whisper.

"An orgy," she whispers back.

She's messing with me, swaying gently in my hands as Coldplay blasts from the speakers, much better than the music when I arrived.

Her friends are chatting about some guy, and Piper is calling him out as a cheater. Their words are exaggerated which is aided by the empty wine bottles beside her.

I rest my chin on Zara's shoulder. "Is this your idea of fun?"

She shakes her head. "I've never been happier to see you."

"Do you want to leave?"

"We can't." She turns her head, and her breath caresses my ear and neck, and goose bumps tingle my skin. "They know I have a boyfriend, so now you're here, we need to role play."

"I hate it and love it," I growl out against her neck, dotting her skin with kisses. She sways in my arms, and I can't help myself. I run a hand up and down her hips.

She takes my hand and brings it to loop through hers. When I grind my dick against her ass, she stiffens in my arms.

Game on, *girlfriend.*

"Why are you here?" she asks again.

*Because I can't get you out of my head.* "I was taking a stroll along the beachfront and heard the music. Decided I'd join the rave."

She laughs. "Liar. You hate every second of being here."

"So let's leave…"

"I can't. I promised I'd stay until tomorrow. What happened with you driving back to London?" She moves her hips in tune with the beat as her ass rubs over me.

I watch as three more guys stroll into the room and sit near Piper and Anna.

"I decided to stay and check out the real estate value." My plan to return to London and work without Zara in my penthouse to distract me got derailed when I imagined some random guy coming on to her. I have taken this protector role that Penny asked of me too far. And now I'm at a fucking gathering of college students getting high on the smoke in the room. "But this is not my scene, and you're having a good time, so I'll go."

"Stay a bit, please," she says softly.

"I have work to do, and after last night, I could do with an early night."

She throws down whatever was left in her glass and turns, kissing me on the fucking lips. Then her hands loop around my neck, and her body leans into me. I should push her off and tell her it's a bad idea, but she tastes so delicious—a mixture of alcohol and Zara. Soft lips, just as I remember. Her kiss is delicate and hesitant, as though any second could push us over the edge. Instead my hands remain on her waist, holding her close.

"What's going on?" I murmur against her lips.

"Sorry. I know I said I wouldn't overstep, but the guys that just walked in…" I sneak a glance without moving too far from her face. "The one in the blue shirt tried to hit on me earlier. It's when I told everyone I had a boyfriend."

Hairs prickle on the back of my neck. "We're leaving."

"We can't… *I* can't," she corrects. "Stay a while then you can leave. *Please.*"

Jesus. "Fine." If that prick comes near her, I'll ram his joint down his throat.

She turns back around, lifts a hand to cup my neck, and grinds her ass over my dick.

"Not amused, Zara," I whisper close to her ear.

"Act like you enjoy it," she purrs.

"I don't need to act," I say between clenched teeth. I kiss her neck and place my hand on her hips, trying to put some air between us.

"Get a room," Piper calls out.

Brilliant. "Show me your room."

"Now?"

"Yes, *now.*"

She takes my hand and leads me out the door along the hallway. We pass two bedrooms and a bathroom, and then she opens the door to a bedroom that has an ocean view.

I quickly close the door behind us. "You're not sharing with anyone?"

"No. Piper and Anna are next door. Though, now, I wish I was sharing."

"Jesus, if you don't feel safe, you need to leave," I state.

"Now you're here... you could stay?"

"Seriously? You want to sleep in the same bed when I have a condo a block away?"

She looks down at her feet. "I'm not sure why I came. I'm trying to fit in *somewhere*..."

There it is. "Hey." I take her in my arms and hold her for a moment. The reason why I check in on her. I encouraged her to come to London, and I don't want her to be alone in a strange country. "Go back out there with your friends, and I'll stay here. I need to get some sleep."

She kisses my cheek and holds my gaze. "Thank you."

"You owe me," I mutter before she closes the door.

When I head down the hall to the bathroom we passed, there's a damn lineup. I nod to the three guys waiting before me.

Finally, the door opens, and a girl walks out. Then, a guy adjusting his fly.

*The fuck?*

It's like being back at college all over again.

Finally, it's my turn. How many people use this bathroom? I stare at the shower floor. It's wet. Did someone shower or...

Despite the fancy décor, I'm not staying in here a second longer than I need.

I head back to the bedroom, strip off, and climb into Zara's bed. I'll grab a few hours' sleep and once she's okay, I'll head back to mine. I have willingly subjected myself to this environment *for Zara.*

I let the meaning of that sink in.

# 11

______

ZARA

My head throbs.

I open one eye. *Shit.* This bed is smaller than expected, and I'm so close to Jobe. Hesitantly, I lift my head and suck in a breath. His eyes are wide open, watching me. "Sorry." I lift the arm that was wrapped around his chest to wipe the drool off his shoulder before wiping my mouth.

"You snore," he states.

"I do not."

He pats my leg, which is a dead weight over his hips. "Regardless, I need to go to that ghastly bathroom."

*What's wrong with the bathroom?* I pry myself off him and feel the cool air that separates us.

*His body was so warm.*

I watch him tug up his trousers, and he turns to...

... oh.

I watch as he struggles with his erection, and I can't take

my eyes away. Then, with the zipper undone, he walks out of the room, grumbling something about morning.

*He has a great dick, maybe the best dick I've ever seen.*

And with that thought, I'm back to thinking about Friday night after dinner when I heard a door bang, and I got up to investigate. I went toward his room to make sure he was okay, and that's when I heard him moaning. Of course, I checked. His door was slightly open, and he was naked on the bed, giving himself a hand as I suggested. I watched him as he pumped his hand up and down his length, the action mesmerizing. Then, when he whispered my name, I assumed I was hearing things.

I ran back to my room before I did something I'd regret—a second time. I convinced myself I didn't hear him right, as he wouldn't be having sexy thoughts about me.

I annoy him. Everything he does for me is because it's part of his business plan or Penny asked him to do it.

*But last night... he stayed for me.*

He rushes back into the room and clicks the door shut. "I need to sterilize my feet."

"What?"

"That bathroom." He grabs his shirt and slips it on, buttoning it. "Fucking mortifying in the morning with an audience outside the door."

I lift the sheet and pat the space beside me. "Come back to bed for a while."

His hands still, and his eyes lock with mine. "You know that's not a great idea."

I roll onto my back and let out a long sigh. "I miss spooning. And now the bed's cold."

He glances up to the ceiling. "I need to leave and do some work." He says it so matter-of-factly, but then he pulls back the sheet and climbs into bed with me, fully clothed.

Surprising me further, he wraps an arm over my stomach. "This is as close to spooning as we're doing, and I'm only here if you tell me what's really troubling you?"

I take another deep breath and let it out slowly. Jobe wants a D and M. I must be stuck in a dream. Yet the more time I spend with him, the more layers I uncover. He's not the stuck-up suit I once thought him to be. And he cares about me. "Sometimes I miss home. I miss *my* friends."

Jobe kisses my shoulder, and I'm starting to enjoy all the little kisses he offers to console me. "It's natural to feel that way."

"I love the adventure of being here, but I miss the closeness of my friends. Being able to speak my mind without judgment and the good times with Penny." I glance sideways at him. "I also miss spooning." He stills but doesn't look at me. "I haven't been with anyone for a long time, and it's not a London problem but a Zara problem. I need the physical touch that my vibrator doesn't offer." This gains a look, but his poker face is set in stone.

"You need sex," I state as the idea strikes me. "I need what comes before and after sex. I like to hold onto those moments for as long as possible. It's why I was never great with one-night stands when they up and leave." I watch the accusation sink in on his face. *Yeah. I'm talking about you too.* At least he has the decency to look away.

"You're the girl who wants breakfast cooked after you fuck."

I roll my eyes. "And lunch and a stroll together and dinner and perhaps another date." He doesn't say anything, only stares at me. "I know I sound crazy, but maybe we can help each other."

His brow tightens. "Careful, Zara."

"I saw you," I whisper. "Giving yourself a hand." He pulls back, but I keep hold of his arm around me. "I enjoyed watching you. Maybe I could help. I have hands and a mouth and—"

He flies out of bed. "No." He finishes doing his shirt buttons.

"And you could cuddle me."

He won't look at me as he slips into his designer leather shoes.

"I thought you liked me touching you," I whisper as he shoves his shirt inside his trousers.

"Of course I liked it. But there was a point where we knew we had to pull back and not cross. If that's taken away..." His eyes lock with mine. "You don't know me," he says in a darker, dangerous voice.

"Yeah, I remember. I don't know why you were out of sorts last night when you'd have preferred two or three women in your bed. Because that is what you like, right?" I roll over so I don't have to look at him.

"I don't sleep with just anyone," he says quietly behind me as he walks past the bed, stopping near the door. "I'll see you back in London later this evening. I'm heading out for dinner with a client."

"Go and fuck them and see if I care," I snap when he closes the door. *Because I was so bad the first time, he doesn't want round two with me.*

*Knock. Knock.*

"Zara?" echoes behind the door.

"Come in."

Piper strolls into my room in her pajamas. "Hey, are you okay?"

"Yeah," I say, deflated.

"Did you two fight? I saw Jobe leave, and he looked pissed."

"Our first one," I lie.

Why do I expect it to be different now? We have clashed since the day I met him.

It's late Sunday night when Piper drops me off. Upstairs, the penthouse is dark, empty, and hot—a freaking sauna. I turn the temperature down and head to my room, stripping out of my jacket as I go. It's not enough. It feels as though I might melt.

Opening the freezer, I frantically search for ice cream, anything to cool me down. Is the heating faulty? I take a bowl of ice cream out to the terrace as I wait for my room to cool down. It's cold out here, but I don't care because it's better than being inside when Jobe comes home.

There's no way I can sleep in there. I've left the windows open so the cool night air will waft into my room and hopefully make it tolerable.

Settling into the padded chair, I stare across the Thames at the twinkling lights. It's a beautiful view, but it's not home. It's another moment where I feel homesick, missing being able to drive over to see my friends and have a good cry.

I check my cell. It's around lunchtime in LA, so I open up my contacts and call Penny.

"Hold Summer, it's Zara," she says, and I hear Summer cry in the background, then rustling. "Zara. Is everything okay?"

"Hi, Pen. Yeah, I'm good. Is this a bad time?"

"No, no, Summer has gas, and we're trying to make her comfortable. She's three and half months and grown so much."

I smile into the phone. "I can't wait to see her. See both of you."

"I've missed you," Penny says in a high, sad voice.

"I've missed you too. Tell me, what else have I missed?"

"There's not a lot to tell. I spend all my time with Summer, and we split our time between Frank's penthouse and the beach house. Mom and Dad are doing well. Have you spoken to Hugh recently?"

"Not yet. I wanted to check in with you first."

"Poor Sienna has been sick almost the entire pregnancy. She is huge. Retaining fluid too. They are monitoring her blood pressure."

"Oh, he never mentioned it."

"It's been a difficult pregnancy, but she only has eight more weeks until her due date."

"Wow, a Christmas baby. How are you, Pen?" I don't want the entire call to be about babies. "Honestly."

"Tired. Sad that I can't see you like we used to."

"I'm sad for that too but even if I were there, it wouldn't be like old times."

"No, I guess not. But babies grow, and life will be easier soon. Anyway, enough about that. Tell me about London. What are your new friends like? Jobe told Franklin you're thriving."

*Thriving.*

"He said he has caught up with you a couple of times, and you've met at a pub for drinks. You introduced him to some of your friends."

"We did. They are my work colleagues and are younger if you know what I mean. We all stayed at a beach house over the weekend at a place south of London. It was fun, but... I've kind of outgrown the things they were doing for entertainment."

Penny giggles. "We're old, babe."

"We are. But they're fun to be around too. We eat together most lunch breaks and meet up on weekends, so it helps with homesickness."

She remains quiet. "Will you be back for Thanksgiving?"

"I hope so. And also for Christmas as the company closes for the holidays."

"Yay, I'm excited."

"I no longer have a place to live in LA, Pen. So I'll probably stay in San Diego with my parents."

"You can come here and stay with us for as long as you like. The penthouse and the beach house have spare bedrooms."

"Thank you. Maybe for a couple of days because I can't wait to cuddle Summer."

"I can't wait to hug you. I've missed you, Zee."

Lowering my head, I smile as I feel her love. "We'll talk soon, okay?"

We end the call, and I hold my phone to my chest. I've missed my friends, and it will be great to see them, but I made the right choice coming here.

Crap, I didn't tell her about my promotion. I'll wait until it happens so I don't jinx my luck. Instead, I decide to send her a photo, knowing she won't know where I am.

I take a photo of the bridge and the river at night, the sparkling lights on the other side. Then I add a text saying how much I love the view.

I head back inside, noting it's still hot as hell. I can't bear it any longer. The heating must be broken as it doesn't feel any cooler. I hit the cool button several times, then head to my room to read a book before bed.

WHAT THE HELL IS HAPPENING?

I wake up unable to breathe.

Tossing the covers aside, I yank off my top. I'm dying here.

I starfish in my undies, tossing and turning. Ugh, it's unbearable. I get up, open *all* my windows, and cold air blows in. Then I open my bedroom door. All lights are off, and Jobe is either in his room or not home yet. I cover my breasts with one hand and tiptoe out to the control pad on the kitchen wall. I hit the temperature button several times until it's a cool level. This damn air conditioner needs a technician.

"Zara." I jump and turn with one arm over my boobs. Jobe is standing behind the kitchen counter, his bare chest glimmering in the dim light. "Leave it, please."

"Are you serious? It's a fucking sauna. I thought it was broken."

"Not broken." He taps on his cell. The fucker is adjusting it from his cell. He tosses his cell on the marble and leans with two arms on the counter. He looks pissed. "I set it high so you wouldn't have the desire to *spoon*." The air crackles with the tension between us.

"Oh, smart ass. You fixed that." Blood rushes to my head as anger flares. "I'm on the bed like a freaking starfish." I throw my arms out wide for emphasis. "Kill me now because I asked Jobe Hendricks for some emotional support. To spoon me with fucking clothes on." I slam my fists onto my hips.

His eyes travel down my body, taking his damn time until his eyes lift and his heated gaze meets mine.

"Yeah, take a good look, fucker, because you had your shot and blew it. You won't get a second chance." I storm back to my room.

"You have no idea, Zara," he shouts, but it's more of a roar.

"Stop messing with the controls," I call back before slamming my door.

At five thirty, I was up and out of that hellhole.

I've been sitting in the café across from the office block for what feels like hours, and there's still another hour before I start work. I keep checking the time, hoping Piper will arrive soon.

I peer up, and she walks in smiling, her long, blonde ponytail swinging behind her. "Hey, how was your night?" I make a face, and before I answer, she adds, "Oh, he's still mad?" I nod, and she slides into the chair opposite me. "Do you want another coffee?" She glances down at the two empty mugs in front of me.

"If I could drink alcohol, I would." I sigh. "I'll have a tea that you all rave about."

Her eyes light up. "Earl Grey?"

"Yeah, whatever," I say and laugh.

Piper orders our beverages and then returns to the table. "So what happened?"

I shrug a shoulder, not knowing how to explain our fake relationship fight. "He was pissed that I didn't leave with him yesterday morning, and it escalated last night."

"Ugh, no one likes a bossy control freak, except..." she cleans closer, "... I find it focking sexy in bed." I smile at the way she cusses in her accent. It doesn't stop me from imagining Jobe in bed, telling me what to do.

Taking a deep breath, I consider that maybe we're not meant to be. Last night, I told him that he wouldn't get a second chance when it was me who didn't get a second chance.

"Ladies," George says as he takes a seat beside Piper. He's wearing a trendy tie with his shirt in an array of pastel colors. "I come with news. Today's the big announcement. What else will be revealed?"

"Then we must go," Piper adds. "I need to sort my emails before the morning meeting."

We head across the road to our office block and take the elevator to the third floor. The staff is talking amongst themselves as we stride past the rows of office cubicles to get to ours.

"Hey." Anna stands from behind her table and joins us. "Did you hear?"

"Hear what?" Piper asks as she unpacks her bag onto her table.

"About the merger. It's happening this week. We are supposed to be meeting the new CEO today."

"Oh. Is this a surprise to everyone?" I ask in curiosity.

"*Yes,*" Anna emphasizes. "Everyone is talking about our jobs and redundancies or a company shake-up. I spoke to Carissa from IT on the entire train ride about what the tech team are saying."

"What are they saying?" Piper folds her arms.

Tim enters the room and remains at the front, where we can all see him. "Can I have everyone's attention?" Everyone takes a seat behind their desks, and the room falls into silence. An anxious anticipation of what comes next fills the air. "While some of you are aware of the announcement today, unfortunately it will have to wait another week or two as there has been a setback, and the new Executive Director of the Board could not make today's meeting. While many of you have questions, please send them in an email. Otherwise, today is work as usual. And please don't start any rumors to make your coworkers unsettled. If you want answers, send your questions my way. When I know more, then you'll be the first to know. We'll speak more about it in the weekly meeting."

"I don't think anyone will lose their job," I whisper to Piper. "The company cannot afford to have unfair dismissal law cases during a merger."

Piper smiles at me. "Right. I already promised myself I wasn't going to stress about it."

"Changing the topic. Are you still looking for a roomie?"

## 12

JOBE

My mother holds me by the shoulders as she studies my face.

"You have dark rings around your eyes, darling. You need to get more sleep."

"Sacrificing sleep is part of the job, as you know," I murmur before I kiss her cheek.

"You sound like your brother." Fine lines crease around her blue eyes. She studies me a moment longer. "Please don't make the same mistake as him."

I smile at Mom. "Get married and have kids? No chance of that." It's not what she implied, but there is no point in causing her worry. My father worked long hours, traveled around the world, and often left her alone with us four kids for weeks at a time. She hated that Franklin followed in his footsteps. It's why she admires Penny. She is the only person to convince him to slow down.

She places a hand on my cheek. "Don't joke about things you have no control over."

I chuckle as though she told a joke. "Trust me. I have complete control over that, and it's not on my radar."

Franklin lands a hand on my back. "Never say never, especially to our mother. Now, can I fix you a drink?"

"Nothing I'd love more. It's been a week."

"Did you see Zara?" he asks. "You know Penny's going to ask."

"Yeah, I caught up with her. She's doing fine. Penny doesn't need to worry."

He nods. "How is the takeover development?"

"It's progressing well. Sir James is starting to believe in our vision." Though juggling two London business dealings at the same time is not ideal.

Franklin hands me a whiskey on ice, and I slip out of my suit jacket, laying it across the leather chair. "Penny will be excited. She has researched London's innovative green building practices and will have a plan for us by the end of the month."

"Sir James' interest piqued when I spoke of Hendricks Real Estate being a visionary leader with focus on sustainability," I say, and Franklin raises his glass toward me. "I'm excited about our vision, and I've already taken the next step in securing property in Dubai."

"Mom was right. You don't have time to sleep."

"Jobe." Penny bounces into the room with Summer on her hip. She already has the dark hair of her parents. "I spoke to Zara." Suddenly, I'm no longer thinking about their baby. "She sent me a photo of the view where she is staying. It looks fabulous."

She hands Franklin her cell to pass to me, and he glances at the image, his eyebrows lowering before he hands it to me. I stiffen seeing the image from the terrace overlooking the Thames because Franklin has stayed at my penthouse. "What's this?" he asks.

"Zara's view, by account." I hold his gaze and give a subtle shake of my head.

*The fuck?* he mouths.

"Lola is waiting for us," Mom says, directing us into the dining room. "Thank you, Lola. We're ready for our starters," she says to our server.

Lola has worked for us for twenty years, and Mom hates keeping her waiting. She reminds us she has her own family to go home to.

We take our seats just as Charlotte and Byron arrive together. My younger siblings have been bickering of late, and I'm not in the mood for it tonight. Mom stands and hugs them both, as she does to all of us, even if it's mere days since she saw us last. "You're training too hard," she tells Byron.

"It's his profession, Mom." I pipe up in defense of Byron's elite basketball career. "No gain without pain."

"You know that's not true, Jobe. It can become a chronic injury." She places a hand on his shoulder. "You need to eat, darling."

"What Jobe means is the pain he feels today is the strength he'll feel tomorrow," Charlotte quips. Mom hugs my sister, who is equally dedicated as Byron to the LA Sharks basketball club my family owns, working in the business side of the team.

"And you're working far too hard. Have you hired an extra assistant yet?"

"Nope, most are there for the glory and for a chance to meet the guys. We're interviewing all week."

"No Aussie today?" I ask. Byron's teammate and best

friend is from Down Under, and he's usually here once a week for the family dinner.

"No, he's FaceTiming his parents tonight," Byron says.

"How is Giana?" Penny asks Byron about his new love interest.

"Good. Her art is flourishing."

"It's not the only thing *flourishing,*" I say.

Byron glares at me. My brother is smitten, and this conversation wouldn't happen if my father were here.

"When is Dad expected home?" I ask Mom.

"On Friday. Hopefully, it's the last time he travels for the year."

I glance at Franklin, expecting a raised eyebrow as we know my father hasn't fully retired, even though Mom wants to hand it all over to Franklin. With the way he's glancing down, I know he's breaking the no-cells-at-the-table rule.

My cell buzzes in my pocket, and I discreetly retrieve it, keeping the cell on my legs to read the screen.

> What the fuck is going on between you and Zara?

I glance up at my brother and mouth, *later.*

"Can we meet tomorrow to discuss the takeover?" Franklin asks in a business-like tone. His serious gaze sends a clear message not to decline him.

"We can chat over lunch. It's the only time I have free," I tell him, not ready to discuss Zara in detail with him or anyone.

"Thank you, Lola," Mom says as dishes are laid in front of us. "Please, no more talk of business at the table."

THE FOLLOWING DAY, I FINISH THE LAST MORNING MEETING over a Zoom call.

I knock, then open my assistant's door. "Cancel my next meeting," I tell Hayley. "I expect lunch with my brother to take longer than I desire."

"Of course. When do you want to reschedule?"

"Later this afternoon. Email me the details." I close her door and head outside to where my driver waits. "Bloom, please, Joseph."

"Meeting your brother, sir?"

"Yes, at his request, not mine."

I check emails and messages, but none from a certain female in London. If I know Zara, I expect the *Fuck you. I've moved out* message any time now. We need to remain civil, at least until the gala. It's enough time to secure some confidence with Sir James to sign the contract. The woman is under my skin, and I'm endeavoring not to think about her while I'm in LA finalizing business contracts. I have to focus, yet here I am, having lunch with my brother, who will open an interrogation about my feelings for her.

Inside Bloom, Franklin sits at the usual table at the back that is always reserved for family, friends, and last-minute reservations. He stands and shakes my hand. "Busy morning?"

"I've managed to survive on air only."

He chuckles. "It's a family trait. I'll order us some food immediately."

"Best you order us a bottle of Blanton's La Maison du Whisky too."

His brow furrows. "What the fuck have you done?"

"Nothing, yet."

My cell lights up with an incoming call. *Venus.* I ignore it and block the number.

Frank raises an eyebrow. "You're not seeing—"

"No," I cut him off. "I must have missed her number."

"You're blocking every woman you fuck?" he asks unbelievably. "Shall we address the elephant in the room first?" he snaps. "Why was Zara at your penthouse? No, why did she tell Penny it's where she is staying?"

"Nothing happened if that's your concern."

He leans forward. "Yet." His serious big brother face warns me not to mess with him.

I glare at him. "Give me some credit. I'm trying fucking hard here."

Franklin holds his temples. "Je-sus."

"I needed a favor. Sir James told me going forward, he didn't trust me. Said my lack of having a wife or girlfriend depicted an irresponsible or untrustworthy nature. He thinks I'm not a man of my word if I'm not capable of committing to a relationship, so I asked Zara to be my fake girlfriend."

"You're fucking delusional," he spits. "Why did she agree to it?"

"She needed somewhere to stay until she sorted out her living arrangement. I said she's welcome to stay at mine indefinitely since I'm only there once a month."

Franklin leans back in his chair and eyes me suspiciously. He links his fingers on the edge of the table. "There is nothing going on between you?"

"Nope."

"So what does this fake dating entail?"

"She accompanies me to dinners with Sir James, and there is a gala ball we need to attend, and then the contracts should be secured. Sir James loves Zara. She's perfect as she talks about Penny and yourself and how she loves Summer and..." Fuck.

"And..."

"And how she can't wait to have babies."

Franklin's eyes round wider than our dinner plates. "Babies. You and Zara? I never got the impression she wanted kids."

"It's part of the charade. She sounded convincing, and Sir James believed her."

He narrows his eyes. "Do you act like you're together in front of him?"

"We hug and touch each other like we're together just for show." He screws up his face as though he's in pain from hearing my words. "And we've..." I hesitate, "... kissed, but not like you think."

"Like I think? What I think is *if* your charade is uncovered, all hell will break loose. He'll never trust us to do business again, and we need his fucking business. We need his trust. So you better not fuck this up." He shakes his head. "And especially not with Zara because you'll have Penny to deal with if I don't murder you first. Why the hell didn't you get one of your booty calls to date?"

"Because they would fuck it up. Zara knows the family, and we trust her. She was perfect for the job."

He rubs at his temples again. "You're going to break her heart."

"What? I told you nothing is going on between us. It'll be fine."

"I know you better than you know yourself. She'll fall for you, and you'll break her heart." He shakes his head at me. Then, his expression changes as though he has a realization. "You like her, don't you?"

"Of course I like her. She's a family friend." Something I continually remind myself every time I want to cross the line.

"No. There's something different about you." Typically, Franklin can see when I'm trying to avoid my feelings. Living with a woman as beautiful as Zara is hard enough without him breaking down the barrier of me wanting something I can't allow myself to touch. And in Sandbanks, I came awfully close to losing all self-control with her.

"Let it go," I warn him. "It's business."

If only I could convince myself.

# 13

JOBE

DAYS AND WEEKS blur into one as I keep myself busy with work from the moment I wake until I fall into bed at night. I send Zara numerous texts, and her responses are the same, citing she is fine. I should sleep on the long-haul flight to London, but I can't stop thinking about her and what I'm going to say since we haven't seen each other for three weeks.

*Stay.*

*I'm sorry.*

*We have one more event...*

It's after ten Sunday night when I arrive at my penthouse, and the entire place is in darkness. I'm dead on my feet as I head straight to my room and collapse on the bed.

The next thing I know, my alarm is sounding at five thirty. As I do most mornings, I head into my gym and work out for the next thirty minutes. Then, with a towel over my shoulder, I walk into the kitchen, where Zara is sitting at the counter, drinking coffee.

"Morning." She barely glances my way.

"Morning. Have you eaten breakfast?"

"Yes, thanks." She stands and grabs her handbag. "I'll see you later." She leaves without another word, and the slam of the front door jolts me like a nonverbal fuck you.

*She's still pissed.*

Understandably so. I need to reconcile matters between us and send her a text.

> Will you have dinner with me tonight?

I don't expect her to reply immediately. More than likely, I'll get the cold shoulder until the last minute. I could take her to one of the finest restaurants, though she was impressed by my cooking skills.

I call the concierge.

"Hi, Trent. I'm sending you a list of groceries to have delivered tonight."

I didn't think about food again with meetings dragging out to midafternoon. I checked my cell like a teenager waiting for a reply, and yet there was not one word from Zara.

Only messages from my mother.

> Byron believes you have a girlfriend in London. Is there any truth to it? Please give me the grace of not being the last to know if you have a love interest. It's not curiosity, more happiness you have found someone to share your life with. Why didn't you mention it when you were here?

I let out a long sigh. The reason my mother is the last to

know is because she is already assuming I have found someone to share my life with. Byron is deflecting the attention from himself, and I'm not chasing any girl around the world as he did by surprising Giana in Italy...yet in a way, I am.

I walk into the last meeting of the day with the new company Board we are taking over. It is Warburton Investments where Zara works. The asset value of their portfolio fell six months ago, and Franklin and I tracked the risk and capitalization rate before taking steps to acquire the majority stake in the company. Culture at the top level has improved with the recent changes in management. Our strategy is to sell off noncore assets in industrial and commercial portfolios and focus on office accommodation in CBD areas. The business was founded on office real estate, and for the next hour, I'm met with arguments about our new direction with ESG activist investors. Thankfully, we have Penny working for the company with her knowledge of current-day ESG issues. We have it under control and want this damn meeting to end.

The debate stretches out to six o'clock. Acquiring this company is something I have kept from Zara. Since she is an employee, my hands were tied to discuss it with her. Franklin and I don't discuss business in conversation with anyone outside the company, and yet I trust Zara. The urge to impart the information about the future of the company out of guilt is a foreign emotion. I have to remind myself it won't affect her, and when decisions are made, we'll have a quiet conversation.

My cell vibrates in my pocket, and I check it without apology.

I won't get home until 8 p.m. Sorry.

I tap a reply.



My thoughts shift away from the meeting to something more interesting—*planning my night with Zara.*

# 14

ZARA

After three weeks apart, Jobe is back, and my thoughts are all over the place. Do I want to go home and have the sight of him tempt me to imagine all the ways he can pleasure me? Ignite my ovaries like no other man can? How can I hate a man and yet be equally attracted to him? And now said man wants to take me to dinner.

God help me.

*It is easier to despise him.*

Instead of going straight to the penthouse after work, I head to the old-time pub in Piccadilly to clear my head. I love this pub. It reminds me of the carefree feeling I had when I arrived in London. Before I reach the bar, I recognize Oscar standing with another guy.

"Big O," I call out and then hug him.

Oscar introduces me to his friend, Baron, as Hollywood. Baron appears unimpressed with my intrusion and leaves us to head outside and stand with the other suits on the sidewalk.

"Did I offend him?" I ask.

Oscar shakes his head. "He's an old flame. One I shouldn't rekindle," he says as though he's already resigned to the fact he will.

"So it was perfect timing?"

"Something like that," he offers with a laugh. "How have you been?"

"Okay. I need a drink to clear my head before going home."

"Are you still at that overpriced hotel?"

"No. I'm living with... it's complicated. Give me a minute." I order a drink and down some of my gin before continuing. "Do you remember the guy from LA?"

"The jealous one?"

"Not jealous, bossy."

"Okay, let's run with that... you're not living with *him*?"

"We made a deal. I help him out, and he gives me somewhere to live since he's only in London once a month. He lives in a penthouse by the Thames, so I think I got the better deal."

His eyes fill with worry. "What did you have to do?"

I love that he's concerned for me. "Be his fake girlfriend for a few dates."

He shakes his head. "He's not faking it, Hollywood."

I laugh as though it's a joke. "Oh, he is. We barely like each other. I don't want to go to his penthouse tonight because I don't want to argue anymore. If we can avoid each other for the few days he is here, then we'll fight less."

"Fight?" His brows arch. "Do you want some advice?"

I pop a shoulder. "Move out?"

"Fuck him."

I laugh. "I tell him to fuck off all the... oh, you actually mean, fuck him?"

"You both need to get it out of your system. Then you can move on. Friends. Friends with benefits. Whatever. But this angst between you is obvious, and there's only one way to fix it."

I shake my head. "Are you high? It's not happening. He can't stand the notion of touching me." The one time he did turned him off for life.

"The time he barged in here, the sexual tension was obvious even to me. If it doesn't mean anything, you'll know soon enough."

"I think it would be a big mistake, and I still don't have anywhere else to live, sooo..." I pop my shoulder again. "It won't happen. Besides, my best friend is married to his brother, and it is freaking weird that I'm even talking about this."

"It's not weird, Hollywood. I mean, what's the worst that can happen?"

I let out a long breath. "It happened once when we were drunk. I don't remember much of the night, and I assume neither does he. It's like it never happened, or I was so bad that he never wants it to happen again. I'm..." I stall, thinking of the right words, "... pastel compared to his vibrant world."

"Have you seen him with anyone else since?"

I shake my head. "I heard the rumors before I jumped into bed with him."

"He doesn't bring women back to his penthouse with you there?"

I shake my head again. "We made a pact. We're faking this relationship for a business merger. The businessman he is dealing with believes integrity, honesty, and commitment come from a personal attribute, and a sworn bachelor for life is untrustworthy. The man has contacts, so we need to act the part *all of the time*. No drunk dancing with random men." I wink at him.

"He's besotted by you, Hollywood. No guy would go that far with a girl he didn't care about."

Oscar's expression is one of understanding. His big, gentle eyes tell me it's okay to have feelings. "I think it's more frustration. With me."

He chuckles to himself. "He's frustrated for sure. Blue balls will do that to a man."

"Eww."

"Besides, I don't think I could ever tell my best friend, and we tell each other everything. It's..." I shake my head, "... I can't explain it."

"You can be each other's dirty little secret."

"Well, thanks for the advice, but I still believe you're wrong." I down the rest of my gin and notice Baron making his way toward us. "I should leave so Baron can make his move."

"Unlike you, *I* have no willpower."

I laugh at Oscar. "Then have a good night, my friend." Pushing up onto my toes, I kiss Oscar's cheek. "See you next time."

I head out of the bar, past all the suits gathered on the street, and head to the Tube. Getting off at Westminster, I walk the few blocks to Jobe's penthouse, and when the elevator doors open, I hold my breath, unlocking the door.

*What do I say to him?*

The first thing I see is a shirtless Jobe in the kitchen. I can't help but stare at his broad, muscular back. Jobe in jeans... it's as though he has peeled a layer back, showing me a rawer version of himself. A version my stupid hormones adore because my stomach flips in excitement. Shit.

He spins and sees me. "Evening, Zara. You're just in time." He focuses on flipping vegetables in the frypan.

I can't help but watch as he holds the pan, his muscles flexing in his arm as he gently shakes it, tossing the vegetables. It's something so simple yet it lights a fire in my body. "It smells good." It's so good that I'm drawn to sit on a stool by the counter and drop my bag on the floor. "What are you cooking?"

"Ahh, my secret recipe." He rounds the counter and takes my hand in a handshake of sorts. "I apologize for my behavior before I left. I treated you poorly, and it was unacceptable."

I smile at him. "I appreciate your saying so. But if we're going to spend time together, it's best we don't fight." *And for the love of God, put some clothes on.*

He gives me a nod and lets go of my hand. Immediately, I feel the space between us.

"We're different, and that's okay," I say in an attempt to explain why we butt heads.

He turns to me and leans both elbows on the counter until his face is close to mine. Unable to look away, those dark eyes make me his prisoner. "Different in a good way or bad?" he asks.

"Good, I guess." I back up, needing to create space. "You're different."

"Different to you?"

I nod. "Very different to me."

"It sounds like a bad thing?" he says in a low, deep voice. "I think we need to be honest with each other."

"You sometimes make me uneasy." He frowns. "Nervous. You're a lot."

He grins at me. "Part of me is." That deserves an eye roll. "I don't want to be that person to you. We're friends, right?"

"Friends?" I raise my eyebrows. "Is that what we are?"

He reaches out and takes my hand in a gentler way than before. "Do you want to be friends?"

My breath quickens along with my heart rate. What is he asking me? "Of course, I want to be friends with you. Your brother is married to my best friend, so it makes sense for us to be nice to each other."

He holds my gaze as though he's waiting for me to say more. He pushes up off the counter and walks around to me. "This is me being nice." He unrolls the tie on the counter. "May I?"

"This is the part where I get nervous." My voice quivers, and my damn heart won't slow down, sending my senses into overdrive.

"Relax, I'm going to blindfold you and give you a taste. I want you to guess what you're eating."

*Oh no, no, no.* His tie around my eyes sends the wrong message, diverting my stomach and straight down to my pussy.

"You're going to feed me?" I squeak. Warmth creeps up my neck. I'm losing control here, and I need to be in control around Jobe. "It's random, especially for you."

"Not random. Spontaneity is not my friend."

"I *know,*" I say, exaggerating the word. "It's why this is random."

"I planned the four courses this morning. Considered how to make it fun."

Fun? It is... seductive. "Okay. If I'm out of my comfort zone, then I think you should also be tested."

"I cooked the food, Zara."

"Not that. I'm going to ask you a question with every dish. You have to answer honestly. I can't see you, so I won't be able to tell if you're lying, but I'll hear it in your voice." He ties the soft material over my eyes, and I take a slow breath through my nose, though it does nothing to calm me.

"This doesn't count as one, but..." my breath hitches because this feels an awful lot like foreplay, "... have you done this with other girls before?"

His answer doesn't come quickly, causing my body to tense. "No..." He pauses, and while his answer should bring relief, I'm still on edge.

I'm not sure what to do with my hands, so I carefully sit on a stool, reaching for the edge of the marble counter and grip hard. Tilting my head, I listen as he handles the cutlery and pans. "Open your mouth, Zara," he commands, and I do.

The aroma of basil and parsley hit my senses as he places the fork on my tongue. I close my lips as he slides it out, leaving something warm and soft in texture. It's a little chewy, and I'm not sure if I swallow or continue chewing as it's definitely seafood. Not oysters, clams, maybe. The notable flavors include tomatoes, basil, seafood, and...

"Are you ready for some more?"

I nod. "Please."

My mouth is open, waiting. It feels odd, yet I like it. A lot.

The fork touches my tongue, and I close my lips as he slides it out. I sense his eyes on me, watching every little detail. How do I look to him? Imagining how his eyes are on my mouth, my hormones send the wrong messages to my brain.

*Calm the hell down. Now.*

*Mmm...* potatoes and rice soaked in the seafood broth and combined with the tomatoes and herbs.

It's a sensory overload.

"Do you like it?" His voice is a soft hum as though he's enjoying it as much as I am.

"I do."

"Do you want some more?"

"Of course I bloody do." More food, more of Jobe's seduction skills. I'm here for all of it. I can't see him, but somehow, I know he's smiling at me.

"Bloody hell, ay. She's already talking like a Brit." He gives me another taste.

I cover my mouth with a hand as I smile and swallow the delicacy melting on my tongue. "I'm ready to guess."

"Go ahead."

I tell him, and then he spoons more into my mouth. "What else?"

"A touch of cream."

"Round one to you."

I grin like a kid after an Easter egg hunt. "Next." I turn in the stool so it's easier for him, and his thigh bumps my knee. He is so close. Too close.

I open my mouth and wait, but then I feel like an idiot and shut it again. What is he doing? He's right there, yet nothing is happening, our heavy breathing echoing around us. The suspense is killing me, and I want to tug at the blindfold.

Finally, his fingers touch my chin, and I open my mouth, no verbal prompt necessary. A nutty, creamy texture jolts my taste buds. The food is again of soft texture... mushrooms. And truffle. Is it truffle butter? "Wow." It's all I can say.

Fingertips brush my lips, and I open again. This time, I taste pasta, soft and smooth. "I'm picturing myself in Italy. The Amalfi Coast." I lick my lips, savoring the salt residue. "A type of pasta, mushrooms, truffle, parsley, a broth, maybe chicken or vegetable, and some sort of cheese."

"You're cheating somehow."

I giggle. "I'm not. I should have been a food critic."

His fingers graze over my lips, but I keep still, fighting the urge to shift. My mouth slowly opens, his fingers lingering on my lips, and I allow him to touch me in a way that sends messages south.

"A flake of parsley," he whispers.

He doesn't need to explain because, damn, I like this game. We're not doing anything sexual, yet it's as intense as foreplay. I imagine him leaning in and kissing my lips, a gentle brush, a delicate kiss.

A groan escapes, and I stiffen.

"Are you okay?" he whispers in my ear.

*Fuck. Is he leaning over me?* I lay my hands in my lap and splay my fingers to sense if he is near. He presses on my hands, pushing my fingers flat to my thighs.

"No touching," he says close to my ear, sending shivers up my spine. He is turning me on, and he knows it.

*Breathe.*

Not too deep because it will sound desperate. "Have you ever been in a relationship?" I say in a breathy whisper. How can a man be so attentive and distance himself from love?

"One in high school."

"Did it end badly?"

"No. I ended it. I felt constrained. Too many rules. She had expectations. No point in making promises you can't keep. Open," he says as the food touches my lips, and I quickly obey. Opening my mouth, it's meat, soft and tender. More herbs. A hint of citrus. Some sweet potato.

I chew carefully, considering his words. *Too many rules.*

"Persian style lamb. Now, do we get to eat because I'm hungry for more?" I'm so hungry for him that I need the food to distract me from the equally delicious Jobe Hendricks.

A gentle hand lands on my shoulder. "Patience, Zara. What dish did you enjoy the best?"

"I can't choose because I loved all of them." *And how it was served.*

He is leaning close. His arms brush past my shoulders, and then I sense him between my thighs.

*Good God.*

Will he kiss me?

His hands are at the back of my head, and he's standing between my thighs instead of standing behind me. I swear it's a ploy to rattle me. The tie slips off, and I'm left ogling his bare chest. Rounded pecs that I could easily lick if I leaned slightly closer.

Slowly, I allow my gaze to slide up to his beautiful face and meet those dark brown eyes. He's watching me intently, and I'm unable to look away. My heart flips with a longing I know I shouldn't be feeling.

There is a sexual magnetism to Jobe, a self-confidence that he knows what he does to me.

I swallow hard. "That was only three dishes."

A slow grin parts his lips. "Right. We'll eat, and then I'm saving the best for last."

What could be better than what I just experienced? I feel fucked by food, and I'm tingling all over. "I'm already sated," I murmur.

His sexy eyes dance at my response. "Don't be so easily satisfied, Zara."

I huff. "I am, so the bar is low."

His brow furrows. "Raise the bar."

I flinch. "Are we talking about sex?"

"We're talking about life," he says in a low voice. "And sex."

Oh boy. "So I lied. I'm starving. And you can take that any way you want."

His hand cups my cheek, and his eyes linger on my lips. "A problem I need to rectify."

"Rectify away," I whisper.

Jobe steps back, and the air separates us, leaving a chill

in his absence. My stomach falls in disappointment when he walks around the counter and stands by the stove to prepare our dishes.

Visually, the food is not as appealing as Jobe's naked torso, and suddenly, my appetite has nothing to do with the meal he's serving.

My ass is numb.

I've been sitting at the counter for God knows how long, eating everything Jobe puts in front of me. He leans on the counter and watches me as he eats. I already told him he is a genius in the kitchen. I should clarify he is a genius at seduction, and I want more.

We have finished a bottle of red, and I'm tingling all over.

"When am I getting the fourth dish?" I tease. I'm full and don't need any more food, but a girl is curious when told there is hype around the save-the-best-to-last dish.

He unties his apron and folds it before placing it in a drawer. Then he leans over the counter and clinks his glass with mine. "Are you ready for it?"

*It?*

I drop my gaze to his pecs bulging before my eyes. I'm overheating again, and not from the thermostat setting. Speaking of... "If you turned the heating down, you could put some clothes on," I note as I peel the jacket from my shoulders.

"Or you could take more off." He quirks an eyebrow.

He is definitely flirting.

"The rule, you can look but not touch. Is that for you or me?" I take another sip and wait for his expression to give me something. He straightens and pours another glass of wine. I wait a few more seconds before I add, "I guess it's for both of us. You didn't want to touch me with clothes on." I straighten in my seat. "And while I'm here admiring all of this..." I circle my hand around him, "... we both know it's a bad idea."

Jobe turns and prepares something on the other counter. "Remind me again why it's bad, Zara?"

"Um... because of your brother and my best friend. What do we tell them?"

"Why is it any of their business?"

"Penny is my best friend, and we tell each other everything."

"I think I rank higher with Frank being my brother, and he doesn't need to know anything unless I wish to tell him." He places a bowl of ice cream and something else in front of me.

"What is this?"

He fires up the coffee machine.

"Ice cream and Nutella."

He spreads Nutella around the top edge, makes a hole in the center of the ice cream and pours half of the shot of coffee into it. Then he picks up the spoon and mixes it gently, scooping it to the edge and collecting some of the smooth, nutty goodness. He then comes to sit at the counter beside me.

Jobe raises the spoon, and it touches my lips. When I open my mouth, he pulls the spoon back. Licking my lips, I let out a sigh when I taste the coffee shot mixed with ice cream and hazelnut. "You'll regret it if you deny me this."

He smiles and places the spoon in my mouth.

I close my eyes, savoring the flavor. "It's divine."

Jobe scoops some more and places the spoon upside down in his mouth, drawing it out slowly, watching me watch him as we give in to the craving of wanting the sweet pleasure in our mouths.

The divine food, the expensive red wine, the stolen glances, the seductive stares, and now finishing with a decadent dessert, the coffee is giving me a boost. "I'm not going to sleep tonight," I whisper. "I have caffeine sensitivity after midday."

He withdraws the spoon from his mouth, licks the edge, and then places it over my lips as if to silence me. "Who said anything about sleeping?"

## 15

———

ZARA

"What are we doing?" I whisper.

His dark eyes hold mine as he leans closer. "Kissing," he whispers as his lips brush over mine.

I close my eyes and gently press my lips to his. He pulls back slightly, his mouth sweeping over mine, his tongue tracing the outline of my mouth slowly, softly. Our breaths mingle, and I don't think dessert has ever tasted so good. "I can taste the coffee," I murmur.

He trails kisses over my cheek, down my neck, and to my shoulder, so I tilt my head, giving him access to my skin. My mind battles... I should tell him to stop.

His lips move to my ear. "I need to taste you, Zara."

My stomach flips, and all my thoughts stop. Arousal rushes through my body, and I'm beyond stopping it. I push up, wrapping my hands around his neck and my legs around his waist, kissing him hard.

With two hands under my ass, Jobe carries me to his

bedroom, where he kicks the door open and places me on his bed. His lips stay on mine as he huddles over me, undoing my shirt buttons. I start from the bottom button and meet him halfway, pulling my shirt over my shoulders, my breasts spilling over my bra. Jobe runs his hands over my skin and bra, trailing his hands behind my back and unclipping my bra. He slowly slides it off, staring at my bare chest, taking all of me in as he does. I sit forward and fiddle with the buttons of his jeans, but Jobe swats my hands away.

"Be patient."

"Not one of my stronger traits," I reply.

He makes light work of my pants and pulls them off. I'm lying on my back in only my panties, staring at the bulge in his jeans pushing against the band.

He moves away from me, his expression now tight. "Is this what you want, Zara?"

I nod, my eyes heavy with desire for him.

"I'm giving you a chance to gather your thoughts and consider what is happening."

*What is happening besides we are about to fuck?*

Oh, he's giving me time to say no. I did tell him multiple times this would be a huge mistake, but the way my body is screaming to be touched means I want him inside me now. Drunk on arousal, I don't care if this is for one night or one week. I *need* him tonight. I meet his gaze and hold it. "I want this."

He nods slowly and waits a few more seconds before sliding his jeans and silk boxers down his glorious thighs. Long, lean, muscular thighs. The best legs I've ever seen. His family's beautiful olive complexion is evident in his legs covered by trousers every day.

When was the last time he sat on a beach and enjoyed the calm in the warmth?

He strokes his beautiful cock. "What is it?"

I shake my head. Why am I thinking about that now? I hold out my arms for him, but he pulls my ankles, so I slide closer to the edge, then he pries my knees open, kneeling beside the bed. He lays one kiss over my clit, and even through the thin material, I feel it. It sends a shudder through my core, the anticipation almost unbearable.

His eyes rake over me, a yearning between us. He slips one finger under the band of my panties and slides it over my wet slit. His touch is torturous, slow, and delicate. When he pushes one finger inside, I arch, seeking more.

"Yes," I moan out, tilting my hips. He withdraws, and before I can whimper in protest, he adds another, my thighs shaking. When he pulls back again, he slides another finger in, then pumps slowly, the stretch exactly what I need, and he hits the spot immediately. "Faster," I demand on a moan.

"Stop telling me what to do," he growls out before leaning up and bracing himself over me, kissing my cheek. Then his mouth is on mine. "I've got this, angel."

*Angel.*

His tongue moves between my lips and twirls with mine. His fingers are working me, and the orgasm is building faster than I want, and I can barely concentrate. He breaks the kiss, his mouth moving to my breast. He toys with one nipple, sucking and nipping before shifting to the other. My back arches, my body surging at the intimacy of his touch. I take his head and hold it between my hands as though I have some control over him. The truth is, I have none. His thumb presses on my clit while his fingers pump and circle at an incredible speed. Lost to the bliss, I cry out as I come, lifting my hips off the bed before I fall limp onto the sheets.

Jobe slips off the bed and slides my drenched panties down my thighs, tossing them toward the wall. He lifts my legs over his shoulders then his hot mouth is on my pussy, licking and groaning as he tastes my orgasm. "So fucking beautiful," he whispers. "So sexy." He licks and sucks my clit and toys with me as though I'm his shiny new toy, and he can't get enough of me. I squirm and bolt my hips as smaller orgasms ripple over me, one after the other.

Sitting up, I run my fingers through his hair and tug. "I need you now," I whisper.

To my relief, he doesn't hesitate. He reaches and opens his drawer, pulling out a condom.

Anxiously, I lay back and wait as I watch him roll it over his thick erection. Since I'm on my back, I consider if this is too vanilla for him. I don't recall much of our first time. All I have to go by is gossip and the fact he mentioned multiple partners at once. My insecurities start to bubble, but before they have time to rise, he kneels between my thighs.

"Open your legs wider, Zara." He stares at my pussy while he strokes himself. I force my legs wide until my inner thighs tighten. He smiles. "Fucking beautiful," he growls out, then he guides himself to my entrance and leans over me, his biceps tensing as he braces his weight, his face strained in what looks like a grimace.

"Are you okay?" I murmur as he slides out slowly and pushes in again, allowing my pussy to adjust to the size of him.

"Are *you* okay?" he counters, and I nod.

He pushes deeper, this time a little faster.

"You looked like you were in pain?"

He drops his head, his muscles clenching like he's holding back. "You have no idea how long I've waited for this."

Oh. I didn't expect him to say that. "It happened before..." I remind him.

"It wasn't memorable for you." He moves faster, instinct taking over.

I run my hands over the planes of his back, forging every detail to my memory. "It's patchy," I admit between breaths.

"Trust me, tonight will not be. You'll remember everything I do to you, and you'll feel it tomorrow."

*Oh my.*

"I live here," I pant out. "It doesn't have to end tonight, so I don't want to be sore for tomorrow."

His face changes.

*Crap.* Did I overstep a mark? "Just saying because it's been a while. I need to get back into the game."

"The game of sex?"

I nod. "You were my last."

Something comes over him. His eyes darken, and he rocks into me harder and faster. He lowers himself onto his elbows and pumps into me until I'm incapable of talking. He rides me deep and hard, and I wrap my arms around him to hang on for dear life. He lifts a leg over his shoulder, and his thrusts are punishing. I close my eyes and give myself to him, trusting him with my body. Something changes in the air between us. He's no longer in control, and neither am I. We are lost to the lust taking us to the edge. My head is in the stars. Then, I'm blinded by the brightness. "Jobe," I call out as a mammoth orgasm rips through me.

He thrusts hard, sinking deep as he shudders, emptying into me. His thrusts slow, his breath coming in loud pants. Then his eyes hold mine, a heart rendering tenderness in his gaze. I give him a satiated smile, completely satisfied while trying to ignore the rush of overwhelming happiness of being with Jobe.

Leaning his forehead against mine, his breath brushes over my face. A hint of coffee and ice cream. My heart flutters, remembering everything. "Thank you," I whisper, kissing his lips.

He pulls back, staring at me, puzzled.

"For everything," I clarify. "Especially the orgasms."

Jobe is behind me in the bed, spooning me when I wake up, and I fail to hide my grin. It's the complete opposite of how I woke up the first time we were together.

That memory dims my good mood, and I whisper into the sheets, "You vanished on me last time."

"I did." His deep voice sounds from behind me. "I shouldn't have."

My face heats. "I assumed I must have been awful for you."

"What? No." His arm tightens around my waist. "I was... out of my depth. It was good, Zara. Better than anything I'd... and I knew how little you thought of me. I didn't want to see your regret, so I left."

"I don't regret it," I say and cup his hand, sliding his fingers toward my clit. I press his hand onto my sex and close my eyes.

"I have breakfast covered," he murmurs, and I smile into the pillow.

Suddenly, I'm flipped, my front on the mattress. He's over me, spreading my thighs apart with his knees. He grabs a pillow and lifts my stomach, pushing it under my hips.

What is happening?

My face is squashed to the side, and he's on his knees behind me, stroking my sex. "Your pussy is fucking perfect," he growls out.

*Oh.* I'm wet already, and he spreads the moisture over my sex and clit. He falls over me, his stomach to my back, and I love the warmth radiating from him. Hot air brushes over my ear. "I'm going to make you come, Zara. Again and again."

I smile as though I'm in sexual heaven. "I'm here for it." *I am back in the game.*

His cock presses at my entrance. Then he shifts, using his hand to guide him all the way in.

I lift my head. "Oh…" I moan. It feels so good at this angle.

"I'm going to fuck you hard, Zara. Are you okay with that?"

I smile goofily. "More than okay."

He starts off slowly, then builds quickly, riding me hard and fast. Desire spreads quickly through my body. I pant with every thrust. Jobe pushes up and circles his hips as he pounds my ass, driving into me at piston pace. Whether it's the angle or the position with my hips tilted up for him, I feel *all* of him. Seconds later, an orgasm rips through me. I let out a moan of pleasure and wait for him to empty inside me.

It doesn't come.

He forces a hand under my stomach and lifts me. "On your knees, Zara," he barks. I do what he asks. One hand cups my neck, and he pushes my face toward the pillows. His knees spread my thighs wider. The other hand grabs my hip to hold my position. Then he gives me everything he has.

I can barely breathe as his cocks drives deeper and deeper into my body's threshold, the pain and pleasure crashing into one. I groan as I build again, my body confused as the sexual pain creates a new brand of bliss of being completely fucked. I come again, loud with a cry of relief and joy, momentarily blinding. Impossibly, he pumps harder, his thrusts owning my body once more until he moans loudly and slumps over my back. He remains still for a few seconds before his loud pants begin to slow.

Jobe kisses my back as he pulls out and falls onto the bed beside me. Every time his gaze meets mine, my heart turns over in response.

I smile, wrapped in a silken cocoon of euphoria. "Hey."

"Hey." He sounds sex drunk, and there is no better sound.

He's on his side, and we take our time, enjoying the sexual haze before it disappears. Then he glances down, and his expression flails.

"What?" I whisper, seeing the shock and horror on his face. My gaze lowers, expecting blood or something. It takes a moment to realize he didn't wear a condom. "I'm on the pill," I reassure him. "And you're..."

"Fine."

But he's not. Something has snapped his control. He jumps up from the bed and heads to the bathroom. Moments later, I hear the shower spray. Do I join him and reassure him it's okay or give him time to process?

I don't want to stay in his bed if he needs space. Collecting my clothes scattered around the room, I head to my bathroom to shower alone. It's probably best because the throb between my legs indicates I couldn't go another round.

After showering and tending to my sore bits, I emerge from my room, hair washed and completely refreshed, wearing my bathrobe. Until I know what the day holds, I haven't planned what to wear. I inhale a familiar smell.

*He's cooking breakfast.*

A positive sign.

I start to say good morning then realize the gesture has passed since our good morning greeting was in his bed. Sliding onto the stool, I watch him standing barefoot in his loose chambray shirt and jeans. His tussled dark hair is still damp from the shower.

I like casual Jobe.

"Are you hungry?" he asks without turning.

*For you? Yes.* "Starving." He turns and eyes me. Yeah, I wasn't only talking about food, and it came out in my tone. "Are you okay?" I ask gently. "After I showered, I wasn't sure what to expect."

He lowers his head and closes his eyes. "I've never had unprotected sex, and it caught me off guard. If I got you pregnant—"

"Jobe, I use contraception," I remind him. "It's fine. Now, what are you cooking?"

He gives me half a smile. "Zucchini fritters."

"Smells good." Eggs, grated zucchini, carrots, and cheese are on a plate on the counter.

"So do you," he murmurs.

I stand and walk over to the other side, closer to him, spring up, and sit on the marble counter. I run my fingers through my hair. "It's my favorite coconut shampoo." He steps closer and leans in to smell my hair.

"It's good, but that's not what I was inferring."

*Oh.*

I open my legs so he can stand between my thighs and tilt my neck. "My new perfume, perhaps?"

"No."

A hand runs along the inside of my thigh, exploring and moving higher. He cups my sex and leans close to my ear. "I can smell *you* from here."

"Oh, I have a smell?"

He nudges my ear and kisses my neck. "Your perfume is good, but Zara is my favorite scent."

The stroking of his fingers over my panties sends a pleasant jolt through me. His nearness overwhelms my demeanor, and I become putty in his hands. As soon as one finger slips under the elastic, I lean back onto my elbows and open my legs for him.

He holds my gaze as he slides my panties down my thighs and lowers his face to my clit. I cover an arm over my eyes as my hips buck with his lips every caress.

Breakfast is served.

**16**

___________

ZARA

MONDAY MORNING, I sit in the café opposite the offices and wait for Piper to arrive.

Jobe and I spent the entire weekend in his penthouse. We fucked in every room. No furniture piece was safe. Even now, there's a gentle throbbing between my legs from shower sex before he left for work.

Piper bounces toward me, wearing a lady's black pantsuit with a hot pink shirt underneath her blazer. The colors accentuate her blonde hair, bright like the sun, her broad smile lighting up her face. She leans in and hugs me, then places a small box on the table. "We missed you yesterday."

*Oh shit.* She messaged me about meeting up to watch the game. "Sorry. I was flat out." Literally. "Time got away from me."

"Is your boyfriend here?"

I smile at her. "He is."

"Then you're forgiven. We can catch up next weekend."

"Sure. I don't have anything else on." It hits me how I'll miss him the weeks he'll be gone.

She orders us both a coffee and then slides the box closer to me. "Have you been to York?"

"Not yet." I open the box. "Yum. What flavor do we have today?"

"Blueberry and apricot." She beams her smile at me. "Shall we plan a weekend for you to visit? It's such a fun and interesting city, yeah?"

I smile. "Yes, let's do it. I don't want to stay in London every weekend because there is so much I haven't seen."

"Right. On the next holiday weekend, we'll visit Scotland."

"That would be awesome." I take a bite of my muffin and groan when the flavor hits my tongue. "These are good," I say with a mouthful.

"What's awesome?" George asks as he slides into a chair beside Piper.

George's hair is perfectly styled, and his pastel lime shirt is accessorized with a lemon-striped tie. Being with them both makes me want to revamp my wardrobe.

"York," I answer. "Piper wants to take me there."

"Count me in," he says jovially. "Zara, did you hear anything more about the merger?"

I shake my head.

"By all accounts, the Board is slowing matters up." She gives George his boxed muffin.

I shrug. "It doesn't faze me as I'm happy in my current position. I just hope they don't make me redundant." I want to share the promotion with my friends, but Tim asked me to keep it quiet. And God knows what might happen. It might not even go ahead.

"Lydia has been promoted." He lifts the lid of the box and then smiles at Piper and mouths, *Thank you.*

I stare at him. "Where are you hearing your information?"

"Gretchen. We had drinks Friday night, and she was pissed about something. Since she is going on maternity leave in a matter of weeks, she spilled the beans on a few things like the executive offices have been painted different shades of blue for each office. She also said you might know more."

"Me?" I say in a high pitch. "Why would she think that?"

He tilts his head in a nod. "No idea. Anyway, we should find out more today. Monday morning meetings are the best."

"You're weird," Piper tells him and sips her coffee. "I won't be here forever, so I don't care a bunch."

The emotional turmoil pulls at me at having to lie until the whole team knows more. My gut twists uncomfortably, torn between loyalty to my friends or to the company and a CEO I have never met. But his words stay in my head, and I mull over his point about the office being painted blue. A reminder of that first night when Jobe spoke about color, and how blue helped to focus, and... what did he say... improves productivity?

Weird.

I smile, thinking how I carried a wounded heart from that same night, and now I'm floating on the clouds. The regret and hurt melted away.

# 17

## JOBE

ANXIOUS FOR THE business day to end, I roll my shoulders, needing a good massage to ease the tension. Like numerous times today, my thoughts head straight to Zara. My cock twitches when I think of her sprawled out on the kitchen counter... in the shower... on my bed.

My cell buzzes. Clive can fuck right off. I'm done for the day. While Sir James' company takeover is a priority, the merger taking place now is settling in with announcements happening as staff reshuffles. Why I believed I could manage both was a dumbass move.

It buzzes again with an incoming call from Franklin. His day is only beginning. I send a reply.

Will call later.

Penny and I are invited to Sir James' gala ball.

The fuck?





I toss my cell on the desk and close my eyes, rolling my shoulders. How am I going to convince Penny not to come and see her best friend? Needing something to take the edge off, I stand, head to the liquor cabinet, and pour myself a double on ice. Then, I return to my desk to continue with the endless emails.

Several bourbons later, I walk out of the office.

Even from the street, I see the penthouse is dark.

*Where is she?*

She can go wherever and do whatever she likes as long as she behaves as though she has a boyfriend.

*Am I taking this too far?*

My thoughts are akin to us as a couple, pretend or not. I have never had feelings like this.

Inside, I flick on the lights. Has she not come home from work? Is she okay? I tap on her number.

"Hey," she answers. "Are you home?"

I smile at the mere sound of her voice. "I am. Just walked in."

"I'm in the pool," she says excitedly. "You should join me. It will ease the tension."

"I know something else that will ease the tension." *Her heels wrapped around my shoulders.*

She laughs. "Are you horny all the time?"

"Do bears shit in the woods?"

She giggles. "Such a romantic."

Her infectious laugh makes me smile. "Stay there. I'll

come right down." I grab a towel and head out the door, taking the elevator to the basement.

Zara is breast-stroking across the pool but stops and paddles when she sees me. "Are you getting in?" She frowns at my suit.

"I am." I strip off and dive in.

"Oh my God." She's laughing when I surface. "I don't think nudity is allowed."

"I own the fucking building, Zara. I can do what I want." Including the security clearance to disable the keypad to enter the pool on my way in so we won't be interrupted. I pull her close and wrap her arms around my neck. Her legs circle me like a monkey.

"You own the building? I assumed you only bought the penthouse."

"I bought the entire complex and rent out the other apartments." I nuzzle her neck. "If anyone has a complaint about their pool access being denied, they can direct their complaints to the owner." I suck on her neck and shoulders while sliding my fingers inside her.

Zara's eyes pop. "Oh. We're doing it here, are we?"

I grin at her. "About the only place we haven't fucked."

She looks over her shoulders. "It's public."

"Not tonight."

"I don't know…"

"I have it under control." I work my fingers inside her, watching her pretty face change as pleasure overtakes her body. She comes for me, hard and fast. I can't resist and smother my mouth over hers. "You're fucking beautiful."

She pulls away, staring at me. "You think so?"

"I know so."

She grinds her pussy over my erection. "Careful," I warn. "I might slip in."

She lets go of my neck, pushes her bathing suit aside,

and takes hold of my dick. "For the record, you will never just slip in."

I smile at her. "Fuck me now, Zara. Because I'm about to blow in the pool."

She eases herself onto my cock and slowly slides up and down. "Best feeling in the world. My cock inside you."

She giggles and tilts her head back as she rides me. The animal in me takes over. I spin her to the side of the pool, hold her hips, and pump into her as hard as my body demands. Her arms spread out over the ledge of the pool. Her head tilts back as I bring her hips forward to meet my every thrust.

*When I'm here, she is mine.*

AN HOUR LATER, WE WRAP TOWELS AROUND OUR DRIPPING WET bodies and take the elevator up to my penthouse. As soon as the door closes, I gently cup her face, kissing her plump lips. "Do you want to go out for dinner?" I murmur, preferring Zara for dinner.

She shakes her head. "I want you to myself. Can we order in?"

I eye her sexy body. "And what will we do while we wait?"

She smiles up at me. "I have it covered."

After ordering Thai food, I place my cell on the counter. She takes my hand and leads me to her bed.

"I want the feeling of wet-bodied sex out of the pool," she purrs. She gives me a little shove, grabbing the towel from my waist. "On your back, Hendricks."

A slow smile parts my lips. Bossy Zara is a turn-on.

She slips off her swimsuit and crawls over me, sitting over my hips. "Hands above your head." I do as she says and watch her caress her breasts. She squeezes and massages, then groans, leaning forward so I can take one in my mouth. Her hands push down on my wrists, ensuring I don't move. Her in control, taking what she wants from me, is fucking erotic.

My dick is hard, and I lift my hips to find her.

"No." She *tsks,* firmly pushing my hips down. Easing up, she slides onto my cock, putting me out of my misery. She slowly rides me, her hands holding my wrists as she stares down at me, watching my reaction. "Is that good?" she murmurs.

"It's perfect. Now speed it up," I grit out, needing more of her.

"When I'm ready," she says, her eyes sparkling with desire.

I take all the pleasure Zara gives, riding me into the mattress until she is bouncing with abandon. She comes, her head tilting back, and I grab both her breasts, pumping into her and riding into my orgasm.

The vision of her blurs as she watches me come. The bliss overrides every thought in my head. A sensation I live for, the pleasure rippling through my body—the pleasure of Zara's body. Then, leaning down, she kisses my cheek and lips, deepening the kiss, sharing the moment with me. "I'm so glad you asked me to move in with you."

I laugh. She is so fucking sweet. "It was always my plan."

She frowns at me. "You didn't know we'd end up like this."

I arch my brows. "I hoped we would. You're all I thought about. I couldn't handle it any longer. I tried not to want you, but it got to a point that I gave up the fight."

She slides her long legs along my body and lays on top of me, her chin resting on her hands splayed on my chest. "What are we going to do?"

"Eat dinner, then fuck some more."

"Not what I meant. Is this going to be our secret?"

"About that." I let out a long breath. "Penny and Franklin are invited to the gala with Sir James. And us. It's the final time we need to pretend in front of him." Her face changes. "It's okay. We don't have to tell them anything except we're pretending for Sir James. Franklin knows what we have to do to get the takeover."

"Franklin knows?"

I nod. "He hasn't mentioned it to Penny. I told him it's merely until the gala."

Pain flickers in her eyes for a moment then she rolls off me. *Was it disappointment?* "I'm going to shower before dinner arrives."

Tilting my head, I admire her sexy ass as she strides out of the room. "Or we could eat naked," I call out, but I don't get a response. "If you don't want Penny to come, I can tell Frank to cancel," I add loud enough for her to hear.

Nothing.

I find my cell and send Franklin a message.

> Zara is nervous about seeing Penny with us faking a relationship in front of her.

It buzzes with a reply.

> Tell her not to be as I told Penny what is required… unless you're not faking it.

Fuck.

## 18

ZARA

AFTER EATING the Thai food in silence, Jobe's cell doesn't stop.

"We agreed on this," he snaps, and I jump out of my skin. My heart races with his anger.

*I could not work for him.*

"Make it happen and check back with me in the morning." His tension rises with endless calls, and it feels wrong to be in the room when he is attending to business. His demeanor has changed, and he needs privacy to deal with whatever went down with his company.

Before I walk out of the room, he says, "Yes, I'll be there tomorrow, and I'll deal with it first thing in the morning."

The one thing I know about the Hendricks family is they won't sleep until they get the job done, so I don't expect Jobe to come to bed any time soon. My sheets remain wet, and while there are other bedrooms, I feel we are in a place where I can sleep in his bed. I stick my ear pods in and play my favorite romantic playlist rather than listen to Jobe's heated conversation.

When I wake the next morning, I'm lying next to an empty space as he's clearly left for the office at some ungodly hour. *Did he even come to bed at all?*

I go through my usual routine and wait for Piper at the café.

George walks in with her. "It's happening today," he says, wide-eyed. He looks smart in a suit jacket.

"Have you been talking to Gretchen again?"

He frowns, his brows pinching. "Maybe."

"Well, I'm heading there now," Piper says, looking at me. "Coming?"

Downing the remainder of my coffee, I walk with them into our office block. My stomach is tense. Not for today's announcement but what Jobe said last night.

*It's the final time we need to pretend* plays over in my mind.

I hoped we were getting somewhere, and now there's a freaking time bomb ticking for when he checks out. I don't know whether to ask him point blank if he's going to end us because I saw him in the moment when we were together. We have something. I heard him admit to the yearning. We have great chemistry, so why end it and not see where this will lead?

Oh crap. Is it you want what you can't have, and now, after I gave myself to him, he's moving on?

I scan my ID as I walk through the building. I'm so distracted I probably won't hear a single word.

Around nine thirty, we gather in a meeting room and wait for Tim, who strides in, hands in pockets, eyes lowered. The door closes with an audible click that echoes the room as we all wait for what comes next.

"Can I please have everyone's attention?" Mindless

chatter stops, and he clears his throat. "Today is my last day at Warburton Investments." Gasps and groans fill the room. "As you know, the company is merging with an LA-based company." His eyes meet mine, and my heart flips. Why does this have anything to do with me? "Over the next week, offers will roll out. Some juggling is inevitable. It's your choice whether you want to stay with the new company or accept your new role. There's not much more I can say than to wish you all the best for the future and thank you for making my role here easier than it should be. You're all a great bunch, and I'm sorry not to host the Monday meeting any longer." Someone sobs at the back of the room. I didn't know him well but he seems like a great guy. "Juliet has my personal number, so if any of you want to reach out for a drink, I'd love to see you. Are there any questions about your future roles, not mine?"

"Who is Juliet?" I whisper to Piper. "We should have a drink with Tim."

She nods. "She's his PA. *Was.*"

I give my focus to Tim. I feel for him as I sense this was unexpected. He glances at his cell. "The new company director is on his way down." He looks at the door.

The guy opposite me raises his hand. "Tim. Was it your choice to leave?"

"It was a mutual agreement."

"Bullshit," George whispers beside me.

The door opens, and a suited guy appears.

Designer suit. Dark hair. Suddenly, I'm wide awake. "What in the holy fuck!" I whisper, though it's more of a quiet shout. His eyes scan the room. I avert my gaze. I cannot look at Jobe Hendricks right now.

Piper leans forward and stares at me. "Is that your boyfriend?"

"Not anymore," I snap.

I can't breathe. Why didn't he tell me this was the *other* merger he was working on? Heat rises up my neck and cheeks, my whole face glowing red. So, this is what he had to deal with first thing this morning. And he didn't mention a damn thing.

"Did you know?" George whispers.

I give him a sideways glance and shake my head. "Did you?"

Jobe clears his throat. "I'll start with introductions. I'm Jobe Hendricks, the new company executive director. Thank you for taking time out of your day to be here."

"Love his accent," whispers come from behind me.

"I'd do him," a woman says, but I don't turn.

*He's not on the market, bitch, but after this meeting, he might be.*

Jobe's eyes find mine, and I narrow mine at him. Bastard. How dare he embarrass me in front of my work friends whom he has met. I understand the secrecy, but he could trust me with this information since it's integral to my career. Because right now, I feel like I'm nothing more to him than a convenience to his business deals. And it really was just sex between us. Nothing more. He never felt close to me on an emotional level. Never considered trusting me with this information. I have tuned him out and don't hear a single word he says.

It clearly cements our fake relationship—he really doesn't see me as anything more than a temporary lover.

He would have known how this would be received.

*Poor fucking form, Jobe, and I don't care that you're my new boss. I really can't stand the sight of you right now.*

"I want to invite you all to be part of the team to revolutionize the London market. Warburton is one of the many companies Hendricks Real Estate is invested in, along with Hendricks Capital Management that my brother,

Franklin, manages." His eyes scan the room, and I lower my gaze, refusing to acknowledge him. "There'll be whispers about the merger but I assure you, if you're in this room, then your job is safe unless your behavior is questionable and your work ethic poor. New contracts will roll out over the next month. I'm employing an extra executive assistant to accelerate the process. If you have any questions, email Gretchen. She'll hand everything over to her replacement when she is on maternity leave." He looks around the room as if assessing everyone's reaction. "Unfortunately, today is not a day that I can stay and answer questions, but we will address everyone soon. So, please excuse me. The Board is waiting for me. I look forward to meeting each of you in the near future." His gaze meets mine, but I give him nothing but my best poker face as I stare through him as though he is a ghost to me.

The fucker.

Jobe leaves the room, and the staff stands, whispers turning into louder conversation. Some people threaten to leave, citing an uncertain future. *He could have handled it differently. Or was it the Board's decision?*

"Are you okay?" Piper whispers. Her blue eyes are full of understanding. I shake my head. "He kept looking at you."

Slowly, I close my eyes before opening them again. "Can we go?"

"Sure." She creates a path through the crowd, and I follow her to the door as we head back to the office. "You know, everyone will be taking their time coming back. Let's head down and get a coffee. Caffeine doesn't fix everything, but it helps when alcohol isn't a choice."

"I'll need fifty fucking cups," I mutter.

She turns and smiles, looping her arm through mine. "You need to vent, and if it takes fifty cups, so be it."

"Thank you." I squeeze her hand as we head out of the

office block and cross the road to the café. I'm old enough to handle the crap the universe throws at me. However, I've never been any good with surprises. From being spooked by my best friend telling me she's pregnant and our lives spiraling in opposite directions, it's unexpected dishonesty that destroys me the most. Furthermore, his lie is an embarrassment I can't handle.

I take a seat while Piper orders the coffee. As soon as she slides into her chair, she stares at me. "Tell me everything because there is a lot going on behind the scenes you haven't told me about."

"You're right."

And I do. I tell her everything.

She reaches across and takes my hand. "So you've fallen for him?"

I swipe a single tear from my cheek. "If I'm being honest, I've always liked him. It was easier to hate him than fall for the bad guy. One who would never be satisfied with monogamy."

"But he did commit to you even though he said it was a fake relationship."

"Then he's a damn good actor. He admitted to a final date when the show ends, so..."

"Hey, I get it. I also fall for the wrong guy. Promises me the world and then does something to ruin everything we had and turn it into something meaningless."

"We're the queens of picking the wrong guy." I force a smile. "Today..." I shake my head, "... he could've mentioned it, then I wouldn't look like an idiot in front of you all. Worst of all, it made me look like I was keeping it from you."

"I didn't think that."

"George did."

She tilts her head. "George is George. He'd sell his soul for gossip."

"Now. If people find out we had something, if we did..." I shake my head to rid the painful thoughts, "... they'll judge me. Believe there is favoritism. You know what people say about women who sleep with the boss."

"You didn't know he was the boss."

I arch my brow for emphasis. "Or if I'll sleep with him again now that he is the boss. But what pisses me off more, there isn't a repercussion for him. I'm over the fucking shaming of women."

"I hear you, girlfriend." Piper smiles. "Then hold your head high as you have done nothing wrong. Before we go down that rabbit hole, here's some advice. Put everything aside. Work. The fake relationship. The past. What happened today. How do you feel about *him*? What does your heart tell you?"

I pick up my second coffee mug and sip it slowly, pondering my feelings for Jobe. "Before he turned up at work, I would have wanted a chance for us and see where a relationship takes us. Because even when we bicker, I enjoy it. He challenges me. Years back, when he upset my best friend because he was looking out for his brother, I was ready to fight him for her. But now that he's betrayed me, not trusted me with this... I feel... insignificant to him. Like my feelings don't matter. And I don't know if I want a relationship with a man who treats me like this.

"Right. But even when you hate them, they attract you in some way. You might want to ride this wave. You might save each other."

I hold up my mug and tilt it toward her to make a point. "First, it's a freaking tsunami, and I don't know where the hell it's carrying me. All I can see is us both drowning and never trusting to love again."

"Whoa, you said love."

*Shit.*

"I meant a relationship. Because it's lust that has trapped us."

Piper assesses me for a moment and then checks her phone. "We better get back because your boyfriend will think our work ethic sucks, and we'll both lose our jobs."

"Fuck him." All I can think is that it's not the worst thing that could happen to me. Maybe I need to update my resume, find another job, and find somewhere else to live after the gala. Because I'm scared of what happens next, scared of Jobe confirming I haven't meant anything more to him than a stepping stone to a business deal.

We walk into the office.

*What is happening?*

Everyone is at their desks, focusing on their screens.

"What have we missed?" Piper whispers to George.

He tilts his head to a camera in the corner of the ceiling. "Security cameras will pick up anyone not working. Read your emails on work ethic." His gaze flicks to mine, and then he looks away without a word.

*What does he know?*

"We'll chat at lunch," Piper whispers to me.

Only we don't. Lunch comes and goes without a word of the takeover, as it appears my work friends no longer trust me.

AT THE END OF THE DAY, I DON'T TOUCH MY PHONE MESSAGES until I'm on the Tube. There's a message from Jobe.

I'm sorry about this morning. I know you're
mad, but my hands were tied. I want to talk
about it, only I'm on my way to the airport
as something has come up in LA. If they
gave me more notice, you could have come
back with me. Penny, for once, would be
excited for the extra emissions if you were
on the jet with me. We'll talk later. I'd rather
be with you tonight than sorting out the
fuckery back home.

Bull-fucking-shit. He is the executive director. Were his hands really tied? It is up to him who he tells, and more importantly, he could have trusted me. Let me inside his fucking armor that blocks all emotion.

Tim looked out for me and my career, and now he has lost his job. Another reason why I am upset and have every right to be when he lets the Board dictate how much he trusts me.

I let out a long sigh. It works out for the best since I did not want to face Jobe tonight. We both need space.

And I need a shit ton of time to work through this.

THE FOLLOWING DAY, EVERYONE IS DISTANT AT WORK AS though I'm a spy. Piper barely speaks in the office, but at lunch, she is back to her chatty self, so it's obvious the mention of the security camera has spooked her.

By the time I head home, I'm overwhelmed and need a quiet night. As soon as I enter the penthouse, I receive a text message.

Wish I was there with you. What are you
having for dinner?

I haven't replied to his texts as I don't know what to say without mentioning how he hurt me. Why do I have to be the girl who wears her heart on her sleeve?

I shower, order takeout, then check my cell.

*Penny.* My heart does a little dance.

> Hi, babe, how is it going? I miss you so much. Franklin told me about your fake relationship with Jobe. If you want to talk about it, I'm here for you because you need a freaking medal. Love you x

I let out an equally disappointed sigh at the acknowledgment of a fake relationship. But she's right. I need a medal, a big fucker, to show I survived. If only she were here so we could talk.

My cell buzzes again.

Jobe.

> By the way, Penny knows.

No shit, dumbass. I'm relieved Penny knows, even if it's fake because I don't like keeping things from her. Checking the time, it's midmorning in LA, so I grab a blanket and head out to the terrace.

My cell makes the weird FaceTime noise.

"Zara!" Penny screams. Her big smile lights up the screen. "How are you?"

"Okay." I force a smile because seeing her has brought on a ripple of emotions. "I miss you."

Her face sags. "I miss you too. Terribly." She looks away and then back to me. "Summer is sleeping. I'm so tired and all I think is Zee would cheer me up. We could have a night out together, and the world would be right again."

"Your world is right," I tell her. "Everything is how it

should be. I won't be away forever, and I'll be back doing those things with you like no time has passed."

"Have you booked a return flight?"

I shake my head. "Everything is uncertain at the moment. I gave myself a year, but we'll see."

"What do you want to achieve in a year?"

She's watching me attentively as I consider my answer. "Originally, I wanted to get my life in some order. Boost my career. Travel some and enjoy the adventure. Make new friends."

Her bottom lip curls under. "You already have great friends."

I laugh at her. "I do. You're my forever friends. But I don't want to be alone here."

"No." She leans closer. "Why didn't you tell me about your arrangement with Jobe?"

I twist my lips, feeling like a shit friend. "I didn't know how you'd react. Besides, it's a short time, and I think we have one more date... a gala to attend together."

"I know." Her eyes widen with excitement. "Franklin and I are also attending. I get to see you, and it will be fun. When your mother told me you won't be home for Thanksgiving, I decided to come to you."

"You spoke to Mom?"

"Yes." Her eyes widen. "I wanted to surprise you if you were coming home. Thank you for doing this for the family. I wasn't happy at first, the dishonesty in business." She shrugs. "I felt sorry for Sir James. Then I understood how our family investment will benefit both businesses, and an older man's opinion could ruin that." She tilts her head as she holds my gaze. "You've always been stronger than me."

My eyes well. "I'm not. I have always admired your strength and doing the right thing in the world. You have your life in order. I'm still floating around the planet, not knowing where I'm going or why."

Her brow furrows. "You just told me your plan. Stick to your goals. Show London what Zara Hart can do."

"I'm glad you have faith in me." I double back. "So you're coming to the gala?" Excitement grows in my chest at seeing my friend. It will be like the old days, but it won't.

"Ah-ha." She beams her beautiful smile at me. "Jobe said it's not necessary, but Franklin thinks we should attend to represent HCM."

"It's so close to Christmas... but I'd love to see you." But not when I'm fake adoring her brother-in-law. Only it's not fake. *She'll notice.* I. Will. Die.

Her head turns. "Babe, I'm sorry I have to go. Can we talk tomorrow? By the time I'm organized, you'll probably be in bed."

"Of course. You can talk to me anytime." We blow each other a kiss before ending the video call.

I hold my cell to my chest. Damn, I have to text him.

> Penny and Franklin are coming to the gala! I can't fake date you in front of them!

I get to my feet, anxiety creeping up my chest as I wait for Jobe to reply.

> I'll convince him not to attend so you don't have to stress.

> Stressed? More like mortified!

Grabbing the blanket, I head inside to pour a red wine to help me sleep. Then, I flop onto the sofa with my wine glass and open my cell.

I wrap the blanket around me, seeking some form of comfort. Now, all I need is a good book—one that ends with a guaranteed happily ever after.

## 19

JOBE

THE LAST FEW days have been hell.

For the first time in years, I'm over the shitshow of business fuckups. Dealing with incompetent dickwads is doing my head in. I have respect for my brother because *this* is Franklin's life, and he is great at it.

Today, I'm grateful for the break and to be with family at Thanksgiving. Pulling into the long circular paved entrance out the front of my parents' home, I park beside Franklin's black Bentley. Penny and her parents emerge from the car.

Frank takes Summer from her baby carrier and places her in a stroller. I'm out of my car, clicking the security button while Penny is still fussing over the bedding. I walk over to them and peer in. Summer is asleep, her tiny lips in a pout.

Penny looks tense. "She doesn't travel well," she whispers, pulling me in for a hug. "Happy Thanksgiving, Jobe." I kiss Penny's cheek and tighten my arms around her, feeling the gentle love. She has brought much warmth into our family and brought us closer in a way.

Franklin shakes my hand and pats my shoulder in a reassuring way. "Happy Thanksgiving, Jobe." I place a hand over his. Franklin is the person I admire the most, even more than our father.

"Happy Thanksgiving, Frank." I turn to greet Penny's parents, Lacey and Ray. Penny walks ahead with the stroller and her parents on either side through the front wooden double doors. Franklin drops back with me, wheeling a large case.

"Is this what you need for one outing with a baby?"

He chuckles. "We are staying overnight. The bag is for Summer and Penny's parents." He cocks a thumb over his shoulder. "Royce is spending time with his family, and with Lacey and Ray with us, we didn't fit in the sedan." He looks around to see if my driver is here. "No Joseph?"

"No. I'm not staying long. Like you, I decided he needed to be with his family." I tap his shoulder twice. "We're softening in our old age."

"Do not elaborate. I refuse to be known as a soft cock." He gives me a sideways glance. "And don't mention anything about Zara unless Penny asks."

"Why would I? It's no one's business but ours."

Frank gives me one of his do-not-fuck-with-me looks. After thirty-five years, I'm immune to his scowls.

We all head into the dining room, where everyone is seated. Mom and Dad stand to greet Penny, Frank, and her parents first, while the staff takes Summer to the nursery.

Mom takes my face in her hands and kisses me on the cheek. "You look tired, darling."

It's an accurate assessment. "I'll be fine. The international flights are catching up with me."

"Are you sleeping, darling, or working the entire journey?"

Before I answer, my father comes to stand with us and shakes my hand. "Happy Thanksgiving, son. While I respect your dedication, your mother is right. The stress will catch up with you, and you'll be forced to rest. Take some time to reset and sleep on the jet."

*Wow. Usually, my father is all work, work, work.*

"If there's anything I can do…" my mother begins.

I shoot her a reassuring smile. "I'm fine, Mom." If she hears the slightest inkling a woman might be involved, then there'll be no stopping her interference. I witnessed her meddling with Penny and Franklin. She has met Zara before and would be on the first fucking flight to London.

I take my seat and read the special Thanksgiving menu printed for each setting.

*Main*
*Whole turkey with seafood bread stuffing (Alaskan king crab,*
*Maine lobster, Southern Bluefin tuna otoro, and golden caviar*
*from the Caspian Sea),*
*seasoned with imported saffron and spices and covered in edible*
*gold flakes*


*Sides*
*Candied sweet potatoes and butternut squash seasoned with*
*spices from India*
*Caramelized onions with spices from Egypt*


*Sauces*
*Cranberry sauce with Sembikiya Queen strawberries and*
*dekopon citrus from Japan*
*Asparagus vinaigrette with Pappy Van Winkle Family Reserve*
*Bourbon*

*Dessert*
*Pumpkin and pecan pies with apple and coconut custard*

My mother's idea of Thanksgiving is firstly about being grateful, and her prayers reflect her appreciation. Our meals are extravagant. Only today, the fancy menu is next level.

Byron makes a face at his best friend and teammate, Brandon, the Aussie who practically lives here. "Jesus," Byron mutters. "We'll need to train five times a day to be ready for our next game."

I grin at him. It is excessive even for my mother. Dad brings out a bottle of Michter's 25-year bourbon whiskey and hands me a glass, which I down quickly.

"I spoke to Zara," Penny tells me. "She looks happy. I mentioned the gala and how Frank and I want to attend," she says with excitement in her voice. "I just want to see her. I think she's as excited as me."

*Is that what Zara told Penny?*

I nod and down more whiskey, ignoring the way Franklin is eyeballing me. "She misses you," I tell her. "I don't see her often, but she is endeavoring to enjoy the time she has there."

"She said she made new friends." The way Penny is staring, I sense it's a quiz on how close we are. I told her I check in on Zara most trips and no one needs to know anything more.

"She was with them once when I messaged her." I'm doing my best to act naïve, but the weight of Franklin's eyes boring into me has me sweating.

"Zara is staying at your penthouse now?"

My gaze flits to Frank, then back at Penny. "Yes, but we come and go at different times. I've barely seen her."

"Jobe's penthouse is huge. His bedroom is at one end, and the other bedrooms are at the other end, along with the media room," Franklin points out.

"And I leave for the office at the crack of dawn and in bed early," I emphasize.

"Oh, right." Realization hits Penny. "Zara likes to sleep in and is a night owl."

*Don't I know it.*

"After talking to Lacey…" Mom begins and looks at Penny's mom sitting at the end of the table, "… we decided next year we'll have a smaller lunch after we volunteer at a soup kitchen." Pride shines in Mom's eyes.

I stare into the empty glass. What's in the fucking whiskey? *My mother announced she will work in a soup kitchen…*

"While I enjoy fundraising and the galas, Lacey has shown me the benefits of helping other charities, especially those that support the homeless. I hope you all can join us for a few hours next year before coming home to be truly thankful for our blessings."

"Wow," I murmur. "I never imagined I'd see the day you would fundraise without being in a ballgown and diamonds. I'm proud of you, Mom." I stand and round the table to hug her. One by one, everyone follows to hug Mom, Dad, and Penny's parents.

Mom fans her hands at her face. "Oh please, you'll make me cry and mess my makeup." She composes herself and whispers, "Let us pray." We link hands since Mom has always asked this of us. "Lord, thank you for all the blessings you grant us every day. May you bless this food, and may it nourish and sustain us and strengthen our hearts and minds to do your work. Thank you for surrounding us with family and friends and for guiding us toward gratitude today and every day. Amen."

"Amen."

Lola starts to serve the food, but Mom says, "Lola, we can manage. Please, you and Sergio should join us and enjoy the meal."

After working with us for as long as I can remember, even when I was a child, Lola and our chef, Sergio, didn't sit with us. Penny's parents' charitable lifestyle has influenced my parents.

Penny's influence on my family is for the better. Her opinions matter. It's why I can't tell my brother everything, as he'll tell his wife, and it will cause complications.

Late afternoon, I apologize for leaving early, citing work commitments—an excuse my father accepts. Instead, I'm heading home to text Zara before I do anything else. It's after midnight in London, and she probably won't see the message until morning, but I can't wait until then. She is continually on my mind, and I need to speak to her... apologize if I upset her with the merger secrecy. I know I could trust her, but what I could not have is her voice in my head if she felt sorry for Tim or any of her workmates. Zara has a kind heart, and empathy cannot interfere with a business decision.

> Just checking how you are. I know it's your first Thanksgiving away from family and friends. I hope you had a good day.

My cell buzzes on the table and hope swells for it to be a reply from Zara.

It's from Hayley. Why is she working on Thanksgiving?

> Contracts are ready to proceed with the takeover. You need to sign off first. Hope you're having a relaxing day.

This major takeover of Sir James' company is a priority

and the main reason for my frequent visits to London. When it's done and dusted, I can cut back on travel. My gut tightens because it's the last thing I want to do. I enjoy being in London. I tap a quick reply.

> Thank you, Hayley. Stop working on a holiday and enjoy time with your husband. FYI, on Monday, I'll explore some residential markets in London. If this takeover happens with Sir James, we'll have potential growth in the real estate sector of the investment company.

My phone buzzes again.

> Take your own advice and relax!

I smile at her reply. Hayley knows me well.

My cell buzzes again, and I sit upright when I see it's not from Hayley.

> Today was just another day in London. I watched a movie and fell asleep early. Do you know when you'll be back?

Is she asking so she can avoid me while I'm there?

> Next week. Looking forward to it.

THE FOLLOWING THURSDAY, I ARRIVE AT THE PENTHOUSE around midday. Instead of heading to the office, I make calls from my study and Zoom into a meeting, blaming jetlag for my physical absence. I want to be here when Zara arrives and not caught up in meetings until seven o'clock tonight.

After barely sleeping on the flight and ignoring my mother's advice, I'll be ready for bed by seven. The more work I completed on the flight, the more time I will have with Zara.

I'm in the kitchen preparing dinner when the door opens.

She is pale as fuck, and my stomach flips. "What's wrong?" I go to her and attempt to take her bag so I can help her sit down.

She holds up her hand. "Don't come near me. I'm sick."

I don't give two fucks if she's sick. She needs help. I place a hand around her back and walk with her to the couch. The heat radiates from her, even through her clothes. "You have a fever," I tell her.

"No shit, Sherlock," she snaps. "So you shouldn't be this close to me."

"I need to be close to help you," I snap back. "Stop worrying about me. Is anyone sick in the office?"

She nods. "Everyone is too scared to miss work after your speech about work ethics. It started before the weekend, and now everyone in the office is coughing."

For fuck's sake. "This is why the staff has sick leave. You're not going back to work."

"I know," she groans out. "I don't have the energy. Hopefully, I'll be over it by Monday."

After removing her shoes, I swing her legs up onto the couch and cover her legs with a blanket, fluffing the pillows behind her. "I'll get you some meds and water."

After setting Zara up with what she needs, I call Trent and ask him to get a doctor to my penthouse as soon as possible.

Zara eats her dinner on the sofa and then falls asleep. I'm concerned for her. Why hasn't anyone reported this? Picking up my phone, I make a call.

"Jobe. What do I owe the honor?"

"Marcus. Have you heard of the staff falling sick on level six?"

"Gretchen mentioned today we had a number call in sick."

"A number? They're all sick and sharing the virus because the staff are afraid to take sick leave for fear of losing their jobs. What the fuck!"

"*You* did speak to them about work ethics."

Dammit. This wasn't what I'd meant. Clearly, I was so worried about the look of betrayal on Zara's face during that meeting that I didn't express myself properly. "Yeah. I get that this is on me. Now I've got to fix it. What is the work-from-home policy? What procedures does HR have in place?"

"This is not something our company offers."

"Well, it is now. Ask Gretchen to update the *Policy and Procedure Manual* and send it to HR. If anyone is contagious and capable of doing some work from home, then it needs to be an option. You do not come to work and spread a virus. We're on the brink of a fucking endemic within our company. The staff is to take sick leave or stay home and work. Surely, everyone has work computers and has Zoom access?"

"Not everyone."

"Then make it happen. Moving forward, we want everyone working at full capacity." Investing in a real estate investment trust company will be profitable, but not if half the staff is sick and making bad decisions.

An hour later, my cell buzzes.

"Trent."

"Hello, Mr. Hendricks. The doctor is downstairs."

"Send him up. I'll wait by the elevator."

I greet him at the entrance to my penthouse.

He nods. "I'm Dr. Edwards. I'm here to see Zara Hart."

"Thank you for visiting. Zara has come home from work unwell. She has a temperature and sore throat." He gives me a look as though I'm overreacting. I'm not.

"Hi," she rasps when he walks in.

"Hello, Zara, I'm Dr. Edwards. May I check your vitals?" She nods, and he takes her temperature and blood pressure and checks her pulse. "I'm going to listen to your chest." I head into the bedroom to get my wallet and hear him ask a series of questions. "Have you been around anyone who has been sick?"

She coughs before answering. "Most people at work. It started with a colleague who caught a bug from her kids." She lays back and closes her eyes.

"From what I hear, current pathology reports are indicating a bacterial chest infection. It is rife in childcare facilities and schools. Your work colleague could have caught it from her children. It affects adults differently."

"I have only been in the country for three months and still adjusting."

"Getting used to different bug strains can take time for you to build immunity. I'll take a blood sample and send it to pathology. I'll also write a script for antibiotics. Don't start the antibiotics until I get the results. I'll call you in two days to confirm." He looks at me. "You can fill the script and have it ready," he tells me as he slides on gloves. "I expect it to be this strain of bacteria," he notes, preparing the needle. He looks at me again. "If it is Mycoplasma pneumoniae, it can remain in the throat for thirteen weeks. Please be mindful with your partner."

"She's not—" I don't bother explaining. "I will."

I contemplate our limitations, but I also think of the staff. I send Gretchen a text.

She sends it through. I'll call her later and ask her to be checked and to remain at home to work.

No one is going to lose their jobs.

The doctor writes a script and leaves it on the table. "If Zara's condition worsens or she has chest pain, you may need to take her to the hospital."

"I'll keep a close eye on her."

There is no way I'll be leaving her side.

ZARA HAS SLEPT MOST OF THE DAY.

Between Zoom meetings, I refill her water and offer more medication, ensuring she is receiving plenty of vitamin C and zinc. Last night, she slept in her room, which I do not like. I checked on her several times and spent part of the night on the lounge chair in her room. Her condition hasn't worsened, nor has she improved. At least the staff has been informed, and measures are in place to prevent this from happening again. Coughs and colds are part of winter, but it should never have gotten this bad.

Trent delivers a bag of groceries, and I fire up the stove to cook her chicken and vegetable soup. It's what Lola did for us when we were sick.

After preparing the vegetables, I check my emails. There is an invite from Sir James to attend dinner this weekend.

I send him a reply.

> Unfortunately, Zara is sick, but we are excited for the gala.

*Two weeks...*

Two weeks, and then we don't need to fake it.

Will she want to continue the charade? Is the sex simply a fun thing for her because she is lonely?

While back in LA, I had time to consider what I want moving forward in my life. If there was a slight chance Zara and I could try as a couple, as weird as it sounds, a long-distance relationship would not work. So our situation is further complicated.

The chicken bones are boiling, and I add the vegetables to the broth and stir. Will she be able to eat bread with her sore throat? All I fed her today were smoothies full of immunity-building nutrients.

*I care for her more than I want to admit. Think about her more than I should.*

How do I explain that I don't want *whatever we have* to end? Especially when there is no clear path to beginning a relationship.

THE FOLLOWING DAY, ZARA IS HAVING SOUP FOR LUNCH.

She received a positive pathology report and commenced the antibiotics.

"I'm already feeling a bit better," she says. "It must be all the care from you and this amazing soup." She gives me an awkward smile before it fades. "It still doesn't make up for what went down before you left."

"Zara." I kneel on the floor beside her. "I should have trusted you." She cocks one eyebrow. "While I made excuses that my hands were tied, I was scared that you had the power to influence my decision."

"Why would I do that?"

"Because you have a good heart and see things differently to me." I reach out and rest a hand on her knee. "You're a refreshing influence. I see that now." She gives me a subtle nod as though she knows it. "Is there something you want me to cook for dinner?"

She smiles appreciatively. "You've done enough, Jobe. Thank you. I feel sorry for the rest of the staff not receiving the same care from the Board director."

It's a dig, yet it also makes me smile. "At least there are now measures for people to stay home if they're sick."

"Thank you for rolling that out."

"To clarify, when I spoke about work ethics, it was to the staff who were on their computer watching sports or playing games. Or the ones who would leave and think no one noticed. It was taken out of context."

She offers a small smile. "To be fair, a shake-up was warranted, so don't feel bad. I'll feel worse if you catch this from me." She pushes her matted hair behind her ears.

"Where's your brush?"

She narrows her eyes at me. "In the bathroom. Why? And for the record, I don't care what I look like."

"That's evident," I say teasingly. "I'm going to brush your hair."

"No way," she calls out. Her bathroom drawers are a mess. After a few minutes of scurrying in her drawers with makeup, jewelry, and God knows what else filled to the brim, I locate her brush and then go and sit behind her. She holds out her hand. "I'm capable of brushing my own hair."

"I know. Allow me to do this for you." She huffs, and for once, she doesn't have the energy to argue. I slowly detangle her long brown hair.

"This is unusually soothing," she whispers. "No one has brushed my hair like this for me since I was a child."

I kiss the top of her head. "I'll do anything to help you get better, baby."

*Baby?*

I never use that word. Yet it feels good saying it to Zara.

**20**

———

ZARA

THREE DAYS BEFORE THE GALA, I am finally feeling like myself again.

To my surprise, Jobe has booked a makeup artist and a hairdresser to come to his penthouse on the day of the gala. Tomorrow night, I have a manicure and pedicure appointment. I feel spoiled beyond anything I have ever known. We haven't been intimate in weeks, and yet, everything he does for me shows me he cares, and it's confusing the hell out of me.

Tomorrow, the cleaners are coming before Penny and Franklin arrive. We spoke a week ago, and I promised her I'd be better by the time they get here. My stomach is in knots over how Jobe will act toward me when they're here because I don't want the pampering to stop.

While they know we are fake dating, they know nothing about our fling—one that will end after the ball.

This week, Jobe returned to the office to work. He never

got sick, which surprised me as he was close to me the entire time. I'm working from home for another week and returning to the office next week. Piper said there is barely any staff in the office, though most of us will be returning on Monday.

My cell makes the familiar FaceTime sound.

Penny.

"Hi, honey." I assume she is calling and about to get on their jet, but her face is pale, and she looks like crap. "Are you okay?"

"Hi, Zara," she says with a hoarse voice. "I have the flu…" She breaks into a coughing fit. "I'm so sorry. I really wanted to be better and come and see you. I need a Zara hug."

"Oh, babe, I'm so sorry." I feel so bad for her and understand how awful it feels when you're unwell. "I was hoping to see you too. At least I'll get to see you soon when I'm home for Christmas."

She forces a smile. "I'm looking forward to it." She rubs at her red eyes. "I have no idea how I caught this. I haven't been this sick in a decade."

"You're a mom and working big hours for Franklin and Jobe. Be kind to yourself, Pen. It's natural to get rundown when you're a new mother."

She smiles, and this time, it reaches her eyes. "I love you, Zee."

"And I love you."

"You'll have to tell me how the gala is. Send photos," she says with a little more enthusiasm.

"I will. Jobe has arranged for makeup and hair to come to the penthouse. It's weird being fussed over."

She smiles. "The Hendricks men like to splash their money around." Her eyes round. "It's weird Jobe is doing it for you."

I laugh to lighten the mood. "I know, right? I only have to

pretend to be his girlfriend for a few more days so Franklin and Jobe can sign the contract."

She scrunches her face. "It's already signed."

"What? Oh, Jobe probably mentioned it, but I didn't absorb it because I've been so sick." He lied again. But then, he could have ended our fake relationship and didn't...

"Yeah, so you don't need to fake-fake it."

"Great." I roll my eyes for her benefit. "I can relax and have a few more champagnes." I wink at her. Only I can't stop thinking that there is no need for me to attend. My presence is no longer required, and I'm filled with conflict about not wanting us to end.

"Ugh, I wish I was there with you." She pulls a sad face.

"We'll make up for it when I'm home. See if Hugh is also free."

She smiles at the screen. "I'd like that." She waves to me. "I'll talk to you after the gala to see how you coped with Jobe being *Jobe*."

I laugh. "Get well, babe."

When the screen goes blank, I let out a long, conflicted sigh. I'm relieved she can't make it and possibly catch on to my true feelings for Jobe, but I also miss my friend.

The makeup artist finally leaves. At times, it felt as though my face was a blank canvas, and she was creating a masterpiece that was going to take days to complete. I asked her several times not to apply it so damn heavy. I'm going to a formal ball, not a nightclub to pick up some random.

I change into my gown, one that Jobe's stylist selected and had delivered here. Either he has great taste, or his stylist is a fashion icon. It's a tasteful low-cut gown, champagne in color, and covered in sequins, heavy around the hem and fading to lightly scattered over my waist and heavy at my chest. I feel like a princess and barely recognize myself in the mirror.

The jeweled accessories are minimal yet make a statement. Drop diamond earrings dangle halfway down my neck and one diamond bracelet, which are on loan. My hair is down and curled perfectly. My reflection fools me that I could be someone who would be on Jobe Hendricks' arm.

I grab the diamond clutch purse and head into the kitchen. Jobe stands from the couch, his eyes all over me. I expect him to say something, but he remains silent.

"Do I look okay?" I twirl on the spot.

"Zara..." he shakes his head, blowing out a breath, "... you look fucking delicious."

*Not what I was expecting.*

"Thank you, I think. But I don't want Sir James having those thoughts."

He comes to stand mere feet away. His eyes hold mine, and there's an intensity I haven't felt in weeks. "Every man in the room will have those thoughts tonight."

I smile at him, flattered in a way. I allow myself the time to check him out. "You look handsome yourself, as you always do in typical Jobe style."

"I'll take that as a good thing," he says in a deep voice, his gaze unwavering.

I grin at him. "It is. It's natural for you to look good."

He frowns at me. Did I say the wrong thing?

"Do you not realize how beautiful you are? Ever since we met, you have mesmerized me to a point where I struggle to take my eyes off you."

*What?*

His eyes darken, and then he holds out his hand. "We better leave because if we stay another second, I'm going to mess up your hair and makeup."

*Oh.* "Let's go then," I say and swiftly head to the door.

I can't let that happen. He sees this as our final night as a fake couple, but my heart is well and truly involved.

If I fall into his arms even one more time...

... I'll never recover.

My heart thumps in my chest as I begin to panic. I'm fucking scared to even fake it with him. It's too much. I could say I'm feeling unwell again. Do I stay or do I go? After everything Jobe has arranged for the night, it would be a waste of money and energy if I backed out. Since Sir James is going to be there, we have to fake it since he believes we are a couple. It's not strictly necessary, and yet, Jobe wants this between us. *He wants me tonight.*

He doesn't know that I know. I keep asking myself, *Is it our last night of faking it?*

He takes my hand and leads me out of the apartment. Then, like a gentleman, he opens the car door and assists me with my dress to slide into the car. Nothing Jobe Hendricks does feels like pretend. His eyes hold mine when we speak, and I catch glimpses of his gaze lowering and checking me out. His voice is deep yet tender and also on the brink of cracking. None of it feels like pretend, especially the way his fingertips trail lightly up and down my arm.

From the moment we arrive, he is right by my side. His hand has a strong hold around my waist when we speak to his business acquaintances in the foyer. Minutes later, his hand clasps onto mine as he leads me into the ballroom. He cannot keep his hands off me. Every touch and stolen glance is very, very real.

The sexual tension between us is about to crack.

We weave past several round tables covered in white linen until we come to the front of the room. Harrison is standing by the table. He shakes Jobe's hand, then mine, introducing us to his wife, Rachel, who is stunning in a navy sequined gown. Her dark hair is styled off her neck with curls pinned in an updo.

"Congratulations," I say to her and Harrison. "You look amazing. I can't believe you're a new mom. What did you name your son?"

She holds my hand and beams a big smile. "Callum. He's two weeks old and so tiny compared to the girls but doing well."

Callum James. "CJ. I love that."

She grins at me. "So do I, though Sir James isn't partial to abbreviated names," she whispers.

As if cued, Sir James comes forward. "Good evening, Jobe," he greets and shakes his hand. Then he turns to me and holds out his hand, his eyes meeting mine, and I struggle to look away. He is different tonight, as though he is unsure of me.

Maybe it's because the contract has been signed, and he's waiting to see what Jobe does with his former company, though it doesn't explain the serious gaze for me.

Natalie stands and holds both my hands, nudging her husband aside. "Zara. You're radiant."

"Thank you. And you're beautiful, Lady James." While she is in her fifties, she could pass for a woman of forty. Elegant, sophisticated, and fun to be around. I imagine she has her work cut out for her with Sir James.

"Please, call me Rachel," she whispers. "No need for formalities here. Unlike Ernest, he always likes to be referred to as *Sir*." She winks at me, and I almost let out a giggle. "I'm sure you're in need of a champagne, darling."

She hands me a flute, and I thank her before taking our seats. Behind us, other guests file in and find their table.

"We have rearranged the seating," Rachel tells me. "Ernest's eldest brother is coming along with our nephew.

They were able to come after your friend, Penny, and Jobe's brother couldn't attend."

"I apologize for the late notice. Penny is very ill and upset they couldn't make it."

"It's fine. Our friends and family are always available and waiting. Ernest has five brothers, none like him," she whispers. "Though Edward, his oldest brother, has a smaller business and does rather well for himself. His son, Oscar, and he run a tight ship."

*Oscar.*

"Here they are. Ernest will introduce you."

*Oh, my fucking God. Big O.*

After being introduced to Edward, Oscar walks over to us and beams his friendly smile at me. "Nice to meet you, Zara," he says after we are introduced. *Do we pretend we don't know each other?*

He shakes Jobe's hand. "Congratulations on the takeover."

"Thank you, Oscar James," he says and gives me a side eye as though I should have known this.

Before we say anything more, the announcer asks everyone to take their seats.

Oscar leans in close. "Your secret is safe with me as long as mine is with you. Though I have to ask, are we still pretending?"

I shake my head. "I'm not," I say honestly.

*Finally,* he mouths and winks at me and then moves to sit with his father.

As I take my seat between Natalie and Jobe, I think about what Oscar said. His secret...

Then it dawns on me. His family is unaware he isn't straight.

Why?

I glance at Harrison, Sir James, and then Edward and

imagine living in their extravagant world. The Hendricks are fancy and extremely wealthy but do not have the royal attitude of the James family.

Away from the opulent balls and formality of the James family, Oscar can be his true self. I loved Oscar's personality from the moment I met him and would rather spend time with him than with his stuffy uncle. A sense of contentment washes over me. I'm okay that the fake dating show can stop tonight. I don't want to have to pander to Sir James' narrow attitude anymore. Come to think of it, I'm not a fan of his opinion that Jobe was unreliable because he was single. People shouldn't be judged on their sexuality or their relationship preferences. *Or whether or not they have children.*

After our main course and auction, the classical music begins and people take to the dance floor. "May I have the first dance?" Oscar asks me.

"Of course," I say, delighted.

He takes my hand and leads me out onto the floor. "Give me a quick rundown. Where are you two at?"

"Well, we stopped pretending and embraced the attraction," I say and smile at him, knowing he was right. "Then I found out he took over the company where I worked. I was mad as hell he didn't tell me. Then, he had to fly back to LA. What I do know is I am done pretending."

Oscar frowns. "Another takeover separate from my uncle's?" I nod. "Fuck, the man's a machine." He eyes me carefully. "Does the workaholic syndrome run in his family?"

"I'm afraid so."

"Huh. Like my uncle." His eyes turn serious. "It's a lonely life, Zara."

"Ha," I joke. "We are not at that stage, so slow down. Not even a couple," I whisper.

Oscar's beautiful, subtle smile is back as though it's imprinted on his resting face.

"Why don't they know?" I ask him.

He shrugs. "It's none of their business. If I find a person I want to spend the rest of my life with, then I'll make it known." He shrugs. "I don't want my personal life to be public."

I smile up at him. "We need to make another pub date."

"Am I invited?" a voice comes from behind me. "Excuse me, Oscar, do you mind if I cut in? I've been waiting to dance with my beautiful partner all night."

Oscar lets go of me. "Of course. She is beautiful," he says in a serious tone. Then he grins. "You make a great couple." He winks at me before he strides away.

Jobe pulls me closer, then he raises my hand in the air and moves side to side, occasionally twirling us as we move. His eyes never wander from my face, staring at me as though I'm the only person in the room. The longer he stares, the faster my heart beats.

"Did you tell Oscar we're a couple?" he asks in a low, deep voice.

There is nowhere to look other than at his intense, dark eyes. "I told him I'm done with faking it," I whisper.

His eyebrows slightly tighten, enough for me to notice. "Done for tonight or done forever?"

"Forever," I murmur.

Shit, he can take it two ways. We are done and finished, or I want to take the next step.

"I don't want what we have to end," he whispers.

My lips part in the biggest smile. "Neither do I."

He leans his forehead to mine as we sway, and it feels so romantic to be doing this with Jobe, the man I believed could never be tamed.

The calm orchestral music switches to modern pop. I

smile at Jobe as we break apart and move with the music, my hips swaying. I'm singing the words and catching glimpses of Jobe's eyes locked on my body. He's barely moving, doing a weird thing with his arms. I smile at him and keep to the beat while only his feet are not moving.

What. Is. Happening?

He looks... dorky.

*He can't dance.*

I take his hands and guide them to my hips, then turn, moving my ass over his crotch.

He stops suddenly, and I turn over my shoulder to see what's wrong. He's staring at my feet. "Are you okay?" he asks, his brows pinched in concern.

*What?* "Yes, I—"

He bends and takes my foot, carefully inspecting it.

"What are you doing?" If we are questioning feet issues, then we should be looking at his.

"You're okay, baby."

*I know I am.*

Suddenly, I'm whisked into his arms. *What the...* "Excuse me. My partner has twisted her ankle," he says as he carries me past couples dancing and twirling.

"Jobe, what is happening?" I say quickly, utterly confused.

"Follow my lead." When we reach our table, he tentatively lowers me to the floor, keeping an arm around my waist. "Keep your foot off the floor, baby."

Everyone at the table is staring at me.

*What is he doing?*

"Unfortunately, we need to leave. Zara twisted her ankle on the dance floor."

*Say what?* I grimace and lift my foot.

"Sorry if I wore you out," Oscar says, his subtle smile in place and clearly onto us.

"I'll be okay," I tell him. "Two left feet." I shrug.

"Oh, I hope you're okay," Natalie says and stands with Rachel beside her. Then I'm surrounded by everyone at the table wanting to check out my sprained ankle.

*I will kill him.*

"I'll take her home and elevate her foot with ice," Jobe announces. "I'm sorry to leave a beautiful ball. You'll receive my donation on Monday," he tells Sir James as he slides his suit jacket down his arms and helps me slip into it.

I narrow my eyes at him. I was having fun.

"I hope to see you all again soon," I say as Jobe whisks me into the air again and carries me toward the large wooden doors. "Was this really necessary?" I ask when we are a good distance away.

"If you knew the thoughts I'm having, then yes." His beautiful dark eyes hold mine.

"You can't dance," I whisper gleefully.

He gives me a sideways glance. "No. I'd rather express myself in other ways. You were grinding your ass on my cock, and I didn't want everyone to see us compromised."

"We were not compromised," I say, amused.

"If I remained there any longer, I'd have to find a side room so you could grind your pussy on my face."

I giggle. "Jobe Hendricks cannot dance. Finally, I found your weakness."

"Zara," he warns. "It is not a weakness. My priorities lie elsewhere, and I'm too busy to hang out in clubs and *dance*." He says it like it's a dirty word.

"No," I say, seeing through him. "But I imagine you in those secret VIP clubs receiving lap dances where the girl dances for you."

"Exactly," he snaps. "And a gala is not an appropriate place for what could happen next."

Jobe has proved to me he is capable of some

commitment, be it short-term. If he needs a kinky lap dance, then I'm here for it as long as it's only me.

On the last night we have to fake it, I see a changed man. "Are you going to ensure I get my ankle treated?" I can't help the smirk on my face.

"I'll be treating you, Zara. Only the ice won't make it to your fucking ankle."

*Oh.*

**21**

———

JOBE

The moment we step inside the penthouse, I have Zara against the wall. My mouth collides with hers, and I sense she wants this as much as me. My hands are all over her, pushing beneath the snug material of her gown to find her breasts. I need it off her before I tear the fucking dress. I spin her to lower the zipper and spin her back around with urgency so I can watch the gown slide down her beautiful body.

All night, I struggled to keep my eyes off her. With the darker makeup, her alluring eyes, and her sexy curves, I barely held it together when having a conversation with Sir James. Then, when I watched her on the dance floor with Oscar—Sir James' *nephew*—I was done with surprises. Done with fucking pretending.

Her big brown eyes hold mine as I slide the material over her shoulders and down her hips. I lower my gaze and suck in air because the sight of her body steals my breath. I take her hand for her to step out of the material pooled at her feet. Her breasts spill over the strapless bra that looks a size too small. My body burns hot with desire for her. I can barely concentrate with my heartbeat pounding in my ears. Her hands rest on my shoulders, and I lift her so those long legs straddle my hips. I could take her against the wall right now.

But she deserves more.

I kiss her hard, open mouthed and tongues clashing, as I walk with her toward my room. Then, lowering her carefully on the bed, I begin to loosen my tie.

"No." She stands.

*Shit, did I read her wrong?*

"Sit." She points to the velvet chair in the corner of the room, and I do as she asks, watching her sexy ass as she walks out of the room. "Don't move."

What is she doing? I loosen my trousers and free my cock because it's so fucking erect it hurts trapped beneath the material.

She returns with her cell, and I raise a brow, wondering if she's texting someone. "Are you going to video us?" I ask, tilting my head. I'm joking, but the thought of watching us fuck has my cock begging for her touch.

She gives me a look as though she likes the idea then music sounds from her cell.

"I have devices with sound wired to every room," I tell her if that's her thing, but then she begins dancing to an acoustic song—a female singer that I can't place but is familiar.

"I love this song," she says and begins to move her hips, swirling her ass in that tiny G-string. She leans over me and finishes what I began with my tie, then begins to unbutton my white shirt. Immediately, my hands are behind her back to remove her bra.

"No." She straightens. "You can't touch me *yet*."

"You're kidding me?"

"I'm giving you a lap dance that you'll never forget."

*Fuck.*

*She is perfect.*

Zara straddles the chair and removes my shirt. Our faces come so close, her sweet breath caressing my lips, her eyes holding mine, alluring me to kiss her. She stands and somehow makes a seductive show of folding my shirt and tie.

My daze is broken by her twerking her ass before dropping to the floor and bouncing up. She turns, touching herself. My heart pounds, trying to pump blood to my brain because I swear most of it is in my dick.

I'm about to tell her things I've never told any woman before. I need to fuck her and regain composure. For months, I have tried not to want her, and yet I didn't want anyone else. My balls had never been heavier.

Her long legs straddle me, and my hands cup her ass as I thrust against her, needing to touch her. She lifts, shaking her head. The music continues to play, and she's singing along, but the words have no meaning. All I hear are the dirty thoughts in my head. "I need to taste your pussy," I tell her.

*I need to smell you, have your scent all over me.*

She smiles, and the power is hers. "Lift," she tells me.

Zara pulls my trousers off and rids every part of my clothing from me. I'm sitting naked in the chair with a hard-on like no other, dying to bury myself deep inside her. Then she drops to her knees and slides those delicious lips of hers over the tip, taking me deep in her throat.

*Fuck yes.*

"Yeah, baby." My fingers thread into her hair and suddenly, she pulls back, staring at me.

Her eyes narrow into a glare. "Do I need to tie your hands behind your head?"

A smirk grows on my face. "No." But fuck, if she likes that sort of thing, I'll bring it. And she'll be begging... *Oh yeah.* I close my eyes, and I want to come faster than I have in years. "Zara," I moan out, not knowing what to do with my hands as her mouth fucks me deeper and faster. I lift my hips and thrust, fucking that sweet mouth.

I come hard, and through a haze, I watch her swallow, her pretty eyes staring up at me. "You're perfect," I murmur.

She stands and continues to dance, slowly removing her bra and commanding my attention. I love her tits. Perfectly round, they bounce slightly, and now I'm imagining fucking her from behind and watching those breasts bounce as my dick pounds into her. As she caresses each breast, she licks her fingers and toys with her nipples, swaying her hips.

I'm not sure where to focus, my eyes tracking each movement. If only I could touch her.

Her hands move lower, fingers splaying over her sex. She slides them beneath the material of her G-string, and she closes her eyes, moaning as she presses her clit. My dick is so fucking hard, I clench my jaw, wanting nothing more than to rip those panties with my teeth so I can see her pussy.

Every stroke of my dick quickens as I watch Zara pleasure herself. She stops with the self-control I lack, her lips parting with an expression of pleasure as she slides the lace down her thighs. She comes closer, one foot lifting to rest on my thigh. Her hand trails down her stomach to her clit, then slides a finger inside. This close, her scent surrounds me.

My imagination goes wild as she pleasures herself inches from my face and with the most perfect view. She pumps a delicate finger inside her pussy, the moisture gleaming on her sex and fingers, her sensual moans filling the air. She has filled my head with erotic thoughts of all the ways I want to take her, and now I'm blinded by her with a carnal urge to fuck her senseless.

"Enough," I snap and pull her down on my lap, devouring her lips. I kiss her with everything I have, desperate to love her and have her, and not only for tonight.

"Get on the bed, Zara," I demand. "Now." Her eyes flick over my face and widen with recognition that I'm serious. I walk to my drawer and find multiple ties. When I turn around, her eyes are an inferno of need. "My turn, princess. Place your hands above your head."

I bind her wrists above her head, loose enough to free herself if she desires and flick another tie over her breasts. She whimpers, and then I trail a hand down her stomach to her pussy, continuing along her inner thigh to her ankle. I give her a look that there is no more pretense—tonight she is mine. I want her, all of her, and I'm done fighting it.

Her beautiful, innocent eyes tug at my heart. *Not tonight.* I release her ankle, move the tie to her face, and cover her eyes. "Lift your head, Zara." She does, and I tie it loosely over her eyes. I take a moment to take in her beautiful body splayed before me, her hands remaining above her head as I asked. "You dance beautifully," I praise, gently pressing my lips to hers. "Are you ready to dance with me?" I ask against her lips.

"More than you'll ever know."

"I believe I do." I kiss her again and again.

Breaking the kiss, I lean back to admire her pussy and run my fingers over her slit, tasting her wetness on each finger. She's ready, and I groan at her laid out for me. Ready *for me.* Lifting her ankles, I place each over my shoulders. "Ready, princess?" She nods quickly, and I love how eager she is.

I steady my cock, close my eyes, reveling in the feel of her as I push inside. Fuck, she's so fucking wet that I slide through the tightness—warm, soft, and perfect. She makes me weak. It's easy to get lost in her, and when I struggle to hold back, I force myself to slow down to enjoy the moment as long as I can.

Tonight, she owned me like no one has before.

Now it's my turn. I build fast and fuck her pussy like it's mine. She cries out when she orgasms, her pussy clenching around my cock, and I curse, not seeing her pretty eyes. I tug the tie off as I pump into her, watching her eyes glaze again. It hits me fast. The world shakes as an orgasm runs through me. I collapse onto her, panting, lost to the brightness blinding me. She pulls her arms out of the ties loosely binding her hands to caress my lower back, her long legs curl around my hips. It's as though she feels everything I do. How I have never felt more alive than when I'm with her. In her arms, the outside world fades away. She is there right beside me while my breathing slows. The pounding in my chest eases, and I close my eyes, enjoying the stillness, the quiet, and the euphoria filling my body and mind.

Why did I believe I needed more than one woman in my bed to satisfy me?

Zara is all that I need.

**22**

———

JOBE

My cell buzzes on the bedside table with an incoming call.

I barely open my eyes to read Franklin's name on the screen. While it's a reasonable time of the evening, it's not even dawn in London.

"This better be good," I murmur in an attempt not to wake Zara, who is sleeping beside me.

"I checked the pilot's schedule with the jet, and there is no mention of you returning this week."

"I have a shit ton of work to do here before I return. I'll be home for Christmas, so if Mom is questioning my absence, you can explain the importance of my presence in London."

"This is the last home game before Christmas, and the entire family is expected to attend. It's important as owners of the team, and you should support your brother."

I groan out a sound of inconvenience. "What day?"

"Tomorrow night."

I sit upright in the bed. "By tomorrow night in LA, are you implying tonight in London time?"

"Why do you think I'm calling? This game should be on your calendar."

"I have other priorities in my calendar, and none are fun," I snap, throwing back the bed sheets and heading to the bathroom. "Do you have the pilot's schedule on your screen?"

"I do, and I have already added a flight that will leave in two hours. Be on it, Jobe," he warns, ending the call, and I toss my cell onto the counter, both hands gripping the marble. I stare into the mirror, then bow my head, taking deep breaths to calm my thoughts. I'm feeling pulled in multiple directions when all I want to do is lie in bed for another hour with my girl.

After showering and throwing a few things in a case, I kiss Zara on the cheek. I'll send a text to her when I'm on the plane explaining why I had to rush away and promise to be back by the end of the week.

THE MOMENT THE JET TOUCHES DOWN IN LA, MY DRIVER IS waiting to take me straight to the LA Sharks arena. I stride past security and receive their nod of acknowledgment. I'm ushered toward the VIP area where the rest of my family awaits. Penny spies me first and waves.

She's sitting beside Franklin, her father on his other side. Her mother, I assume, is home with their baby. In the row of seats behind them is Charlotte and my parents. After greeting everybody and shaking hands, I take a seat beside Charlotte. She takes my hand and squeezes it.

"I'm so glad you made it, Jobe." Her eyes dart over my face, an anxiousness rarely seen in her.

Fuck. I forgot about the shitshow that went down here while I was away. Charlotte and the Aussie were hooking up behind Byron's back. Byron had one rule. No one on the team was to touch his sister. It was the way he discovered their secret that pissed him off. They were the two people he trusted most, and from all accounts, he has barely spoken to either of them since.

I place my other hand over hers. "How are you holding up?" I imagine how hard it is for her being caught in the middle of a feud between our brother and her boyfriend.

"I'm nervous as hell for both of them, but we need this win. As long as they are professionals on the court, I'll deal with everything later." She's not looking at me, her gaze is directed at Brandon.

"You like him a lot?" I ask.

Her gaze flicks back to me, and she looks puzzled. "Of course. We were planning a future together."

Already?

"Hasn't it only been a few months?"

She shakes her head. "We've been seeing each other on and off over the years. We only became serious in the past six months. We were friends first, remember? It was an easy transition because we already knew each other."

Charlotte is not even twenty-five, and yet she knows what she wants in love. I understand why she kept their relationship a secret. I'm protecting what Zara and I have without the influence or interference of anyone else or their opinion on the matter. While we explore our feelings, it has to be about us and no one else.

The music ramps up, and lights flash around the arena, skimming over the crowd screaming with delight at the Los Angeles home team. It's a full house, and the noise is deafening. Charlotte screams out for her brother. She gives equal cheer to Brandon Johns.

"How is BJ?" I ask her. I know my brother is pissed, but he has the support of his family and the team. The Aussie only had us, and if I were to make a choice, it would be family.

"He's okay. He's focused on the win."

I nod. While I don't follow sports, when my family became the team's owners, I understood the importance of supporting the LA Sharks because a premiership would be a huge financial gain. And my brother would reach a milestone in his professional basketball career.

For the next two quarters, I clap and cheer, watching my brother and the Aussie dominate the court. While they are both stars in their own right, there is something off tonight. It's like they are competing against each other.

Halfway through the third quarter, we are up by eleven points. Byron attempts to pass it to Brandon, but then our big guy, Jye, rolls toward the basket.

"Pass it to BJ," Charlotte says in a desperate plea as though it would make everything between them right.

Even I can see the better pass was to Jye. Byron twists his body to pass him the ball. His opponent runs at him, leaping into the air to block his pass.

His knees buckle, and his leg gives way. His opponent lands with a heavy thud before Byron manages to align his body.

*Oh fuck.*

He falls awkwardly, the opponent's foot lands on his, then his ankle twists. I grimace and groan for him. The crowd gasps loudly, a collective, "Oh."

Byron shouts out in pain as he grabs at his foot, slamming his hand onto the hardwood.

"Fuck, this is not good." Charlotte grabs my arm, concern etched into her face.

"*Nooo,*" she whimpers. "Not Byron."

I stop breathing as we wait.

My parents and Franklin are out of their seats.

The umpire blows his whistle to stop the game. Byron scrambles backward to get off the court holding his leg out straight. The doctor runs around the court and drops to his knees.

Franklin turns and looks at our father then at Charlotte. "You need to be the one to go to him," he tells her. She nods and heads down the stairs toward the tunnel leading to the medical room. Byron is carried off the court, and as he approaches the tunnel, the journalists surround him, cameras flashing in his face.

For the next ten minutes, we watch the game, anxiously awaiting Charlotte's return. It's the beginning of the last quarter when she does, leans across the seat to Franklin, and shakes her head, speaking to him in a low voice. She takes her seat next to me and speaks to our parents first before turning to me.

"It's not good. He has asked the doctor to tape his ankle so he can come out and finish the game only the doctor has decided to send him for an MRI."

"Wise doctor."

She nods at me. "It's more than a basic sprain."

"Fuck," I say under my breath, knowing how much the game means to my brother. The air has changed as fear lingers with what will happen now. The team gets the win, yet no one feels like celebrating the victory.

I send a text to Zara.

Hey, I need to stay in LA until the weekend. Byron has suffered an injury on the court, and there is a chance he'll need surgery so it's best I remain here until we know more.

I miss you already.

For the next few days, I work from my LA office and text Zara daily. Unfortunately, Byron didn't receive good news and had surgery on his ankle today.

When we receive the okay from the orthopedic surgeon, I drive to the hospital with Franklin and my parents. Charlotte is already there by his side. The nurse directs us into the room, and my parents stride ahead of Franklin and me. Mom has not let go of Dad's hand in the last hour. She has maintained a brave expression, but I know how she is hurting and worried for her son.

I want to tell her that Byron will recover. He is strong and determined and has the Hendricks genes. She already knows this, and yet the moment we enter his room and find him hunched over a bowl vomiting his guts up, I realize his journey is harder than I assumed.

The jet arrives in London early Monday morning, so I head straight to my new office, and the entire morning is filled with meeting after meeting.

I attempt to tick off the shitload of emails waiting for me. Most of the staff has returned to work. Lydia has been promoted to succeed Gretchen when she leaves and is currently in training as my executive assistant. A man can't focus when he knows there is someone in the building, and he needs her right now.

I press the call button on my call box.

"Yes, Mr. Hendricks?"

"Lydia, could you please have Ms. Hart come to my office? There is an HR issue I need to discuss."

"Of course, sir."

I wait for her by my office window and stare out to the city surrounding me. It's a city so different from LA, and yet it is growing on me. Despite the financial opportunities and real estate investments, being here with Zara feels right, and I'm making excuses why I want to return more often in the future than the business requires.

There's a knock at the door.

"Come in."

Zara walks in, turning to close the door behind her. I'm first drawn to her long legs in black pants and her tight rounded ass. *Focus.* Her perfect breasts are covered with a pink blouse and a black suit jacket. Classy.

"You're back," she says with a big smile and moves toward me. "I've missed you. How is Byron?"

"We'll talk about him later." Unable to stop myself, I go to her and take her in my arms, kissing her long and deep. My dick twitches, knowing what comes next with her.

"We should be discreet," she murmurs against my lips.

"We are. It's my office. And besides, you're wearing fucking pants. If I call you here, I expect you in a skirt. Especially when I haven't seen you in a week." I continue kissing her plump lips.

She pulls away, her eyes shocked. "You want to fuck me here?"

"Yes, Zara, everywhere and all the time," I say, amused.

"Is this common for you with your assistants?" she snaps.

"Of course not," I retort. "I never touch my staff."

"Because you're a professional?" she says mockingly, and I narrow my eyes at her. "So what am I?"

"You're ruining the moment," I grunt out. "And you're my girl and happen to work here."

The words slipped out, and she is surprised as much as me.

"Am I?" she whispers. "Is that what we're telling people?"

"Your friends already know," I say dryly. "Since you were faking it."

"Piper knows the truth."

"You told Piper and not Penny... how close are you to Piper?"

"Close enough. I reasoned, if I had to move out of yours, we could share somewhere together since her roomie is leaving."

"Luckily, you don't have to move out of mine." I stare at her. "Unless you want to."

She shakes her head, bewildered. "Did you call me here to discuss our living arrangements?"

"No. It's been a hell of a fucking day." I push a hand over the top of my head to ease the headache. "The one person who can calm my mind happens to be in the same building, so being the selfish prick that I am, I called her into my office away from her work."

She finally smiles, and it does something to ease the tension inside me. "You might be questioned on your work ethics, Mr. Hendricks."

"Who is going to question me, Ms. Hart?"

She pops one shoulder. "Your staff, if I'm continually asked to come to your office to relieve your tension."

"Since I'm their boss, it's a matter that is beyond their pay grade. What *is* of interest is how the tension will be eased."

Zara cups my face and gently kisses my lips. "Sit at your desk, Mr. Hendricks."

I arch a brow, moving to my desk. I relax back into my chair, and Zara steps in behind me. Her hands rest on my shoulders as she begins to massage the muscles, and the tightness in my neck slowly eases. Not what I had in mind, but it's doing the trick.

"Is your wardrobe all long pants?" I mutter as I envision

her sprawled on my desk, her skirt bunched around her waist as I fuck her hard.

Her fingers still, and before I can protest, she spins my chair, dropping to her knees. Her hands are on the zipper of my pants as she says, "No. But there are other ways to pleasure my man."

I'm smiling at those words coming from her pretty lips. She knows I want to fuck her mouth, and without another word, her tongue teases the tip of my dick before she takes me all the way in.

I close my eyes, the stress temporarily fading, and the only thought in my head is *Zara*.

THE NEXT THREE DAYS WERE FILLED WITH BACK-TO-BACK meetings. Even with Zara in my bed, I've struggled to sleep, the endless pressure to succeed keeping me awake. By Friday morning, my eyes are red and not the appearance I want when meeting the lawyer to finalize the developments for Sir James' company and the proposal Penny has for greener, sustainable buildings. But all I can think about is a quiet night with Zara.

She's had a busy week with her new human resources role. It's finally happening for her, and seeing her happy, listening to her discuss her ideas for the company, gives me equal happiness. We are similar in some ways.

Before I enter the meeting, her name flashes on the screen.

> I'm heading out with Piper and George. I'll see you at home later tonight.

*George.* I rub circles over my temples. It's not that I don't like her friend. I don't trust him. I was warned he is a gossiper and has caused trouble by spreading rumors in the past. He doesn't hide the fact he is not a fan of mine. Not that I want the staff to like me. I need them to do their fucking job.

Piper, on the other hand, is good for Zara.

Okay, Zara Hart, I'll see you at home.

Zara Hart. If I were being cheesy, I could replace her name with the heart emoji. *The fuck?* Why would I do that? A notification crosses my screen.

Harrison James.

Would you like to meet for a drink tonight?

Interesting. Harrison made it known he wants to move forward with my company after the takeover with him as the CEO. I like Harrison and respect his value to the company.

Name the place, and I'll be there.

**23**

_______

ZARA

GEORGE HAS BEEN GIVING me odd vibes all night, and I sense he is judging me.

When I clink my glass against Piper's glass, he comes to sit beside me. "Did you know your boyfriend was going to take over the company?" His expression has soured while the rest of us have become tipsier by the glass and laughing out loud at any trivial joke.

"Of course I didn't," I snap. "And don't come at me. I'm not in the mood for your jealous bullshit."

"Zara," Piper gasps, shaking her head so as not to antagonize him.

"We are having a casual fling, and I know nothing about his business dealings," I confirm. "When it was announced, I was also pissed, but I have no right to know any of his business dealings, nor should he tell me as I'm with him on a personal emotional level and not a professional one."

"Yet you were selected for a promotion despite working

at the company for a matter of weeks. It's obvious you received special treatment."

"What's obvious is my experience and past record of competency since you're ten years younger than me." *Douchebag.*

"You're being a touch mean," Piper whispers.

"Seriously?" I shake my head.

"Anyway, darlings, I must go." George stands and blows fake kisses toward Piper and me.

"Are you watching the game tomorrow?" she asks him.

"Of course. See you there." He gives me a sideways glance before sauntering away.

"You're watching the game tomorrow? Where?" It hurts not to get an invite.

Piper lets out a loud sigh. "You're caught up on weekends with your boyfriend when he's in town. We assumed you wouldn't be available," she says apologetically.

"You can always ask. At night, Jobe is often busy with business matters and spends hours talking on his cell."

Piper tilts her head at me. Her eyes hold understanding. "How serious are you?" I frown at her. "What feelings do you have for him? Can you see a future with him?"

"We all hope for a future with a partner we like. So yeah, when we're together, we're great, but he's so busy, and the weeks he is away, I also enjoy my time alone." I shrug. "So I have no idea where it's leading, but for now, it works."

"Right." Her eyes flick over my face as if searching for an answer. I'm not hiding anything. "When you're together, do you have long and meaningful conversations?"

*What is she getting at?*

"Or is it about the sex? What is great about your time together?"

I spin away from her, feeling exposed. Jobe and I talk, but it's not long and meaningful discussions because we are similar and like the same things. It's quite the opposite. Our connection is great sex. I down the rest of my drink before turning back to her.

"I'm not attacking you, my friend," she says. "I'm pointing out what the rest of us have noticed. I care about you."

"The rest of you noticed? Am I a subject of gossip between our work colleagues?" When she doesn't say anything, a bubble of anger grows in my chest.

"For fuck's sake," I mutter. "Our relationship is no one's business. If it's about the sex, so what? I'm an adult and in my mid-thirties and don't need to answer to a bunch of twenty-somethings who have barely any experience with the world beyond their schooling." I stand and grab my bag and coat. "Thanks for the concern. Have a fun day watching *the game* tomorrow." I storm out of the bar, still in disbelief that everyone at work thinks Jobe gives me preferential treatment. I suddenly have lost all cheer about being in London.

Her words play out in my head until I exit the taxi. I look up to the terrace and tighten my coat around my neck. Too cold for him to be sitting outside tonight. Piper said it can snow over the holidays. I imagine there will be ample when I return.

The penthouse is dark, and I wonder if he is even home. I head to my room to change, and my first impulse is to search for Jobe, first in his room since that is where I spend my nights.

Piper's words keep playing out in my head. Should I feel guilty that I love having sex with Jobe? Does it matter if we don't have anything else in common and are just having fun? I flop onto the bed and close my eyes. Whenever I think about a future with him, I push it out of my head because I believe it would never happen. I snort out a laugh to myself. *Ridiculous thoughts.* I picture myself in the future, my career intact, no Jobe. My chest hollows. Suddenly, I'm overwhelmed with sadness. My chest is tight, and my throat is dry.

We're only having fun, and nothing has to change.

I cannot control my emotions. Ugh, it must be that time of the month. Speaking of, I'm sure I'm due. With that thought, I climb under the covers to prove to myself I don't need to be with Jobe tonight.

Hours later, I wake feeling warm.

Safe.

An arm drapes over my waist, and the heat is radiating from behind me.

He climbed into my bed and didn't wake me for sex. Jobe wanted only to hold me. A stupid grin creeps over my lips.

We *are* good together, and we don't need long conversations to prove it.

It feels *right.*

# 24

ZARA

Monday morning, I head into the office without first stopping by the café. There is a long list of tasks to complete before I fly home on Wednesday. Jobe and I remained in his penthouse on Saturday and Sunday. We watched movies, ordered food to be delivered from his favorite restaurants, and, in between, had sex, which sometimes led to staying in bed for hours.

"I need your help," Trisha asks. She points to a box of tinsel. "This place needs some Christmas cheer, so wanna help me decorate the walls?"

"Sure."

We take the elevator to the fifth floor. "Are you coming to the Christmas party on Friday night?" she asks.

"No, I'm heading back to California for the holidays to see my family. I heard the office party is the best."

She giggles. "It's a lot. Everyone gets drunk and basically spills all their secrets."

"Office secrets or about their personal lives?"

"Personal," she clarifies. "Not office gossip as most the time… nothing interesting happens here."

"I'm sad to miss it." Not the gossip part.

We loop the tinsel around handrails and over paintings on the walls. "We'll have the workmen come in with ladders to finish decorating tomorrow. I wanted to get a start and gauge everyone's mood."

"No one has mentioned gifts. Does the Board give us a bonus or gift?"

She chuckles. "Not since I have worked here."

We head up the elevator to level six. "I think I might take it up with Mr. Hendricks."

"If anyone can convince him, it's you," she says mindlessly as the doors open.

"Why do you say that?"

"Because you're his girlfriend and all that."

We step out of the elevator, and I grab her arm. "Trisha, what's *all that*?"

She shrugs. "You're together."

"We're not together-together," I defend.

She frowns at me. "What's the difference?"

I shake my head, unable to answer. I turn to Piper, who is staring at me. She gives me a pointed look and then focuses on her screen.

It's uncomfortable being in the office where I used to work. Piper and I understood each other. I regret saying those things to her, especially after a half-dozen drinks, and now wish I could take it back. She doesn't glance my way again, so I decide not to hang around.

My stomach turns, and I'm overcome with nausea. I burp, and it doesn't feel good. "I'm heading back to the office," I tell Trisha. "If you need help, please ask someone here to give you a hand, as I'm—" I cover my mouth with my hand and don't quite make it to my office before rushing to the restrooms. I drop to my knees and puke in the toilet. Thank God no one is in here to hear me. I splash water on my neck and dab a paper towel around my eyes before rinsing my mouth. The end cubicle door opens, and my stomach drops. Lydia walks out and stares at me.

"Are you okay, Zara?"

I nod quickly. "Yeah. My stomach has been in knots since starting the new position. I don't want to mess up."

She eyes me in an understanding way. "I know what you mean. I've felt the same way, and my youngest kept me awake all night last night." She checks herself in the mirror. "It's why I look like I'm on the set of *The Walking Dead*."

I giggle at Lydia. "It's how I feel."

"You might have eaten something to upset you," she suggests. I've barely eaten today. "But if it continues, you might need to get checked out. Or you could test—" She stops herself. "Please get checked out, Zara."

"I will if I'm not any better by tomorrow."

It turns out I'm no better by Tuesday and decide to work from home. Jobe is in the office, keeping his distance in case I am contagious. With most viruses, the contagious period is a few days before, and since we didn't get out of bed most of Sunday because we couldn't get enough of each other, I suspect he is already doomed.

On Tuesday afternoon, I receive a text from him.

Sorry, but I won't make it home for dinner. I'm meeting Harrison James after the next meeting and having dinner with him. We have much to discuss moving forward. How are you feeling?

A little better. Enjoy your dinner. Please say hello to him from me.

I haven't told Jobe how upset I was with Piper. Or anything about the gossip. Yet I feel awful at what went down. I quickly send a text to Piper and George apologizing for my outburst the other night.

*Oh God, here it comes again*. I run into the bathroom and heave.

A few hours later, the door bangs shut.

How long have I been asleep? I check the time, and it's almost midnight. I listen out but Jobe doesn't come into my room. I'm too tired to dwell on why he didn't check in on me so I roll over and go straight back to sleep.

"Zara. Zara."

Gentle shaking.

I open my eyes to Jobe, dressed in a business suit, standing over me. Sunlight breaks through the drapes. "Hi."

"Hi. How are you feeling?"

"Better, I think." I squeeze my eyes closed and open them again. "Yeah, a lot better."

"Are you coming into the office?"

"I am." *I'll try.*

He smiles at me. "Sleepy Zara is adorable."

Why can't I keep my eyes open? I smile goofily at him. "Do you want to get lunch together?"

"If I get a break," he groans out. "What time is your flight tonight? I'll arrange for Ben to drive you." He pulls out a card from his wallet and places it on the bedside table.

"It's at nine, but I need to be at Heathrow by six o'clock."

He nods slowly. "Call Ben and inform him of a time, and I'll accompany you to the airport."

I hold out my hand from the covers, and Jobe squeezes it. "It's after seven. I have to get going, and you should be up."

"Shit. You go. I'll see you at lunch."

Jobe leans in and kisses my forehead before leaving the

room. He glances at my half-packed suitcase on the floor. "Do I need to call someone up to arrange your luggage for you?"

"Have a good day, Jobe," I shoot back. I sit up and laugh at how my suitcase bothers him. Before I swing my legs over the edge, the nausea hits me again. I don't make it to the shower. I'm back leaning over the toilet bowl. After I freshen up, I decide not to return to the office after all.

I open my cell. "Trisha."

"Zara, how are you?"

"Better but not one hundred percent. I'm not coming in today. Please give everyone my best wishes for the holidays and tell them I'm sad to miss the Christmas party."

"I will. Rest up. Are you well enough to catch your flight?"

"I am. I'm already feeling a touch better, and by tonight, I hope to be over the worst of it."

After I end the call, I send Piper and George texts wishing them a Merry Christmas and looking forward to going out for a drink in the new year. I wait for twenty minutes, then toss my cell onto the bed.

I wake to my phone buzzing. I've been asleep for two hours. Crap, I have to tell Jobe that I won't make it to lunch. Then my heart sinks. We haven't discussed Christmas or meeting up while I'm back in California. He booked the jet Friday night, and while he offered me a seat, I had already paid for my flight home.

I already miss him. I turn on the television to the news channel. The screen is filled with snowstorm images in New York. Heathrow has canceled flights, with some being redirected to Orlando and Dallas. I log into my flight app on my cell and read the warnings about arriving early. There is an opening on a flight tonight. Crap. I make a call to Jobe— it goes straight to voicemail.

"Hi, Jobe. I'm not coming into the office as I'm heading straight to Heathrow. I'm sorry to miss lunch. Enjoy the Christmas party on Friday night. Please don't be a stranger when we're home. I—" *I what?* "I miss you already."

My stomach turns over, but I ignore it and pack my suitcase like a woman possessed, then call Ben.

"Hey, Ben. I hope you don't mind me calling, but Jobe said you might have time to drive me to Heathrow?"

"Of course, Ms. Hart. What time do you need to be there?"

"As soon as possible… if that's okay?"

"I'm on my way."

"Thank you."

I take one last look around Jobe's penthouse. Running my fingers along the marble counter, I can almost smell the aroma of herbs as he cooks. I'm going to miss being here.

I take the elevator to the foyer, and a cold blast of air hits me from the open doors. I already need to wear a thick coat, so I slip it on and stand by the glass doors, watching brown and red leaves twirl and scatter in the wind. The sky is gray, threatening to rain, and I'm ready to go home to a somewhat warmer climate.

After a few minutes, Ben parks the black Bentley near the door, and I head out, clutching my coat around my neck, my suitcase in tow.

"Allow me to help, Ms. Hart."

"Thank you." He takes my luggage, and I rush into the warmth of the car's back seat. He slams his door and pats his hands together. "Thank you again, Ben. I didn't want to brave the Tube today."

His eyes meet mine in the rearview mirror. "Mr. Hendricks would never forgive me if I allowed you to take the train."

I smile at him. "Thank you, most days I enjoy it. Not today with a suitcase and in this weather."

He gives me a nod before steering the car toward Heathrow.

The news channel didn't exaggerate a word of the report. The airport is the busiest I have ever witnessed, and I'm now regretting not canceling my flight and flying in comfort on Jobe's private jet. I couldn't accept his offer when he's already doing so much for me. I can stand on my own two feet. I don't need the comfort of his wealth to enjoy being with him.

"Excuse me, Miss." The guy behind me urges me to move forward in the line.

*Focus.*

I send Penny a message.

> I'm at the airport. I can't wait to see you and Summer x

By the time I land and am through customs, it's midnight in Los Angeles and eight in the morning in London.

With my cell in my hand, I attempt to read the messages, and as I head through the terminal, I hear, "Zara," my mother calling out to me.

"Mom." She pulls me in for a hug, and Dad is right beside her, wrapping his arms around both of us.

"I've missed you." She sobs, and I tighten my squeeze.

"It's only been four months, Mom." I love that she misses me, but I've been living away from home for almost two decades.

"I know, but it's the longest we have gone without seeing you, and it's not great for my nerves knowing you're in a foreign country."

"England is barely foreign, Mom."

Dad gives me a gentle smile. "You were too far away for your mother's liking." He takes the handle of my suitcase while Mom keeps her arm linked with mine as we head toward the car. "You can tell us all about your adventures on the way home."

Inside my parents' fifteen-year-old sedan, I continue to read the messages. Three from Penny with ideas of catchups over the holidays. One from Jobe hoping I have recovered and to call him as soon as I arrive. One from Piper. It's a voice message.

"Hi, Zara. I hoped to see you before you left. I wish you a happy Christmas with your family, and we'll catch up when you return to London. I'm going to miss my American friend. Big hugs, my love."

I smile and send her a text.

> Hi, Piper. Thank you for the voice message. I'm going to miss you too. I already do. I would like that very much and look forward to catching up, especially for a girl's night after the holidays. Sending a big hug and kiss to you xx

I lay my head back on the seat's headrest and close my eyes. I barely slept since the plane was a full flight, and the neck pillow just didn't cut it.

"Can we tell her?" Mom asks Dad.

I open my eyes. "Tell me what?"

"We have booked a few days away," Dad says, catching my gaze in the rearview mirror.

"Away? Where?" All I can think about is how far away from Jobe and Penny will we be? I expected Christmas day to be at our home in San Diego, and then I'd drive to Los Angeles to see my friends for a few days.

"Mexico," Mom almost sings it.

I sit upright. "What?"

"Your mom has saved enough for us to spend a few days at a resort since you said how cold London is in December."

"You'll be able to spend time by the pool and relax for a few days," she says as though she has given me a wonderful gift.

I can't be upset with them as it's so kind. But while I love my parents, I don't want them organizing my life, especially not when I'm in my mid-thirties. Dad is eyeing me in the mirror, so I force a smile and nod. "It sounds wonderful." I could do with some sunshine. "Only a few days?" I say, sounding disappointed.

"Yes, darling. We leave the day before Christmas for four days. It was a great special. We'll have to forgo our traditional Christmas lunch, but it's worth it to do this with you."

"Thank you both," I say sincerely now that the shock has settled. "I appreciate it."

I send Penny another text to give her the heads up.

> My parents have arranged a 'secret' vacation to Mexico for four days. It leaves two days to see you before I return to London. Any chance you want to drive to San Diego before we leave? So sorry to cancel our plans. I didn't know x

THE FOLLOWING MORNING, I WAKE TO A STRING OF MESSAGES.

The first is from Jobe. Then Penny.

One from Hugh. *Shit, has his wife had the baby?*

One from George.

*Jobe is calling...*

My heart does a little flip seeing his name, and I smile at my impatient man.

"Good morning, Mr. Hendricks."

"Zara." His voice is strained.

I sit upright and lift the covers to my chest. "Hey. Is everything okay?"

"Piper died in an accident last night."

"What?" I gasp. "What do you mean *died*?"

"She was in a car with a guy, and he crashed the car. A date apparently with someone she met on a dating app."

"What the fuck?" I croak. My heart is racing, and I can't breathe. "She's really dead?"

Silence.

I hold my breath. This can't be real.

"I'm so sorry. It's not how I wanted to tell you, but I didn't want you to hear from anyone else. Is there anything I can do?"

My eyes burn, and tears roll down my cheeks. The nausea is back, and with it, my gut tightens. I'm going to be sick. "When are you coming home?"

"Tonight. I have commitments with my family. Some things have happened at home and I promised Mom I'd be there for Christmas Eve. I'll drive down to San Diego and see you the day after Christmas."

I shake my head. My throat is on fire, and I can barely speak. I keep seeing images of Piper laughing at something I said at the bar. Joking around together. I'm struggling to accept she is gone. "My parents have surprised me with four days in Mexico for Christmas. I'll call you when I get home." I sob.

"Zara. I know this is hard, but she didn't suffer. The

reports indicate she died instantly. An object in the back seat flew into the front when the car rolled. It hit her in the head, a fatal blow."

I sob louder. "What about the driver?"

"He didn't make it. He was taken to hospital but died a few hours later."

I can't catch my breath.

"I need you to breathe slowly. In and out," he says in a calm voice. "I'm here for you, Zara."

"You're not. You're over five thousand miles away," I moan.

"I'm a phone call away if you need me. You can talk to me anytime. I care about you."

Nice. "I care about you too, but my heart is broken, and I need someone to hold me in their arms and reassure me everything is going to be okay," I croak on the last words.

"Imagine my arms around you. I'm holding you ti—"

"I gotta go," I say quickly, interrupting him. I need to cry alone. "I'll talk to you later, Jobe."

I turn my cell to silent, unable to speak to anyone else today. I curl up in a ball, crying myself back to sleep.

THE FOLLOWING DAY, I BRIEFLY SPEAK TO GEORGE.

Everyone at work is a mess. Understandable. I wish I were there to mourn my friend with them. My heart is hurting so bad. Overwhelmed with uncontrollable emotion, Piper's death has triggered me to think about loss on other levels. Like what I'll be like when Jobe decides I'm no longer fun.

I wipe my nose with the back of my hand. It drips as much as tears fall off my cheeks. I'm on a downward spiral, and I'm at a loss to protect myself from the pain. I keep seeing images in my head of Piper. My heart hurts in a way I have never felt before.

I haven't checked my cell all morning. I don't want to see any more messages or be obliged to reply. I can't look at social media with a flood of images of Piper smiling and enjoying life. I don't want to speak to anyone, not even my friends.

We leave for the airport in an hour, and I hope getting away will clear my head.

Dad comes and wraps an arm around my shoulders. He pulls me close and plants a kiss on the top of my head. "Is there anything I can do?"

I shake my head. It's a common question, but what can anyone do? A heart transplant free of pain and a brain without memories, thanks.

The entire way to the airport, my parents peer over their shoulders, stealing glances and checking on me. I fake being asleep on the flight, then hold a book in my lap on the drive to the beachside resort. Yet I don't read a single word.

## 25

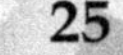

JOBE

What a fucking Christmas Eve.

My sister is walking around like a ghost after having her heart trampled by Brandon. Their relationship came as a surprise to all of us. We all loved the Aussie. He was part of our family. Now he's fucked off to Chicago, and Franklin signed the contract for the transfer. Business is business. I know it better than most. But when it comes to family, I presumed Franklin would have prevented the deal from going through.

Franklin has barely said a word about it. Maybe he knows more than he's willing to reveal. We're on tenterhooks, but it's nothing compared to how Zara is feeling.

Brandon is alive and scored a great NBA deal. Piper will not get another Christmas with her family, and when I think about that reality, it fills me with gratitude for what I have.

Mom hands out the ghastly sweaters we all pretend to

like. I slip it on over my shirt and watch Mom and Charlotte decorate the tree. Byron is on crutches, his injury healing, but he's lost as much as Charlotte since Brandon was his best friend.

*Why the fuck did Brandon want out?*

Franklin and Dad have their glasses full of whiskey, and I overhear them discussing business. That's the last thing on my mind, so I take Summer from Penny's arms and give my niece a big kiss on the cheek. She squirms, and I place her on the floor, watching as she crawls over to my father, and he sets her on his knee.

"Have you spoken to her?" Penny asks, taking the seat beside me.

I shake my head. "Not since I told her about Piper." I stare at Penny. "Have you spoken to her?"

"No. We talked after she heard the news, then everything was in text. She's stopped replying now she's in Mexico."

"I'm worried about her."

"So am I." Penny gives me an understanding look, and it confirms my concern.

"The day after she gets back, I'm driving down to see her. It won't be until the afternoon. Then Summer and I will stay the night at Mom and Dad's, and we'll drive back to LA the following morning."

"I think it's a good idea to check in on her," I say quietly. Penny and I agreed not to share what happened with the family as there is enough sadness in the room already.

My gut is tight with concern, and I don't want to wait until Penny can drive to San Diego. I'll drive down the morning after she returns and speak to Zara first. No one else has to know.

CHRISTMAS PASSES IN A BLUR OF DECADENT FOOD, extravagant gifts, and bad cracker jokes that make some of us pretend to laugh. With the somber mood, it's all a bit of a waste.

Three days later, I wake up thinking about Zara.

She and her family flew back home last night. I have tried to call every day while she was away. It went straight to her voicemail. I open my cell.

> Morning, Zara. I hope you enjoyed the sunshine and spent some valuable time with your family. I'm driving down to San Diego this morning, hoping we can chat. I miss you

Not expecting a reply, I head to my parents' home. This time of year, breakfast at theirs is a casual walk-in affair as we all try to spend more time together as a family. I find Dad and Franklin at the breakfast table discussing the game that was played on Christmas Day.

"Is that all he said?" Dad asks Franklin.

"Morning," I greet and take a seat, helping myself to the almond croissants on the table. "What are we discussing?"

"BJ. He told Lottie at the game that it was fate that he was transferred to Chicago, and they're not meant to be. He changed his cell and his number so she couldn't contact him. She called him a coward, and then Byron said something about seeing him on the court next year."

"This all happened at the game on Christmas Day?"

Franklin nods.

"It wasn't fate, though, was it, since you signed him off."

Franklin glares at me. "He demanded it. Said he had to go and wouldn't give a reason. He said our family was holding him back from being his best."

"The fuck? We've given him everything."

Franklin agrees. "And now there's whispers he'll make the Australian Olympic team. Something Byron will not achieve with setbacks from his injury."

"It is what it is. There are worse things that can happen." I eye Franklin to see if Penny has mentioned anything to him. Dad frowns at me as though nothing is worse than his star basketball son with a near career-ending injury.

Franklin gives a subtle nod. "I need to get home and be with Summer and Pen before they drive down to San Diego for the night."

"You're not going with them?" Dad asks.

"No, I'm flying to Florida for a couple of nights. Lottie is staying over with Penny."

"It will help take her mind off a broken heart."

I also stand. "I'm heading into the office for the day. I'll see Mom and you later tonight."

I head out the door, get on the road, and take the freeway heading south of Los Angeles, not in the direction of my office.

For the next two hours, I listen to a podcast on the real estate market to distract my anxious mind. Maps direct me to a small house with vinyl siding and French windows. It has a white picket fence, and a cat is on the porch, curled up, enjoying the morning sun.

I jog up the steps, knocking on the door.

Silence.

*Knock. Knock.*

Is that footsteps?

The wooden door swings open, and a small woman appears with salt and pepper hair. She has the same brown eyes as Zara. "May I help you? If you're here to talk about the bible, then we're not interested. We are Christians and have our own church."

Stunned, I glance down at my white shirt, black pants,

and suit jacket. "No, ma'am, I'm here to see Zara. I hope you all had a lovely Christmas in Mexico."

She nods slowly, eyeing me from head to toe. "We did, thank you."

I hold out my hand. "Jobe Hendricks."

"Oh, you're the kind young man who offered his apartment for her to stay in." She takes my hand and leads me inside. "We appreciate what you've done for our Zara. Please take a seat. I'm Ruby, and this is my husband, Leroy," she introduces as a tall man enters through the backdoor with a bag in his hand. He stops moving when he lays eyes on me.

"Leroy, come and meet Jobe Hendricks," Ruby calls out.

Leroy wipes his hands on his trousers first before shaking my hand. "Good to meet you, son." They thank me again for helping Zara out, though something tells me they are unaware that I sometimes stay there as well.

"Is Zara here?"

"I'm so sorry," Ruby begins. "She left an hour ago and didn't say where she was headed. Have you tried her cell?"

"It goes straight to voicemail."

"I expect she won't be long, so you're welcome to stay."

"I wanted to check in on her after hearing about her friend, Piper. The two of them were close."

"It hit her hard for the first few days. She seems more herself now. Going about her day quietly. She really enjoyed her days at the beach. A bit of sunshine cures everything."

Her mother should remove her rose-colored glasses.

I stay and listen to their stories about the trip to Mexico and an hour later, I decide to leave. If Zara read my message, then she knew I was coming. I have a sinking suspicion she isn't home because I'm here.

"Thank you for the water. Please tell Zara I came by to see her."

The moment I'm in my car, I call Penny.

"Jobe. I'm almost at my parents' house."

"I decided to come and see Zara first." I veer the car into the street and set the map toward the freeway.

"Oh. How is she?"

"She's not here. I sent her a text to let her know I was coming to see her." Silence. "She didn't tell her parents where she was going."

"Right," she says softly.

"I'm worried about her, Pen."

"I think I know where she might be. I'll leave Summer with Mom and see if I can find her."

My stomach twists, knowing she is in pain. "Please call me as soon as you do. I need to know she is okay."

## 26

ZARA

TWO HOURS HAVE PASSED, and I assume it's safe to go home.

I stare out to the ocean one last time, memories playing through my mind of Penny and me sitting here as teenagers, planning our lives, discussing colleges and our dreams. Then there were the difficult times when guys treated us like crap, and we needed the calm the Cabrillo Tidepools provided.

The sun is directly above me. The warmth touches my skin yet fails to warm my heart. I am cold inside. Lifeless.

My friend is gone. We didn't get to see each other before Christmas, even though we made peace. I mull over her words in my head. Her warnings of Jobe and what she was implying without trying to hurt me. She was being a good friend. I've had days to think about it, and she was right. Sex is not a foundation to build a relationship on, especially when we have nothing else in common.

"Hey."

I turn, not expecting to see Penny. But then, as best friends, we always had a sense when one of our lives turned to crap—the other would know, and we would find each other here.

"Hey," I murmur. "I was about to go home and be ready for you when you arrived."

She's panting a little from the one-mile hike up from the parking lot. She squats down on the rock beside me and removes her Jimmy Choo boots, hiking up the hem of her Armani skirt. I know the designers as I went on a shopping spree with her after she married Franklin, the first time she allowed herself to splurge.

Her bare feet dangle in the shallow water alongside mine as we stare out over the ocean, something we have done many times together.

"You're avoiding Jobe," she whispers. "He's worried about you."

I nod. "Remember the times when we knew someone wasn't right for us?" I begin. "So we rip off the Band-Aid, the pain at its worst in the beginning, but then you heal?" She stares at me, but I don't turn to meet her caring eyes. I need to finish telling her everything, even if it hurts. "It's what I do. Why I rushed off to London even though it pained me to be away from you and Hugh. And that I wouldn't get to see Summer for a while. In my heart, I needed a year to sort out my life, go somewhere new, be someone different."

"Has it worked out for you?" she murmurs.

"It did for a while. Then Jobe happened. Completely unexpected." This time, I meet her gaze. "I fell for him." I see the shock in her eyes. "We weren't faking it." I make a noise in my throat and shake my head, feeling like an idiot. "We both know what an ass he is and that he'll never commit to one person. But I saw a different man. A kind, caring man, and yeah, all those rumors were true."

"Eww."

I smile and look out to the sea and not at my friend. "We were good together. Only before I left, Piper and I had a misunderstanding. She attempted to warn me about Jobe. Mentioned people were talking about my preferential treatment at work. Questioned me about our relationship and if we had long and meaningful discussions. Of course, we never do. We're different, and I can't think of a single thing we have in common except we both like being single, and we love dining out, and sex fuels our souls. And neither of us..." I hesitate. I've never had the courage to tell Penny this before. "Neither of us wants children."

She stares at me. "Oh. You never want..."

I shake my head. "Please don't tell me that I just need to meet the right guy. I couldn't bear you not believing me."

"It's... I won't. There's nothing wrong with being different. Many men don't want to be with someone who is the female version of themselves. They need an escape and appreciate the difference. And I never thought you liked being single. You have grown to accept it. Even in school, you loved being in a relationship. What I disagreed with was how you tried to change yourself to be more of what the guy preferred in a relationship."

Her green eyes hold understanding. Penny gets me.

"Have you changed for Jobe in any way?"

I shake my head. "But it's pointless. It's not going anywhere. I'm not a fool to believe he'll settle for me. It hurts a lot. Even now. But time will heal the hurt. It just sucks that it's a double hit with Piper." My throat burns thinking about her. Tears fall onto my cheeks, and I swipe them away. "She was my closest friend in London, and I'm not sure I want to go back."

Penny places her arm around me and pulls me close to

her side, leaning her head on my shoulder. "I'm here for you."

"I'm also late."

She lifts her head. "What?"

"I've been vomiting, and I assumed it was stress, and then I realized *I'm late.*"

She takes my hand and squeezes it. "What are you going to do?"

I shake my head. "Pray I'm not pregnant. I'm not ready, Pen. I'm not like you. And I'm not sure I'd even tell Jobe."

"Whatever happens, you'll have all of our support."

More tears blur my eyes. "Thank you."

"We're not going to do this. Worry about something unnecessarily. We're getting a test *now.*" She stands and holds out her hand. "I'm doing this with you."

"Are you going to pee on the stick for me?" We both giggle.

"No," she says, pulling me to my feet. "But I'll be there when you see the result. I'll always be by your side when you need me. Always."

Penny keeps an arm around me as we walk back to the cars. "I'll buy the pregnancy kit and meet you back at Mom's." She hugs me before opening the door of her Bentley.

On the drive to Penny's San Diego home, where I spent most of my childhood, I bite my nails and imagine the worst outcome. What will I do if I'm... no. Stop. I need to push out the thoughts until I know the result.

I park the car and wave to Penny's parents who are outside with Summer enjoying the winter sunshine. Penny meets me at the gate. "We'll talk to them later," she whispers. "We'll head upstairs to the bathroom." She turns to her parents. "Zara and I will chat with you soon. She needs the restroom."

"Sorry," I call back and follow Penny up the stairs, the brown paper bag in her grasp. She hands it to me before I shut the bathroom door. This is not my first rodeo. Penny and I have tested on many occasions, often when we were panicked in our early twenties at being a day late.

She knocks on the door as I'm washing my hands, and I open it for her. We sit on the floor with the stick between us.

"How many days late are you?"

This is the part where we stare at each other and chat rather than watch the stick for any change while the timer ticks away.

"I think a week. Ten days, maybe."

She nods, holding my gaze. "Have you any other symptoms?"

"Vomiting. I was ill recently and had antibiotics. But then when we, you know, the timing doesn't align."

She arches her brow. "So it happened more than a couple of times..."

I lower my gaze. "If you call it a couple of times a night, then yeah."

"Oh my fucking God," she whispers.

I peer up, and our eyes meet. "I'm sorry, Pen. I should've told you."

She reaches and takes my hand. "It's fine. I know he's a charmer. Most girls can't resist him."

"I could. I did. But then he..." I shrug. "He was nice to me. And I hated that I fell because I remember how much of an ass he was to you when you first met Frank."

She giggles. "Yeah, but he really is a gentle soul when you get to know him." She narrows her eyes. "Does Frank know?"

"I don't think so." I close my eyes momentarily and open them again. "This is one way to take my mind off Piper. It's weird that I had an image in my head of holding a baby girl, and I named her Piper. But I know it's because I want to honor Piper and not because I want a baby."

She lowers her gaze and then looks at me and shakes her head. "You can honor her in other ways." She holds up the stick. "You're not pregnant, Zara."

I throw myself at her, and she hugs me. I cry quietly onto her shoulder. "Finally, some good news."

She pats my back. "We would have figured it out." We stay like this for a few more seconds. "Now what?"

When I arrive home from Penny's, I find my parents sitting on the couch watching a basketball game. "Franklin's team, the LA Sharks, are playing," Dad tells me.

I nod. "That's great. Are they winning?" I ask, even though I've never been interested in sports. Neither were my parents, but since my best friend's husband's family owns the team, they have supported them. I guess Penny's excitement has rubbed off on them.

My cell vibrates with a message. George.

Hi Zara. Piper's funeral is on Friday. I'm not sure if you'll be back here but I thought you would want to know.

The air freezes in my lungs.

Thank you. I will be attending. You know how much I loved her.

"You had a visitor," Dad announces. "Jobe Hendricks came by to see you." Dad is studying me.

I nod again. "Yeah, he's a nice *friend*," I emphasize. "I'll catch up with him another time." I sit with my parents on

239

the couch. "Do you mind turning the television off? I need to talk with you."

"Of course, love." Mom and Dad stare at me. "What is it?"

"I'm struggling to accept I'll never see my friend, Piper, again." My throat burns again as the tears fall easily. I don't have to do much. It's like a faucet, one thought, and the water flows. "Her funeral is on Friday, and I want to attend. It means leaving early."

Mom places her arms around my waist. Her head pushed into my chest. "We understand, honey. I have loved having you home, but you also need closure."

"The problem is I don't know if I want to stay... I promised myself a year to make something of a career for myself, discover a new country, and find myself. Now, going back there, it will remind me of her. Everything we did together, and it's going to hurt. I don't know if I can," I rasp out the last words.

"You're stronger than you give yourself credit, my girl. You can do this. Take it month by month. It's going to hurt, but you don't want to forget your friend either."

I nod at Dad and wipe away the tears.

"I agree with your father. While I would prefer you to be in the States, I'm so proud you have traveled abroad and are doing things outside your comfort zone."

I snort. "It was hard as I was never brave."

"You are. You need to do this for yourself. Set goals. Book a flight home for Mother's Day. That way, you have something to look forward to and then you can reassess after that."

I nod. "Sienna and Hugh's baby is due next week. I'm going to miss it. So I'll be able to see their baby in May."

"You can't put your life on hold for other people," Dad

offers gently. "Your friends will be here when you come home."

Another three hours until we land.

It's been a long flight, preparing myself for the funeral. I haven't spoken to Jobe. While I feel bad for ignoring his calls, I sent him a text telling him I'm okay, but I think it's best not to see each other for now. I need time, and I hope he understands by giving me space. What I didn't tell him is that I'm devastated he's incapable of settling down with me, and my heart just doesn't need any more reason to ache right now.

I'll make plans to move out after I chat with George and see if he knows of anyone needing someone to share since George seems to know everyone.

I have thought about work and keeping my association with Jobe at a professional level. I don't need to see him, and hopefully, his visits will remain once a month.

Closing my eyes, I try to get some sleep for the last part of the flight, but all I see is Piper's beautiful smile and the way she used to play with her long blonde ponytail. I tell myself not to cry but cherish the fact I can still see her in my mind, and I never want to let her memory go.

International flights are crap, and arriving at six in the morning on the day of a funeral is the worst.

Jobe's penthouse is oddly quiet. Someone has been here to clean the apartment, and the books on my bedside table are in a neat stack. It's weird to have a stranger in my room, but if Jobe trusts someone, then I have no reason not to.

I just admitted to trusting his judgment. Trusting him. I'm not going to explore those thoughts and head to the shower to try and wake myself up instead of walking around, putting one foot in front of the other like a zombie.

After showering, I dab on some light makeup. Pointless, really, because as soon as I see everyone, I'll lose it. I'm wearing a black dress to the knee, tight fitting, but I wore it out a couple of times with Piper, so I think it's right for the day.

After calling an Uber, I head downstairs to wait. Inside the rideshare, I stare out the window, noting the buildings and places where I've visited or passed when I was with Piper. Tears pool and I somehow manage to push the emotion away.

We stop outside the church, and I head inside with a crowd of people I have never seen before. The church is full. The music is depressing and not what I believe Piper would choose for her funeral. Halfway along the aisles, I notice some people from work.

Slowly, I make my way along the side of the church, trying not to hear the sobs or notice people wiping their eyes. The coffin comes into view, and I stop walking, too scared to walk closer, knowing it will break my resolve.

In the front row, men and women huddle together. One glance and I can tell it's Piper's parents and grandparents and other family members by the wailing. *Oh. My. Heart.*

"Zara." A whisper. I turn, and George discreetly waves me over to him. Lydia is on his other side. I slide into the seat beside him, he reaches out, takes my hand, and squeezes it. "I got you, babe." His swollen red eyes hold mine before he looks to the front of the church, where a priest comes to stand. "She'd fucking hate this music," he murmurs. "It's killing me."

"I thought the same thing."

He squeezes my hand again.

We listen to relatives speak about Piper's life and her kind soul. While I didn't know much about her life before we met, I know everything about her gentle soul. For the next half hour, I listen to prayers and words that cause my endless tears to flow. My throat burns, as do my eyes, and I'm not sure how much more sadness I can endure.

Some people choose to leave after the church service, but George, Lydia, and I are bundled up in our coats, gloves, and thick scarves to go to the cemetery.

It's beautiful, with memorials lining some paths, some in the garden beds, and others with headstones. We are at a grave site, a gaping hole in the ground. The other graves are covered with grass surrounding the headstones. A rosebush with tiny yellow buds is in a pot at the end of the site.

We all gather around as the coffin is secured over the hole. The priest begins to speak, though I don't hear a word. I'm forever wiping my eyes, my nose running like a river. I manage to keep the sobs quiet, sucking in each breath though it's difficult listening to Piper's mom's cries over everyone else. George squeezes my gloved hand, and I bow my head. It's too painful to watch. He squeezes again, a double squeeze, trying to alert me to something. I look at him, and he tips his head to the left. On the other side of the grave, to our left, Jobe is standing a few feet away from everyone else.

My heart stops.

*He came.*

He is wearing his standard black suit and white shirt with a long, tailored black coat over his suit and a black scarf draped around his neck. Jobe is all class, but as his eyes meet mine, I see the sadness even from here. It takes everything I have not to run into his arms.

Not here.

I don't have the energy for more emotion.

Averting my gaze, I watch as they lower Piper's coffin into the grave. The finality is too much. I let out a sob, and like a chain reaction, an echo of sobbing sounds around me. Then, we're asked to come forward to throw a rose into the grave. There are red, white, and yellow roses.

"We should choose yellow," George whispers. "It signifies friendship and love between friends." I nod and take the rose, but the moment I look down, my head spins. It's too much. I throw the rose into the grave, move to the back of the line, and squat down on my haunches. I need a minute.

"Zara." His gentle hand rests on my shoulder. "Do you need me to take you home?" I glance up into Jobe's bloodshot eyes and shake my head, forcing myself to stand. He places a soft hand on my lower back. "Take some deep breaths. It will help."

The priest says a final word and welcomes everyone to a special room on the grounds. The crowd disperses until I'm left standing with Lydia, George, and Jobe.

"I'm going to have a drink for Piper. Are you all coming?" George asks.

Lydia nods. "I can for a while."

Jobe looks at me, and I glance back to George. "I want to but, I don't think I can. It was a long flight, and I'm struggling with it all. Can we do something special for her tomorrow night?"

"Of course." He leans in and kisses my cheek, then shakes Jobe's hand before he and Lydia follow behind the rest of Piper's family and friends.

I turn to Jobe, and before I say anything, he wraps his arms around me and pulls me into his chest. I let go of everything and cry for a few minutes before I come up for air. "This is the first funeral I have attended for someone under eighty years of age," I mumble. "It's so unfair. She had everything to live for."

"She really did. I have no doubt she would have been a close friend of yours for life, even across oceans. I wish it weren't true, but that's life. We know little of the sadness many families go through. Death is not only about old age. It's why I choose to live my best life, for we never know our fate. What will happen tomorrow..."

"I'm going to miss her," I sob again.

"I know. But I'll be here for you for as long as you need me to stay."

*What?*

I step away from him. "Jobe, I—" I shake my head. It would be easy to slide back into his arms, but it would make my broken heart even worse.

"Can we please go home and talk?"

I nod, but the last thing I want to do is talk. I need to sleep the entire weekend and when I wake up, I want this nightmare to be over.

27

―――

JOBE

We drive home in silence, and I don't let go of Zara's hand. I thank Ben and inform him we won't require his services until Monday.

I lead Zara to the elevator, then inside the penthouse.

"I'm going to my room," she murmurs, releasing my hand and closing her bedroom door.

I walk to my bedroom, slip off my coat, and change out of my suit into something more casual. It's only five o'clock and too early for her to sleep. I don't want her to think she is alone through this.

*Knock. Knock.*

Silence.

I open the door a crack. Zara is lying on her side, her back to me, with her same clothes on. I take a hesitant seat on the edge of the bed and pick up her hand, holding it firmly in mine. The tears silently cascade down her cheeks, and it fucking crushes me to see her like this.

"Can I make you something to eat?" Zara shakes her head. "Something warm to drink?"

"No, thank you," she rasps, staring straight ahead to the window.

"Do you want me to help you change out of your clothes?" Her gaze flicks to mine, her beautiful eyes narrow. "Think what you want, but I'm not leaving you alone. It's not the first time I've seen you without clothes."

She doesn't say a word, stands, and hangs up her coat. Then she removes her gloves and scarf before sliding off her dress and stockings. She leaves her bra and panties on and then slips on pink silk pajamas.

Silently, I hold back the covers for her to climb under. As soon as she is settled, I go to the other side, step out of my jeans, and climb under the covers with her. I wasn't lying when I said I wasn't going to leave her.

"Nothing is going to happen," she murmurs.

"I know." I slide closer to spoon her. "I only want to lie here with you."

"She didn't trust you," she whispers.

"Who?"

"Piper. She asked me about us before she died. It was like she was giving me a warning, and I should listen. She said that you can't base a relationship on great sex."

"This is true." I search for her hand under the blankets and hold her delicate fingers.

"She also asked if we had meaningful conversations and then I realized we didn't because we have nothing in common."

I now see where she is headed with this. "We are different, Zara, but we also talk. I like being with you. Really like being with you."

"I don't think we should be together." She turns her head and looks me directly in the eye. "We both know it's not going to last, and I can't go through the pain of losing someone I care for again."

"Why do you think we won't last?" Her bloodshot eyes search mine as though I should know the answer. "Because your work friends said so?" I can't help being pissed off because whatever they said, Zara is beginning to believe them.

"No. Because of your history," she murmurs. "Please go. It will be harder if we drag this out."

*No way in hell am I going to let this slide.*

"Everybody has a history. It doesn't depict our future. Your past helps define the path you take and moving forward, I know what I don't want. To keep repeating the past. Especially when, for most of my life, I searched for the comfort of the physical kind from women to who I'd never make promises. Never commit to." I take it one step further. "Maybe it was my upbringing..."

She makes a noise that I'm making this up.

"While people see my family's wealth, they don't see children who are left to be raised by nannies and other staff since my father's priority was work, and he was absent most nights. My mother did the best she could but often accompanied him on his business trips. She was also lonely." I clear my throat. "I'm not making excuses for my past sexual preferences, but I need you to understand that I like you, Zara, a lot. And I have absolutely no desire to be with anyone else." She stares at me, but my words fail to soften her expression.

"Really? Enough to have a baby with me?"

I swallow hard. "That's a big jump from liking someone."

"Tell me about it. The week before Christmas, when I was vomiting, I was also *late*." She sits up with more fire in her eyes. "I had to deal with the notion I could be pregnant and then to find out my friend died. All I could think about was how you'd react. And then, when I lost Piper, the one person who told me to be careful of you, I took it as a warning. It gave me a glimpse into the future."

"And what did you see?" I shoot back because I didn't get a chance to defend myself in her scenarios.

"I was alone with a baby. You couldn't commit to me, and I understood because I knew the deal when I met you. I was a good mom." She gives me a long look before turning back to her side.

"I believe you would be a good mom. And if I knew about the baby, I wouldn't have deserted you."

"That's exactly why I didn't tell you and chose to be a single mother," she murmurs. "I didn't want to force you into anything. I wanted you to love me for me. And it didn't happen."

*Fuck this.*

"Firstly, think all you want, but it's not how it would play out in reality. I would be by your side because..." I let out a long sigh, needing this. Th—the moment of truth. I hope I don't spook her. "I love you, Zara." She turns her head, eyes wide. "I fucking love you."

She rolls over to face me. Tears streaming down her cheek. "Do you mean it? Because I can't play any more games of pretend."

My thumbs stroke her beautiful face, feeling the emotion her big brown eyes hold. "I do mean it. You're the reason I'm here."

"I'm the reason you're here... in London?"

I nod once. "While there were viable business deals, the appeal broadened the day you accepted the job offer. At first, I made a promise to help boost your career and find yourself again because you looked fucking done with everything that night we first... anyway, it became clear to me that I wanted to try with you. Being here in London gave us a chance to be together without the influence or opinions of our family and friends back home."

Her mouth falls open. "Even so, we still fought."

I smile at her. "The way you tried to push me away made me want you more. But I knew my brother wouldn't approve. Or Penny." I round my eyes for emphasis. "She would have had my balls."

Finally, she smiles. "And I promised myself never to fall for someone like you."

"Fall for me?" I kiss her nose. "Is that what happened?"

"You'll have to stick around to find out." Her grin grows.

I wrap an arm around her side and slide close enough so our bodies align. "I intend to for a fucking long time. Do you think you can tolerate me?"

She kisses my lips. Just the once, it's not enough. It will never be enough. I want more with her.

"This morning, I wanted this nightmare to be over, and I didn't want to feel anymore. You were a light in the darkness. So yes, I can tolerate you. Thank you for giving me hope."

I nuzzle her cheek. "I offer you more than hope, Zara. I can give you my world."

# EPILOGUE

## ZARA

### FEBRUARY

THE CAFÉ WHERE PIPER AND I WOULD MEET HOLDS TOO MANY memories. It's been two months, and my heart has not healed, not even a little. I still see her at the same table, her long blonde hair sitting perfectly over her shoulder, and hear her sweet laugh that could light up the room.

When Jobe is in London, Ben drives us to work. When he is in Los Angeles or anywhere else in the world, I take the Tube and meet George at a new café around the corner.

Today is one of those days Jobe is in LA. I'm grateful to spend the time with him when he is here, but I know he needs to be in LA for most of the time. And he mentioned something about setting up a business surprise for Byron to give to Giana as a gift.

When he's not here, life is harder. I struggle not having him home to hold me at night.



I'm already at the café when I receive the message from George. I finish my cup since I arrived earlier than usual. Even Jobe's penthouse was eerily quiet, so I needed to be around people to stop my mind from analyzing a thousand thoughts threatening to undo me.

Slipping on my coat and scarf, I head out to the street toward our office block. Winter has been tough. The blistery winds make my gray mood even darker. As I ride the elevator to the fifth floor, I change my mind and press the button for the floor where Piper used to work. I take one step out of the elevator and stop. Not a soul is here. I walk around the desks to her desk, still vacant until the company employs someone.

How will I cope with seeing someone sitting at her desk?

My heart hollows out, remembering our conversations while sitting here. The first day when she brought me chocolate muffins, how she would whisper to me and plan our weekends from this table. I run my fingers along the bare wood, flatten my hand on the table, and close my eyes. I imagine Piper is here with me, us working side by side. It was a time when she was happy.

So was I.

My stomach bottoms out at the thought of moving on without her. I have come to accept coming to work reminds me of Piper, the happy times, and I don't want to let the memory go. I turn to the window where I used to gaze out in a dream and think about my friends back home.

Today, I'm thinking about Piper.

The elevator door opens, and Vanessa walks in.

"Oh." She stares at me. "You're at work early." She eyes the desk where I'm standing. "Is everything okay?"

I nod and head to the elevator. She probably thinks I'm spying. "Yeah." I force a smile. "I miss her, that's all."

"Oh, right." She turns to Piper's desk. "Of course."

*Yeah, you never spoke to her, so I don't think you would understand.*

"Have a good day." I get in the elevator and ride to my floor. I need to do something fun, so I get out my phone and message George.

> I want to do something exciting this weekend. Something Piper would also enjoy. Any ideas?

> Darling, I am the king of ideas. We'll make plans over lunch. And let's dine somewhere exquisite. I'll take you to the Ritz.

I pop my cell away and smile as I head to my office. Jobe is going to hate that I'll be dining at the Ritz without him.

We have come so far as a couple. I'm smiling because I still love to tease him.

Though he'll be glad I am with George. So much has changed over the past two months. George and Jobe are friends and get on like a house on fire. I needed them to be because George reminds me of the good times with Piper and how fun it is to live in London.

I really couldn't have gotten through the pain without him.

An incoming call vibrates inside my bag.

My heart flips seeing Jobe's name on the screen. "Hey, I was just thinking of you."

"Good. You'll be more than thinking about me tonight when I make you scream my name as you come. I've missed you, Zee. I've missed your mouth around my—"

I cut him off. "I'm at work," I whisper as my cheeks flame. No one can hear us, only I don't want to go the entire day thinking about what Jobe will do to me tonight. Who am I kidding? Of course I will. "Tonight?" I track back. "What time is it in LA?"

"Eleven p.m. I'm about to board the jet. I secured the contracts with Byron for this new art studio he is planning for Giana, so there is no reason for me to stay a second longer. I need you."

My toes curl the way he says, *I need you.*

"I need you too." So much it scares me. "Oh. I made plans for the weekend not realizing you would be here. George is taking me to The Ritz," I say excitedly.

"George will not get a table at the Ritz at such short notice. Looks like you both need my help. Tell him I'll make a booking... for three."

I laugh. There is no chance Jobe will let me out of his sight while he is in London. And George will be equally thrilled to be dining with both of us, especially when Jobe orders his favorite expensive whiskey. "See you tonight," I whisper.

"I love you."

"And I love you."

In a matter of minutes, my day is already brighter, and my weekend is going to be even better. I have survived my first English winter, and I can't wait for summer.

JOBE

. . .

OCTOBER

ZARA TAKES A SIP OF HER CHAMPAGNE AND PLACES IT ON THE
white tablecloth.

A harpist plays on the balcony above us. Succulents and ivy hang from the potted garden strung above us in the lush hotel. It's romantic, and there is no one else I'd rather be with at a fancy high tea. She takes a bite of her sandwich and looks at her watch.

"Is there somewhere else you need to be?" She beams that beautiful smile at me, and I'm ready to agree with whatever she asks of me.

"Your brother's game starts in another hour," she says as though I should know this.

I check my watch. It's Byron's first game in almost a year. It happens to be against his former best friend and teammate, Brandon's team, Chicago. The Chicago team is not the focus as much as Brandon Johns. My sister is running the LA Sharks and more than anything, she wants us to crush Chicago and for Byron to outclass Brandon in skill on every inch of the court. It's more than a game. More than winning. It's about pride.

My family expected me to be there, except I had already committed to be in London to finalize the new executive director to replace me. And to be with my girl.

Zara handed in her resignation, and we are returning to Los Angeles in three weeks. We are packing up our London lives and, with it, a shitload of emotion. She is my lotus flower rising from a dark place, beautiful, strong, and resilient.

She has made a life for herself in London and has fallen

in love with the city. But she misses her friends and wants to be part of their children's lives as they grow.

If this is what Zara wants, then I'll do everything to make it happen. Zara is my future, and I'll go wherever she goes.

We have invested in a new business as partners. A hotel in Beverly Hills where Zara will manage the staff and HR Department, and I will oversee the executive team. We have plans to style it similar to the hotels we love in London, which has brought us to the famous hotel in Edinburgh, especially since Zara never got to see much of Scotland.

I cock an eyebrow at her. "Our dessert is yet to be served."

A sexy smile slowly grows on her lips. "Wouldn't you prefer dessert in our room?"

I lift the napkin from my lap and place it on the table. I lift a finger to the waiter and down the rest of my whiskey. "The bill, please, sir."

I pay for the bill, take Zara's hand, and don't let it go as we take the elevator to the fourth floor, and only let go to fetch the key to open our door. I hold it open for her to enter first, and she walks directly to the window, staring toward the view of Edinburgh Castle, situated high on Castle Hill. It is one of the oldest fortified places in Europe, and Zara loved the tour yesterday and hearing about the rich history from royalty to the military and 'the prison'. It evoked an emotional sadness in her as we walked through the Scottish National War Memorial.

She hasn't gotten over losing Piper, and now with her life changing again, her tears well in her eyes, and I don't know if she's happy or sad. All I want to do is to create happy memories for her. Especially when she visited Piper's memorial site last weekend and said she didn't want to leave

London as she was leaving Piper. I have made it my mission to turn every day into a positive memory until we leave.

I start the open fire in our hotel suite then go and stand behind Zara by the window. I wrap my arms around her shoulders and pull her close to me.

"There is so much of this country I haven't explored yet," she murmurs.

"No. But we can return any time. Plan short vacations during the year. And not just here. We can travel anywhere and even more of the US and Canada," I tell her. "Places closer to home."

Zara turns and loops her arms around my neck. Her brown eyes dance with amusement. "Look at Jobe Hendricks planning vacations for fun and not business."

I kiss her forehead. "I blame you, Ms. Hart. You have changed me."

"To want to take vacations like normal people do," she says in jest.

"To want to take a vacation, period. Before you, there was no time for these things. You have given me perspective, and just so you know, I'll go anywhere with you."

"You're so romantic." She kisses my lips in a peck. Only I keep her there, hold her face, and kiss her deeply. Her hands go to my chest, unbuttoning my shirt. I let go of her cheeks to shrug my jacket off my shoulders. I toss it toward the chair and focus my attention on removing Zara's tight silk dress. It slides down her body and pools on the carpet at her feet. She carefully steps out of it in her heels.

"Be careful with that..." I toss it toward my coat, "... it's delicate material," she mutters.

I grin at my girl. "I'll buy you another." Scooping her up in my arms, I lay her on the bed and kiss her soft skin at the back of her neck. "I love you, Zara," I whisper. "With all my being."

"And I love you," she says with the gentleness I love in her.

I kiss her all over, make love to her, and adore every inch of her body. There is nothing I love more than the sound of my name coming from her lips as I bring her to orgasm over and over. After lying in each other's arms while we simply listen to the other breathe, she heads to the shower and emerges in a robe.

"We should watch the game," she says, bringing me out of a satisfied daze.

We should. It's the least I can do to support Byron since I'm not present at the game. He understood my absence when I promised him to be there for the majority of home games once we return to Los Angeles.

The commentators are talking, yet we barely hear them over the music as the atmosphere intensifies while the players are about to run out of the tunnel. The camera flips to our team seats, where Charlotte stands beside Coach. She is clapping in time with the music with her back turned to the opposition. The camera flips back to the tunnel where the lights are flashing. The team runs out, and the crowd cheers, the chanting louder when Byron appears. He bounces up and down on the spot, looking good, then grabs the ball, runs toward the basket, and dunks it. The crowd goes bananas, and it's only the warm-up.

The fans have missed my brother.

"Can I fix you a drink?" I stand and pour myself a whiskey while the team continues to warm up. The camera angle flicks to the Chicago team.

"No, thank you," Zara says, invested in watching the television. "I feel for Lottie. It must be hard to watch her ex."

Charlotte is a survivor and as determined as the rest of us. "BJ is not only Lottie's ex. He was part of our family for more than six years. He spent more time with us than his Australian family."

The camera focuses in on Brandon's face. "He doesn't have the Hendricks' poker face," she muses. "He looks worried."

"It's because he's not a Hendricks," I retort. "He didn't learn a damn thing by running away. Everything would have worked out fine if he gave it time. Now he has to face the consequences of being a coward."

"Time," Zara repeats in a softer voice. "It takes longer for some to heal."

Before I respond, we are both confused, watching my brother. He has run up the stands to his girlfriend, Giana.

"What is he doing?" Zara asks.

"She normally wishes him good luck, and he kisses her." But there is something else happening.

"Aw... that's so romantic," she says with a sigh.

What is he doing? The crowd is cheering. Byron runs down the stairs and leaps onto the court. His smile is huge and not the determined I-will-win-at-all-cost expression we witnessed only minutes ago.

"What is happening?" the commentators say as they focus on the fans. It's what everyone watching live wants to know.

"I believe Byron Hendricks just asked his girlfriend to marry him," another commentator exclaims. "And she said yes!"

"The fuck?" *At the game?*

"Oh my God!" Zara screams. "That is the most romantic thing I have ever seen."

Oh no, my brother does not get to steal the limelight of the romantic weekend I had planned for my girl. "The most romantic?" I grab Zara and pull her onto me, and she screams as we roll over the bed. "You think that's romantic?" She giggles as I tickle her.

I have her on her back, her hands fixed by her head. I stare into those brown eyes as she catches her breath. "It was romantic. You have to admit it," she puffs out the words.

It was. I have witnessed him giving his heart to Giana from the day he asked me to help him buy the entire first floor of Franklin's high-rise office block so Giana could have her own art studio. Then he surprised her with a vacation to the Maldives, and they flew with me on the private jet, and I made a stopover for them on my return trip to London. He has always been a romantic, and his gestures never inspired me until now. I see his proposal as a challenge because it's in my DNA.

If showing the world how much you love someone is the ultimate trademark in romance, then I want to do something just as magical for Zara.

NOVEMBER

*WHEN YOU KNOW, YOU KNOW.*

I open the box to admire the canary yellow diamonds on the necklace and gently close the velvet lid. "Thank you, it's perfect," I tell the jeweler, a renowned specialist in New York. It's the first piece of exquisite jewelry I intend to give to Zara with a new piece every week leading up to Christmas to help her settle back into life in LA.

He places the box with three other boxes in the same bag. Ever since Piper's death, Zara holds anything yellow in a special place in her heart because it reminds her of their friendship.

"We'll see you next month, Mr. Hendricks."

"Yes, you will." I smile at him, then pass the security guards as I step out onto the street. The street is full of people going about their day. A little way along the street, I stop to check the time and hesitate on whether to go back to the hotel or straight to the airport to catch the jet back to LA. The wind whips around my head, and I tighten the scarf around my neck. I have been here three days, and it's three days too long away from Zara. Catching my reflection in the glass window, I peer inside the small bar.

"I didn't expect to see you here," a familiar voice says from behind me. He steps to my side and offers a lopsided smile as though he is nervous about speaking to me.

Holding out a leather-gloved hand, I give him a smile in return. "BJ. What brings you to New York?"

He smirks. "We had a game yesterday, and I needed some time alone before flying back with the team."

*Time alone.* He is troubled, and if his performance is anything like the game against the LA Sharks when my brother whooped his sorry ass, then he needs a fucking month of isolation.

He pulls his shoulders up to his ears. Clearly, he hasn't adapted to the East Coast winter.

I nod toward the bar. "Do you want to get a drink?"

"Sure." He follows me inside, and I order at the bar before finding a small table in the corner. He runs a hand over his long blond locks to tame them from the wind. "What brings you to New York?"

"I had a meeting with a potential client." He glances down at the gift bag by my feet. His brow creases then he composes himself. "I have bought a gift for someone special," I say before he starts to guess who it's for.

"Anyone I know," he says with a grin, and when I nod, his eyes round slightly.

"Zara. Penny's friend."

He nods. "Nice girl." The bartender places two whiskeys on ice in front of us. Brandon stares into his glass before he takes a sip. "How is Charlotte?" he asks without looking away from the warmth of his drink.

"Lottie is doing well. As I assume you are."

He nods slowly. "Things worked out as they should have."

"Is that what you believe?" I question dryly.

His blue eyes meet mine briefly before he averts his gaze downward. "You know it is," he says in a low voice as though there was no other solution.

I take a mouthful of the whiskey before I speak. "What I know is you hurt my family, crushed my sister's heart, and betrayed my brother's trust," I say in a low even tone. "Yet they would've forgiven you." Brandon has hands on his whiskey glass, his elbows on the table. His head is bowed, yet his gaze meets mine with a heavy brow. "You were part of the family, and yet you ran like a dog with your tail between your legs. No explanation, and then cut everyone off. After all my family did for you, you shut us out." My heart is thumping in my chest, but the little prick needs to hear me out.

"It was my fault," he murmurs and lowers his gaze once more. I give him points for staying and not walking out on me. "Byron hated me because it was my fault, and I couldn't handle your family being disappointed in me. Lottie..." he shakes his head, "... Byron..." he tilts his head back and stares at the ceiling. "It's so fucked up."

"What is?" I snap.

"Life." He downs his drink and stands.

"Sit down, BJ. Give me one more minute of your time."

He remains standing for a few more seconds before he lowers his rear to the chair.

"I met someone. Almost lost her. When you realize there is a person for you out there, don't blow it with pride or by being a coward and running away when an obstacle is thrown across your path. And I know some obstacles are like boulders, and some are fucking megaliths. Either way, your life will never be as good without these people in your world. So you'll move Heaven and Earth to fix whatever damage you have done. Clear the path. Time heals. When the hurt may not be forgotten, it will be forgiven."

He shakes his head gently, three times, then he lets out a loud sigh. "I dunno."

"You don't know what?"

"I dunno if she'll ever forgive me?" He stands. "Too much time has passed."

"Sometimes, the longer the time between meetings, the better."

"I saw her last month. Briefly, but her eyes told me everything I needed to know."

"You're still a coward."

He stands beside me. "I'm heading back to Australia at Christmas to train in the Olympic team. Then, my contract with Chicago is done. I have no plans other than to return to Australia to play."

"So you're putting as much distance between you and Lottie as you can?" I already know this is not about mates but about love.

"It is what it is," he murmurs. He pats my shoulder three times. "I hope the family has a happy Thanksgiving." He takes a step toward the door.

"It's not the same without you."

He turns and stares at me. "Has she been seeing anyone?" he asks quietly.

I shake my head. "No one notable."

He nods once and opens the door. It closes slowly behind him, and all I think is, *BJ, you're a fool.*

Several hours later, I'm in the car heading to my home in Pacific Palisades.

"I'll see you on Monday, Joseph," I tell my driver. "Zara and I will not need you over the weekend."

"Very well, sir." He waits until I have unlocked the gate before he drives away. The house is quiet. No music playing. No romantic movie coming from the theater room. I take the stairs two at a time, open the bedroom door to find Zara curled up on the bed reading a book.

"You're home." She jumps into my arms, and I stumble back, juggling her and my case. She kisses me as though I have been gone for months.

"If this is the treatment I receive after a few days, imagine the reception after a month."

"There will not be a month where we'll be apart," she says against my lips. "We're a team, and where you go, I'll go."

I drop my case and twirl with her until we land on the bed together. "I have something for you," I whisper against her lips.

She pulls back. Her eyes study mine. "You're my everything, Jobe. I don't need anything else."

"And you're my entire world. This is about wanting to give you gifts, not about needing anything." I rub the tip of my nose with hers.

"Well, it's very sweet. Thank you." She kisses me again.

"You need to promise me something," I add. She tilts her head at me. "If anything ever goes pear-shaped, we talk about it. We discuss it, and if it can't be fixed, then we act. But we don't make hasty decisions without consulting the other."

"Of course. It goes without saying. We're not teenagers

acting on a whim." I nod at her, and she strokes my cheek to calm me. "Has something happened I should know about?"

I kiss her on the lips, then again and again. "I imagined a life without you because I was stubborn and allowed pride to interfere. Dignity is not worth a penny if it means letting you go. The pain is unimaginable..."

"Hey." Her lips stop me from saying more. "I love you, Jobe Hendricks, and I'm not going anywhere."

I roll until she is lying on me. "Wherever you go, I go."

She rests her chin on my chest. Her brown eyes full of love. "I promise."

THANK YOU FOR READING ZARA AND JOBE'S STORY

If you want to read more you can download the
**BONUS EPILOGUE:** https://dl.bookfunnel.com/v7wtystzig

You can read more about Zara & Jobe in the *The Wrong Time* (Book #4 in The Hendricks Billionaires Series) it is Charlotte Hendricks story.

*Want more of the characters in this book?*
*You first meet Zara and Jobe in The Wrong Proposal Book #1 in the series. If you haven't already read it you can grab it now.*

*Brandon Johns (BJ) is originally from my Australian sports series. You can read about Brandon in Winning the Player.*

If you want more of my books please follow me on Amazon, and be notified about my next book release.

If you are on Facebook please join my Reader group. We
have a lot of fun talking about books.

Please join my <u>mailing list</u> to be notified of my next release.

You can learn more about me on my website
www.leesabow.com

# ALSO BY LEESA BOW

### *THE HENDRICKS BILLIONAIRES*

*The Wrong Proposal #1*

*The Wrong Move #2*

*The Wrong Promise #3*

*The Wrong Time #4*

### *Beautifully Wild Series*

*Beautifully Wild*

*Hopelessly Wild*

*Perfectly Wild*

*WILD BOXSET*

### *The Player Series*

*Winning the Player*

*Winning the Game*

*Playing for Time*

### *Caught Out Series*

*Jardine*

*Caught Out*

### *Standalones*

*Charming the Outback*

*Cocky Notes (A Hero Club Novel)*

*Note: Velocity is being retitled and coming soon.*

*www.leesabow.com*

# PLAYLIST

- *SPOTIFY LINK - https://bit.ly/3XuKUWd*
- Summertime Sadness - Lana Del Rey
- Illusion - Dua Lipa
- Fly Away - Tones and I
- London Calling - The Clash
- Flowers- Miley Cyrus
- Lighthouse - Hey Holly
- As It Was - Harry Styles
- Set Fire to the Rain - Adele
- I Can Do It With A Broken Heart- Taylor Swift
- Look At Us Now - Daisy Jones & The Six
- Fallout - Hey Holly
- Without You - The Kid LAROI
- Yellow - Coldplay
- Just Give Me A Reason - Pink - ft. Nate Ruess
- So Long, London - Taylor Swift
- A Sky Full Of Stars - Coldplay

# ACKNOWLEDGMENTS

First and foremost, to my husband. Thank you for your encouragement, love, and support of my writing journey. And thank you for taking me to the UK and experiencing all the wonderful things. To my family for all your support.

My gratitude extends to my amazing editors. To Kaylene Osborn at Swish Design and Editing. Thank you for all your expertise, for answering endless questions, and for making my book shine. You are my rock! And a big thank you to Chantell and Nicki!

To Lauren and Madeline at Creating Ink, you always point me in the right direction so early in writing my story. I appreciate you!

To Letitia Hasser at RBA Designs, thank you for my beautiful cover.

My appreciation extends to my Facebook reader group, and all the blogging community for helping to get my book out to the world, especially Give Me Books. You all make the book world a much better place.

To my author friends, I can't express enough gratitude for all your advice and inspiration. Especially to Jodi, Beth, Nina, Maggie, and Kim who are always ready to offer any advice and support.

To my beta readers, Carol, and Robyn. Thank you for reading on short notice and finding the little things to help my story be the best it can. And to my FBBF ladies, Amo and Jo for helping with the UK terms.

To my readers. Thank you for your endless support, and

most of all, for loving my stories. Some of you have been with me from the start of my author journey, and to others, I'm a new author. What I love most is you all embrace my characters and stories and love them as much as I do. Thank you for reading, reviewing, and talking about my books to your families and friends in book clubs and blogs.

I appreciate everything you do for me.

# ABOUT THE AUTHOR

*Best selling Australian author, Leesa Bow lives in sunny Queensland, Australia. She spends her spare time with her family, and catching up with girlfriends for coffee or a wine.*

*Leesa loves to keep fit at the gym, in the pool, and walking surrounded by nature. Importantly, Leesa keeps it fun with laughter in her life.*

*She loves nothing more than to curl up with a good book, and a glass of South Australian wine. Leesa's love of travel inspires the next story. She hopes her books transport the reader around the world by the words on the page.*

www.leesabow.com